SOMEWHERE beside the canyon walls Logan drove past a small oval piece of metal, gave it a cursory glance, then continued down Merida wash. He'd gone some sixty yards before he stopped, shifted angrily into reverse and spun back up the wash. . . . His resentment of the small piece of metal and the implication that someone had been in *his* wash sent him shoveling violently at the earth. The white skeleton of a human arm was lifted in the air by the tip of the shovel. He dug until he saw the buried jeep, the steering column deeply imbedded in the rib cage. Returning to the rusted metal box resting against the driver's seat, he dug it free. The contents sent him sprawling on the sand in disbelief and shock. Bundles of money were tightly packed into the container, some six packets long and five packages wide. Tens and twenties, wrapped with paper binders, a foot deep . . .

Home Box Office

in Association with

Silver Screen Partners

Presents

Kris Kristofferson and Treat Williams

in Flashpoint

Rip Torn
and Tess Harper as Ellen

A William Tannen-Skip Short Production

Music by Tangerine Dream

Screenplay by Dennis Shryack
& Michael Butler

Produced by Skip Short
Directed by William Tannen

A Tri-Star Release

FLASHPOINT

George
La Fountaine

FAWCETT CREST • NEW YORK

*To my wife, Rita, who managed
to make it all work.
And for Dennis Shryack,
my agent and friend,
who managed to sell what was written.*

FLASHPOINT

1

"I don't think I can make it, Ern."

"Yes, you can . . . you have to try, Bob."

"I can't make it. . . ."

Chief Patrol Inspector Stan Hudson yelled, "Okay, let's go! Everybody into the squad room!"

Ernie pulled the belt tight on Logan's uniform, adjusted the collar, checked his own image in Logan's dark glasses. "There—good as new."

Logan held the metal cabinet unsteadily. Patrolman Richart rattled his lock shut; the sound sent Logan off-balance and he grasped Ernie with his free hand. "Tell 'em . . . I passed away at three A.M."

"Nobody will know," Ernie assured him.

"Are my eyes open? Jesus, Ern, I can't tell if my eyes are open!"

Ernie reached forward to lift the sunglasses. "Don't," Logan warned. "One of my eyes may fall out."

"We'll get us some coffee and you'll be all right."

"Does it look like I've been drinking?" Logan asked his partner as Ernie led him down the line of metal lockers.

"No," Ernie laughed, steering Logan to the coffee urn. "You look like George Shearing on his way to a concert."

The squad room was crowded with easels, pictures, diagrams, and sixteen seated border patrolmen and investigators. Ernie held his coffee high in the air as he dragged Logan to an empty seat.

"Why don't they ever have cream?" Logan cried.

Ernie forced a smile. "Learn to drink it black."

"I hate it black!" Logan wailed. "I hate that powdered

shit! Whatever happened to half-and-half or plain ordinary milk?"

District Supervisor Brook announced "good morning" as he hurried into the room. The assembly muttered a reply.

"What about plain old cream?" Logan insisted.

"Sssh." Ernie stopped him as the room broke out in laughter.

"I assume we're all here," Brook began. "Without further delay, I'd like you to meet our visiting VIP, Ron Lacy. Ron's here to tell you what this is all about."

"You know Lacy?" Logan asked Ernie under his breath.

"Heard of him. Some candy ass with a headful of bullshit," Ernie whispered. "Going to tell us how this bureau should be run."

"Gentlemen," Lacy began, flashing a smile to gain their confidence. He was a tiny man, his scalp completely hairless, eyes hidden behind thick lenses. "The information that I've brought today will be of interest to all of you. Many of you may know me. I've spent several years in the Chula Vista District perfecting these devices you see about me. I'm very happy to say the bureau is very excited about the results. So much so," he added confidently, "that I can say quite honestly you men in the Del Amo area will be the first to benefit from these breakthroughs."

The men were already restless; feet scuffed the floor, chairs squeaked as their occupants shifted in annoyance. Lacy sensed this and went immediately to the first easel. He struck a pointer into the line separating the United States and Mexico. "Two thousand and thirteen miles of border. Patrolled by almost as many men." The pointer moved up the coast to California. "Chula Vista, seventy miles of border patrolled by just a *handful* of men. Security more effective than a hundred men in jeeps and planes. Gentlemen"—Lacy paused dramatically—"the new electronic fence!" He whipped the card from the easel, beneath it, the same map but with a large fence drawn along the international boundary.

Lacy was clearly surprised by the moans of disgust. "I know what you're going to say," he cried, trying to recover the group's attention. "It's been proved far more effective than any equipment or plan ever devised in the past."

"Isn't that just the old equipment from the McNamara line in Nam?" Patrolman Richart shot out.

"It's far more effective," Lacy repeated quickly.

"We had that son of a bitch in Nam," Richart snorted to his companions, "on the Ho Chi Minh Trail. It didn't work then, and it probably won't work now!"

Brook took a step to the center of the room. "It *is* working!" he announced sternly, dismissing any further objections.

Richart slumped in his seat. "It didn't work in Vietnam and it cost a bundle," he grumbled.

"Knock it off!" Brock called out.

Lacy cleared his throat before continuing. "Infrared equipment, pressure-sensitive devices, underground wires, and highly sensitive microphones go into making it the 'electronic fence' of the future. To give you just a small idea of how it works, we'll look at the geophone." Lacy crossed to the far easel, nearest Brook, and used the pointer again. "This is a microphone—a seismic microphone, to be exact—buried in the earth." Lacy moved rapidly to the next easel. "These are pressure-sensitive cables. Anything that moves within one hundred and fifty feet of either of these devices will send a signal to the control center here at Del Amo. The microphone—or should I say the geophone—can discern a footstep within thirty-eight paces of its perimeter." Lacy moved to yet another easel. "This metal detector will detect a coin in a man's pocket."

"They don't *have* any coins in their pockets," Logan announced, toasting Lacy with his coffee cup. "That's why they run the border." Logan was rewarded by the cheering of his companions. He tried to rise for a bow, but was still too unsteady to do so.

"It will detect guns," Lacy continued bravely, "anything metal, and send a signal or blip to the control room here in Del Amo."

Ewing, one of the two pilots assigned to the district, asked, "What happens after we get this blip?"

Encouraged, Lacy went immediately to another easel and flipped the card over. "Helicopters!" he announced triumphantly. "Aircraft that can fly in minutes to any location, hold the suspects until a vehicle can pick them up for transport back across the border."

Ewing's loud groan was heard above Lacy's move to the next easel. Logan looked at the back of Ewing's head; he realized the pilot did not have a helicopter rating. Leaning forward, he whispered, "Kiss your soft touch good-bye baby."

"Let me get this straight," Ernie said, rising to his feet. "What happens to guys like us that are patrolmen? What the hell do we do?"

Lacy held a finger aloft, a bright smile spreading across his face. "Schooling!" He beamed. "*You're* the men who will benefit most by this. You will be trained to work with the equipment and taught to recognize the electronic signs of entry. You men will be the crux of this new plan!"

"Wait a minute!" Ernie demanded, waving Lacy silent. "I turned down Immigration investigator to stay out there on patrol! Are you telling me I'm going to have to sit in a little room somewhere looking at little red fucking lights?"

Lacy explained lamely, "There will be fewer hazards!"

Logan pulled himself erect, clutching the back of Ewing's chair for support. "What my partner is trying to say, Chief, is this. We like what we're doing. We *like* riding patrol in a jeep. We've turned down promotions to stay out there on the desert . . . shit . . . we could have been patrol inspectors or Immigration investigators a long time ago. But that wasn't what we wanted! You see, it's important that you know what we wanted. I mean, you're telling us we don't have any choice in the damn thing!"

"Right, Patrolman Logan," Brook interjected firmly. "You have no choice in this."

"Well, sir, may I say for the record—that's bullshit."

"That'll be enough!" Brook warned as the men cheered Logan. "Our job is to close the border to wetbacks and greaseballs, and if this equipment will help us, then we'll use it and like it."

Seeing that the demonstration he'd so carefully prepared was in dire need of justification, Lacy shouted, "The fence caught over ninety thousand aliens last year!"

Ernie announced, "You caught ten thousand guys nine times! That's all you did!"

"All right!" Brook yelled. "The meeting's over! You guys want to act like some girls' boarding school, then the meeting's over!"

The men filed out quickly, leaving Lacy with his charts and diagrams, bewildered by the unanimously hostile reception of his pet project.

The men grouped outside in little knots, angrily discussing the signifiance of Lacy's demo. Ernie and Logan went straight to the maintenance shed, disconnecting the battery chargers on their respective vehicles, checking the radiator levels.

"Chickenshit! That's what it is!" Ernie called from his jeep. "They're bound and determined to shut us up in some little room or have us checking green cards at the border."

"I can't believe they're going to dump us for some goddam computer!" Logan groaned.

"I ain't seen a computer yet that could track a man forty miles!"

The pilot, Ewing, dropped his clipboard on the seat of Logan's vehicle. "The shit's in the fire," he said.

"That's for sure." Logan grinned. "What about you?"

"I can get checked out in the chopper. But they may be using that as an excuse to dump me. I don't know. . . ."

"How long do you think we have?" Logan asked.

"A year, maybe—maybe two."

"If that ain't the cat's ass!" Ernie answered, slamming the hood of his jeep.

"Well"—Ewing shrugged—"*que serra serra,* as Doris Day used to say."

"I screwed her last night," Logan offered.

"Oh, did you?" Ewing asked in amusement.

"Yeah," Logan said indifferently, "I screwed Doris Day but I had to pretend she was Ann-Margret to get it off."

"He doesn't know what the hell he did last night." Ernie laughed. "All the girls at Alicia's cathouse look like Ann-Margret to him."

"She was there!" Logan insisted. "We were counting goldfish in her water bed when this big goddamn shark came along and ate 'em."

Ewing had the clipboard clutched to his chest, laughing at the two patrolmen.

"I knew I could make you laugh," Logan said.

Ewing shook his head. "I don't know how the hell you guys do it, night after night like that."

"It isn't easy," Ernie said. "Sheer willpower, that's all."

"By the way," Ewing remembered, going to his clipboard, "we have a set of tracks at the Paseo wash. Looks like an abandoned vehicle. Brook wants you boys to check it out."

14

"Sure." Logan sighed. "When did it come in?"

"This morning. I spotted it just before the meeting. I didn't see any life in the vicinity, but you should be careful."

"We'll get on it," Logan replied.

The desert was dry; the temperature gauge on the dash read 105 degrees. Logan peered through the binoculars at the dust-covered auto below. He dropped the glasses to his chest as Ernie's jeep crept quietly into position.

"What do you make of it?" Ernie asked.

"No sign of activity."

"They crossed the drag road about six miles back. Could be a couple of coyotes waiting for wetbacks," Ernie suggested, referring to the smugglers who occasionally wandered into section seven, leaving their tracks on a wide sandy belt that paralleled the border, known as the drag road.

"Maybe, but it's got to be goddamn hot down in that car," Logan whispered, putting the glasses to his eyes once again. "Lookee here. . . ." He whistled softly as a slender arm was extended from the front-seat passenger window, searching the air for a hint of cool breeze. "I'll take the passenger side," Logan said quickly.

Ernie moaned. "And I get the fucking sun."

"We can't all be in the shade," Logan said from behind the glasses. He slipped the binoculars into the case. Removing his hat, Logan ran his fingers through his hair several times, then placed the stiff-brimmed stetson back in position. He leaned into the rearview mirror and examined himself closely.

"You're so pretty I can't stand it!" Ernie fluttered in a high-pitched falsetto. "Which side is your good side? It's so hard to choose. . . ."

"I ain't got no bad sides," Logan grinned, exposing spectacularly white teeth.

They left their jeeps on the crest of the hill, picking their way cautiously down to the wash. Logan unsnapped the leather restrainer from the hammer of his magnum revolver.

Ernie Wheeler slipped his weapon in and out of his holster as they split up and moved to the rear of the auto. Ernie's attention was fixed on the side mirror, watching for the slightest movement from inside. He gave a quick glance to the rear seat and was relieved to see it empty.

The tops of two heads were visible in the front seat, both crowns low and cushioned between the seats and the doorjamb. The driver's window had been covered with material to keep out the sun. The passenger window was open to catch any suggestion of a breeze. With one hand ready on the revolver, Logan came abreast of the window.

She had her eyes closed against the heat. Her blouse had been removed, leaving her bra straps hanging loosely at her elbows. Perspiration ran down the mounds of exposed breasts, disappearing into the startling white bra, only to emerge on her stomach in a thin wet river.

Logan studied the face, the hair hanging limply against the damp forehead, the long blond strands tucked behind the ears. The upper lip was damp and the pockets of the closed eyes were moist and pooled with sweat.

Logan glanced across at the driver, leaning against the door. She had taken off her blouse, too, and placed it over the window for shade. Both girls appeared to be in their middle twenties, blond, stripped of excess clothing. Logan exhaled silently, his hand slipping from the butt of the magnum. He knew anything he would do would startle them, but he dropped his voice to a gentle register and said, "Good morning, ladies."

Both girls screamed in fright. The passenger went wide-eyed in terror, her large brown eyes searching the front windshield before she dared herself to look in Logan's direction. Logan grinned broadly, keeping his uniform in view. The passenger sagged in relief against the seat.

"You scared the shit out of us!" the driver shrieked, her relief turning to anger as Ernie smiled through the windshield. "What *are* you guys, cops?"

Logan noticed that the passenger was much prettier than the driver, so he turned his attention to the girl at his elbow. "No, ma'am."

"I'll bet they came all the way out here to sell us a ticket to the policemen's ball." The passenger smiled.

Logan replied, "We belong to the Border Patrol, ma'am, we don't have any balls."

"And that's God's truth," Ernie announced as he poked his head in through the material covering the window. The girls started to laugh, but it grew rapidly, too rapidly, and suddenly hysteria had taken control of them. It was something Logan and Wheeler had witnessed many times before. People overcompensated for their relief, and laughter, any laughter, took on a hysterical ring.

"We're just here to help, ma'am," Ernie added quickly.

The passenger recovered first. Her laughter died in her chest. "I'll be damned!"

"What seems to be the trouble?" Logan asked, taking in her damp cleavage.

"We're lost!" the driver said suddenly. "What the hell does it look like!"

"Something went wrong with the car, too," her friend added. "It just stopped. . . ."

Logan examined the lovely shoulders she shrugged. "What made you take the wash?" he asked.

"She wanted to take a shortcut to Durbin," the driver said in annoyance to Ernie.

"I was born in Durbin. I thought we could save time by taking a shortcut. Then the car overheated or some-

17

thing, and we were already lost. . . ." She lifted the damp hair off her face.

"You guys work for Smokey the Bear?" the driver asked.

"No, ma'am, Border Patrol." Now Ernie was exasperated. "Our job is to keep the borders of the good old U.S. of A. safe for people like you."

"Yeah?" she countered, unimpressed. "I'll sleep real good tonight knowing you yo-yos are on the job. Hey, you! Smokey!" she called across to Logan. "You know anything about cars?"

"A little." Logan grinned. "I'll take a look."

Ernie met him at the grille. He flashed a fist toward the driver before he popped the hood and gazed inside. "Fan belt," he mumbled.

"Fan belt," Logan called to the girls.

"We can take the belt off the generator and put it on the water pump," Ernie continued. "At least they'll be able to make it into Durbin."

Logan relayed this information to the passenger. "We'll take the fan belt off the generator and put it on the water pump. That way you'll be able to drive into Durbin."

"There's an echo in here," Ernie's muffled voice called from beneath the hood.

"Thank you." The passenger smiled, one finger tracing the dampness under the edge of her bra.

Logan leaned on the sill, watching the finger with unconcealed delight.

"Do you have any tools?" Ernie called.

"Don't *you* have any?" the driver retorted accusingly.

Ernie came out from under the hood, started to explain to the driver that his were a long way off, then decided against it, and began the long uphill trek to his jeep.

Logan watched Ernie hurry off, mumbling to himself as he struggled to climb out of the wash. Several times Ernie threw a clenched fist back toward the auto.

"My name's Bob Logan, and that," he said, indicating Ernie, puffing up the hill, "is Ernie Wheeler. We're at your disposal."

"That's an apt way to put it," the driver answered curtly.

"I'm Emily," the passenger said softly, "and this is Ellen."

Logan touched the brim of his hat to both women.

"You work out here?" Emily asked as she slid closer to the door and Logan's elbow. She made no attempt to raise the straps or cover herself, but settled into a comfortable position in which she could see his face and watch his eyes.

"Yes, ma'am. This is where I work. This is the last frontier," he said expansively, his head swinging in the direction of the desert that lay ahead. "This is where the last confrontation between man and the elements will be held. It'll be out there, without spectators or a cheering crowd to urge us on. This . . . is where man's last battle will be fought." He allowed the solemnity of the picture to overcome him.

"My. . . ." Emily sighed.

"Crap!" Ellen sniffed.

Logan threw the driver a quick, scorching glare, but she was studying her nails superciliously.

The jeep came to life on the hill. Logan heard Ernie angrily grind the transmission into gear. "He's one of my responsibilities. He's new to this and I have to be sure he isn't bitten by a rattlesnake or a scorpion. Their bite's fatal, you know." Logan snapped his fingers to show how quickly it would be over. "But years of training are hard to pass along. If it hadn't been for the Apaches, well. . . ."

Logan allowed his words to hang there, waiting patiently until Emily picked up the thread and said, "The Apaches?" before he resumed.

"They raised me. They taught me the way of the Indian. They taught me how to survive in this wasteland. If it wasn't for them. . . ." He let his head fall to his chest. He need not say more; Emily fully understood the implications.

"You're very fortunate," she whispered, her hand resting lightly on his arm. Logan nodded modestly as he placed his hand solemnly over hers.

Ernie slid to a halt on the soft sand, his face wet with the exertion of climbing the wash. He gave Logan a withering glare as he yanked the tool container out of his jeep.

"You must be thirsty," Logan said. Crossing to Ernie's jeep, Logan retrieved the canteen and poncho, walked right on past Ernie's outstretched hand, and passed the canteen inside the car. "It'll be cooler out here," he told the girls as he spread the poncho in the shade of the auto.

Ernie watched the girls slide from the car, sipping from his canteen. He selected a large crescent wrench, attacked the generator mount, let out a howl of pain as the wrench slipped from the nut, tearing the skin from several knuckles.

"We'll get you back to civilization somehow," Logan promised the girls.

". . . where the deer and the antelope play," Ernie said aloud.

"Of course"—Logan ignored the voice coming from under the hood—"these are only temporary repairs we're making."

"We!" Ernie screamed.

"You'll have to have the car attended to once we reach Durbin, but I shall personally escort you to the highway and see you safe in the city."

"You call Durbin a city?" Emily asked as she wiped the moisture from her lips and passed the canteen to Ellen. "I left there when I was seven. I just want to see if it's as dreary as I remember."

"Drearier than you could possibly have remembered," Logan corrected her.

"Isn't there any action at all?" Ellen asked hesitantly.

Ernie's dark, perspiring head slid out from beneath the hood, his hat perched on the ornament, his sleeves rolled to the elbows. "There's a great steak house in Durbin, the Rio Grande. Good food, fine liquor, other than that, D-E-A-D."

"Swell!" Ellen moaned. "Typical Texas nightlife. Pull up a chair and watch the sun set."

Emily explained, "Ellen's tired of Texas and Texans . . . she's from Los Angeles."

"Just once I'd like to meet some son of a bitch who has time to take his hat off!" Ellen exclaimed angrily.

"I always take my hat off." Ernie grinned from under the hood.

"That's probably the slowest thing you do," Ellen shot back.

"He can hum 'The Star-Spangled Banner' while drinking a can of beer," Logan offered.

"Swell." Ellen yawned. "You have anything to eat?"

Ernie's head came out from under the hood, a mischievous smile on his face.

"Not *that*, prevert," Ellen grumbled. "Food, sandwiches, something along those lines."

Ernie watched as Logan went to the jeep and brought back Ernie's lunch. The girls wolfed both sandwiches and washed them down with water from Ernie's canteen.

Ernie attacked the fan belt, made the final adjustments, filled the radiator with water from a five-gallon can he carried in his jeep, threw the hood down, and announced heatedly, "It's done!"

"Swell," Ellen responded without enthusiasm.

Logan assisted Emily into the car, folded Ernie's poncho, and said, "I'll get my jeep and you can follow me out of here."

"They ate my goddam lunch!" Ernie screamed as he drove Logan back to the jeep on the hill.

"I'll pick you up a couple of sandwiches in Durbin. I'll also talk to Joe at the Gulf station and make sure he doesn't have a fan belt to fit their car. That'll keep 'em in Durbin for the night. Don't worry, Ern. Old Bob's looking out for us."

"What the hell am I supposed to do while you're taking them to town?"

"Cover for me, what else? If Brook tries to reach me, tell him I blew the fuse on my radio."

"He's not going to buy that again!"

"Ernie, Ernie, two grateful maidens hang in the balance. I'm telling you, sport, we'll be sleeping in the arms of sensual bliss tonight."

"Let me guess. You get the passenger, Emily—and I get Ellen the mouth, right?"

"Ernie!" Logan cried in pain. "I wanted Ellen for myself! But she only has eyes for you! What was I to do?"

"You get beauty and I get the Hun. Where do I meet you?"

Logan thought for a moment. "I'll find a shortcut past the old Kaufman place and meet you at the stone survey marker near the Merida wash."

"And don't forget my lunch!" Ernie called as Logan shifted into gear.

"Ernie?"

"Yeah?"

"You've got some shit on your nose."

2

The old Kaufman place, located halfway between Durbin and the border, was a simple stone chimney standing against the sky. That there ever was or had been a Kaufman family no one locally could remember for sure. The chimney was the sole tribute to the plucky courage of some pioneer named Kaufman.

The structure itself was gone. The winds and rain had washed and blown away all traces of its existence. The sand had crept over its vitals, hiding the foundation from prying eyes. Burned to the ground by hostile Indians, some said. An unfinished dream that began and ended with the stone chimney, said others. Logan had never met anyone who had known for sure or even cared. That a Kaufman left a stone sentinel in the desert for them to wonder about was satisfaction enough.

The chimney stood alone on the vast Kearney Plateau, bordered on the west by the steep, inaccessible Merida wash, on the east, cut off from the desert by the precipitous Seguin wash. As with most of the area's mesas, access by vehicle was from the north, the readily available highway.

Logan rolled southward past the chimney, Hank Williams singing plaintively of her cheating heart, the portable radio swinging from Logan's rearview mirror. He knew that thirty miles away Ernie would be tuned to the same station, bumping along the desert floor, singing at the top of his lungs.

The disastrous morning had been avenged. The two girls were firmly ensconced in the Durbin Motel, the replacement fan belt to be bused in from Stone Hill the following morning. Everything had gone exactly as Logan had planned. By eight thirty that evening the two patrolmen would be sipping cocktails and enjoying the ladies' company over the preliminary dinner and drinks. By ten that evening . . . who could say, Logan thought as he whistled the tune spilling from the transistor.

Braking the jeep at the edge of the mesa, Logan climbed upright in the cab, scanning the drop to the wash. He had never negotiated the dry riverbed or the steep side of the canyon. He'd flown over the area several times as a spotter for Ewing in the Cessna, had noted several possible paths of exit. The Merida wash was a barren gully, ignored by the wetbacks for the more negotiable ravines east and west of the area. Logan knew he could save himself over twenty miles of hard driving if he could find a path off the mesa. He cruised several hundred yards along the plateau lip before deciding on a route he thought he could navigate.

He eased the front wheels over the edge, half standing in the jeep as the vehicle began to roll down the hill. The front tires hung momentarily in the soft sand, spinning the steering wheel from his grip. He felt the rear end start to come around and fought to head the jeep nose-first into the wash, feeling just a moment's panic when he thought he'd lost it and might have to jump clear. He fought the wheel, whipping it rapidly around to compensate for the drift, feeling relief when the front end responded and he regained control over his direction. Upon reaching the bottom, Logan found himself dripping with perspiration. He lit a cigarette with his Zippo, noting the way his fingers trembled. He allowed himself one swallow of water, rolling it around in his mouth before downing it.

The gully was peppered with large boulders. Round and smooth, they had been tumbled about by the spring rains until their surfaces were as fine as polished marble.

Logan drove slowly down the twisting dry bed, tires humming on the exposed stone flooring. He had to climb the banks in places to avoid the large squat boulders that challenged him. The area itself was virginal. No man had left his mark on the wash. This in itself was a pleasurable experience. Logan thought of it as the feeling that must have accompanied the first moon walk. The pleasure of knowing no one had been there before him, possibly since time had begun. He knew prospectors sometimes entered the area, that Indians may have taken refuge in the ravine, but there was just the possibility they had all missed this wash, that he had been the first to navigate its canyon. The thought pleased him tremendously, for it enabled him to strike modern man from this gully.

Section seven belonged to Logan and Wheeler; it was their country, their private domain. It belonged to them as the cities of glass and cement belonged to other men. It angered them to discover the fresh print of an intruder, especially when the violator was a coyote, a two-legged predator who fed off the desperation of the wetbacks. The coyotes used to invade their domain with false papers, promising the illegal aliens work and wealth, dragging the dehydrated bodies of the poor behind them, then abandoning them to the bureau's patrolmen at the first sign of trouble. Escaping with their two- and three-hundred-dollar fees intact, these coyotes were the real enemy.

Every Border Patrolman had seen the dead bodies of Mexico's fine young men, casually left to perish in the desert, discarded by the coyotes because the situation had suddenly turned risky. Left without food or water, trusting childishly to the saints and the coyotes to return and save them. Patient young men claimed by the desert, tolerant, forgiving, serenely confident of their chances, even when death whispered its hot breath in their faces.

Now the coyotes avoided section seven. The risk of capture was too great, Logan and Wheeler's anger too terrible, the rewards too uncertain. All of them now came in through sections six and eight. Only the aliens who attempted to cross the border on their own made their way into section seven. And few ever made the safety of the highway.

"Yellow Bird" echoed off the closeness of the canyon walls as Logan sang along with the vocalist. He drove past a small oval piece of metal protruding from the bank, gave it a cursory glance, then continued down the wash. He'd gone some sixty yards before his curiosity overwhelmed him. He stopped the jeep, shoved it angrily into reverse, and spun back up the wash.

It was a curiously shaped piece of metal, barely noticeable in the undercut of the bank. He sat in the jeep for a long moment contemplating this first sign of man. Logan was furious at the man who'd defiled the wash. He set the brake and walked forward to touch the rusted metal. He cleared a fingerhold in the sand, gave it a tug only to find it unyielding. Raging at the metal, he cleared a hole large enough for both hands, gave it a mighty pull, but still it resisted him. There had been no shifting of the sand, no give to it at all. The piece of metal appeared welded to the earth itself.

Logan went back to the jeep, unstrapped the shovel, and stabbed it into the rain-packed earth. He was rewarded with a hard metallic clink. Logan gave the object one last hard look before he began to dig the sand away. His resentment of the small piece of metal and the implications that someone had been in his wash sent him shoveling violently at the earth. He exposed a small gas can holder, similar to the ones mounted on the rear of the Immigration Patrol jeeps. Further digging unearthed the bumper to which it was still attached. Anger left him; curiosity took its place. He began to dig in earnest now, throwing large chunks of hard-packed dirt over his shoulder as he slowly uncovered the rear end of a jeep.

The effort left him panting in the shade. He shed his shirt and hat, taking his shovel to the driver's side of the vehicle. Logan ignored the tires and the lower half of the jeep, concentrating on what should have been the driver's position. He struck what appeared to be the side of the seat, but further shoveling revealed it to be a large metal box that had been resting against the driver's seat. Logan shifted forward a foot and scooped at the hard-packed earth. The white skeleton of a human arm was lifted in the air by the tip of the shovel. Logan dropped it quickly and moved off to study the two white bleached bones.

After the calming influence of a Marlboro, he returned to digging, using his hands now, scooping the dirt away from the arm and chest. It took several minutes before he could see the upper torso, the neck vertebral column, bent obliquely forward, and finally the head.

Logan was grateful that the face was turned away from him. He went back to the chest and dug until he saw that the steering column was deeply embedded in the rib cage. Logan shook off the shiver that raced through his body. He backed away momentarily, marshaling the courage to continue. After several deep breaths, he took the shovel to the passenger side of the vehicle, where he put it to use in search of another body. Logan felt relief when he saw that only sand occupied the other seat.

Returning to the box resting against the driver's seat, he dug it free and pulled it to the ground. It was a large three- by two-foot metal container, slightly more than a foot deep. The corners were rusted; the combination lock broke off easily when he applied the tip of the shovel to it. He was on one knee when the lid was pried back. The contents sent him sprawling on the sand in disbelief and shock. Bundles of money were tightly packed into the container some six packets long and five packages wide. Tens and twenties, wrapped with paper binders, a foot deep.

Logan snapped the lid down. Backing away from the container, he rose to his feet. He went to the radio to call Ernie, then thought better of it, as the dispatchers in Del

Amo would be able to hear everything he said. Even Brook, who monitored all calls from his office radio, would know he was back in commission. Logan turned away from his jeep, walked slowly around the closed box, lifted the lid cautiously with his foot, almost surprised when the money was still there.

He removed a packet of tens and twenties, weighed them in his palms as he paced nervously back and forth. Bending over the fender of his jeep, he flipped through each packet. The paper band came loose in his hand and the bills spilled to the ground. Logan leaned against the jeep with both hands, his head hanging between his arms, his attention on the money lying at his feet.

The first surge of excitement began in his stomach. He closed his eyes to halt the dizziness that took hold of him, sucking rapidly at the hot desert air. He rolled his head to the sky and smiled. The smile gave way to laughter. The exquisite joy of it took control of him; his laughter reverberated off the canyon walls until there were a hundred of him echoing excitedly back and forth. The hundreds became thousands of Robert Logans laughing deliriously at one another and their secret.

At the last possible moment Ernie scribbled a note for Logan and left it atop the stone survey marker. Even as he raced to the highway crossing of the West Texas Railroad, he was dreading the assignment. Turning the portable transistor up loudly failed to drive it from his mind. Racing across the hot desert floor only served to justify his anger at Logan. His partner had failed to return to the marker, had failed to bring Ernie's much-needed lunch, had failed to answer Brook's repeatedly angry calls, had in fact placed Ernie in a position of alibiing yet another time, another lie to infuriate Brook. Now Logan had left him alone to handle this assignment by himself. That was possibly the worst offense of all.

Forty minutes later Ernie threaded his jeep through the long line of traffic to the wreckage. He gave Sheriff Paul Kirkland of Moss County a brief nod as he parked on the shoulder and emerged from his jeep, the clipboard in his hand.

A deputy was sending traffic around the rear of the train. Two hundred yards north lay the front of the bus, carried forward under the wheels, spilling its once-live cargo on both sides of the track. At one time it had been a faded green farm bus; now it lay broken and split down the center. The front lay on one side of the train's heaving engine; the tail section sat on its rear wheels near the crossing marker. The area was strewn with parts of bodies—limbs lay under train wheels, torsos drained into the dry desert floor, large brown stains pinned the bodies to their last moment of mortality.

A well-dressed elderly Mexican with ornately tooled Western boots stood beside his Cadillac passively smoking while Sheriff Kirkland raged at him. Ernie knew the Mexican. Ernesto Pedroza had been the chief farm-labor contractor in the area for many years. Each morning and evening his battered buses traveled the highways, supplying local farmers with Mexican laborers from across the border. The buses were always ill-equipped, mechanically unsafe, and overloaded. The Texas Department of Public Safety had fined the man on numerous occasions, but each morning, before daylight, Pedroza's buses rolled north, east, and west unmolested. "He's got a lot of clout," Ewing had once explained. Pedroza's firm was paid for each man supplied; it stood to reason that the buses left the border filled to overflowing.

A young highway patrolman emerged from the front half of the bus, his mouth pulled down in revulsion. Ernie asked, "How many do you make it to be, Steve?"

"Sixty . . . maybe seventy, Ern." The young man was

fighting nausea and waved fresh air to his mouth. "There's really no way of telling yet."

"Any survivors?"

"Two. One lost a leg—he'll never make the hospital. The other one's over near Kirkland. He's pretty shook up. . . . You won't get much from him."

"Did you talk to the engineer on the train?"

"Yeah. The bus tried to beat him across—and lost."

Ernie forced himself to look inside the front half of the bus. The bodies were huddled together in a pile. It was impossible to tell whether they numbered twenty or fifty. The seats were rickety old slat benches, nailed to rotten flooring. They had pulled loose instantly, throwing each man against the seat in front. The bus had been forced down the track sideways, pitching its occupants out the open windows to the tracks and steel wheels. Those that escaped the grinding death of the train were crushed by their comrades.

Ernie backed out of the wreckage and the humming of busy flies. He walked away into the sunlight before he exhaled.

"Pretty ugly," the highway patrolman offered.

Ernie nodded silently; he wanted Logan's support and quick mind to help him with the report. He didn't want to handle it alone, to count the bodies and search for the green work permits. Logan would figure out a means to have others do it for them. That was something Ernie just couldn't do by himself.

Turning back to the train, Ernie sketched the scene quickly, drawing an arrow from the railway crossing to the front half of the bus. Then he paced the distance, carefully avoiding the limbs lying in his path. He wrote the figure above the arrow, drew the train, and listed the number of cars. He started to draw in the slight gully and the pieces of human debris lying about, but they were too numerous, too confusingly alike. He satisfied himself by dotting the surrounding area with a myriad of black specks.

Pedroza had now been joined by a dignified gray-haired Anglo when Ernie walked over to the group.

"You keep those goddamn buses out of Moss County, Pedroza," Kirkland snarled, "or I'm going to stop every damn one of them and shake them down for vehicle safety!"

The gray-haired gentleman, clutching the briefcase, said smoothly, "Then I'm afraid we'll have to file a complaint of undue harassment."

Kirkland was several inches taller than either of the two men and he leaned in menacingly close. "You slimy bastard!" he spat. "Don't pull that shit with me! You keep those fucking junk heaps out of Moss County or I'll personally take a sledgehammer to every one I stop!"

"I might remind you," the lawyer said, unruffled by Kirkland's towering frame, "Mr. Pedroza is an American citizen and pays his taxes. . . ."

"*Mister* Pedroza is *shit! Mister* Pedroza isn't worth one of these poor bastards! Those junk heaps account for twenty percent of all fatalities, *Mister* Pedroza!"

"Will there be anything further, Sheriff?"

Kirkland held a fist up to the lawyer's nose, then swung it toward Pedroza. "I want a list of everyone who was on that bus!"

The lawyer agreed. "Your office will be given a complete list, as will Immigration, but it will take some time. Mr. Pedroza is not in the habit of listing every passenger who rides in his conveyances. Even the Dallas public-transportation system does not require identification to ride the public buses. We shall be glad to oblige you, but it will take some time."

Ernie could sense the angry frustration welling up in the sheriff. He also recognized that Pedroza's attorney had won the battle of the hot afternoon.

Kirkland placed both hands on his hips. "I'm going over this thing with a toothbrush! If the brakes are bad . . . if there's *one* infraction of vehicle safety, I'm coming down around your ears like wet cowshit!"

"There's also negligence," Ernie offered.

The lawyer regarded him for a disdainful moment. "My client cannot be held responsible for the foolish decision of the bus driver."

"*Somebody's* responsible for overloading that bus," Ernie added.

The lawyer almost smiled, but realized that to do so might provoke both men. He forced a grim sobriety to mask his face as he said knowingly, "Each driver holds that responsibility."

The first vehicle from the county coroner's office arrived, its siren winding down as it pulled into the crossing. Ernie started to say something, then lost the thread of his argument. He knew he hadn't helped Kirkland in the slightest, so he turned away from the group to seek out the survivor.

The man was old, huddled in a sheriff's blanket against the side of the car, even though the temperature was in the high nineties. Ernie squatted in front of the man before asking, "*Cómo se llama?*"

The man stared vacantly at the ground—he neither heard nor saw anything. "*Cómo se llama?*"

The man's hat was gone, the dark leathery skin changing to light pink above the eyebrows, the tanned face dark with years of toil, lined with seasons of trouble and pain, making it impossible to determine his age.

Ernie started to repeat the question for the third time, then concluded that there was nothing to be gained by it. The old man's mind was far away, possibly reliving that fateful second when he knew all was lost. Ernie patted the man's shoulder, stroking it gently before he lit a cigarette and stuck it between the wide dry lips. "Take it easy, old shoe," he whispered as he rose, looking aimlessly around before joining Kirkland.

The sheriff was watching Pedroza and his attorney conferring at the contractor's El Dorado. "Tricky son of a bitch," Ernie broke in.

"Slime." Kirkland sighed. "Just slime. . . ."

"They didn't have a chance," Ernie said as he picked up a battered lunch pail. He held it to his nose, inhaling traces of *jalapeños* and *nopalitis,* the pear cactus leaves. He thought he caught a whiff of olive oil and *cilantro.* That it was somebody's lunch somebody spilled along the road in sections made him drop it quickly. Ernie slapped his hands free of the dust, shaking the man's life away, ridding himself of the kitchen smells of hot peppers and oil.

Kirkland's boot went to a mangled pear, toeing it over. "They were picking pears up near Diamond. . . ."

"It could take a couple of weeks to identify them." Ernie shrugged helplessly.

"If we can't find their green work cards, we may *never* identify any of them. . . ."

"Lousy fucking buses," Ernie cursed.

"Lousy fucking business," Kirkland stated as the first of the black plastic bags was carried out of the mangled bus.

Ernie sat in his jeep, one leg hanging to the ground, the clipboard stuck in the steering wheel. Another dark sack was hurried to the coroner's van; the attendant held up two fingers for Ernie to see. He nodded and made two more marks at the top of his report, counted quickly to find that there were sixty-three scratches and the men still hadn't finished with their task.

Ernie felt an arm lean on his shoulder; he looked up to see Logan staring at the carnage.

"Jesus." Logan whistled. "Pedroza?"

"Again . . ." Ernie said wearily.

"How many?"

"Sixty-three—so far."

"All green cards?"

"I guess so. I'm not about to dig in there and find out."

Logan withdrew his arm from Ernie's shoulder and went forward to inspect the scene. Ernie glanced at his wristwatch. It was about five; the first of the Pedroza buses would be rolling into the border crossing at Del Amo. Nervous women would be waiting at the border while their children raced about. He was certain the Mexican community was now aware there would be one bus missing this fateful evening The Mexican border guards would be deluged with questions from anxious wives and relatives, loved ones who'd sent their men off before dawn, unaware whether they were headed north, east, or west. That the bus from Diamond, Texas, met with disaster had little meaning for them except to warn them, to raise their fears, to send them searching frantically through each arriving busload. Mothers, wives, and sweethearts of the Diamond run would wait well into the night, stoic now, tired, hungry children clutching their skirts, mouths working silently in prayer to some favorite saint.

Other families would still not be aware that their husbands or sons slept in dark plastic bags at some shed in Moss County, for many of them came by yet another bus, which brought them from as far inland as a hundred miles. These men might not be reported missing for two to three days.

One of the coroner's men held up a finger, then a half finger. Ernie made a mark on the report for the one man, grew angry with himself when he found he was unable to mark a half man. The thought of the half man made him snatch up the clipboard and fling it onto the empty seat. Suddenly he wished for Pedroza's face to be near so that he could reach out and smash it. He wanted to feel the man's nose crunch under the hammer of his fist. He wanted to feel the satisfaction of cartilage crackling into tiny pieces from the fury of his blows. He wanted satisfaction for these half bodies that could not defend themselves against the Pedrozas of the world.

"That's a hell of a mess, old sport," Logan said.

Ernie jerked the clipboard across the jeep and stuck it in Logan's chest. "You finish this!" he hissed as he kicked the jeep to life and backed quickly away from the scene. He left Logan standing, bewildered, with the clipboard in his hands.

Ernie drove rapidly, forcing a hole in traffic with his insistent horn, racing to the south and the Rio Grande. Silently he sped across the desert, punching the gas to the floor for more speed, savagely jamming the pedal, insistent on putting the area behind him. After he had gone several miles, when the sounds of the train were far gone, he reached forward and shut off the ignition. The jeep coasted slowly to a halt, and he closed his eyes against the day.

He had always thought the bureau ideally suited his small ambition. He had never asked for much, content to be alone in section seven, able to work without supervision, satisfied with Logan's companionship. But this horrible day had begun with the fence, which had abruptly shattered his plan for the future, as insignificant and simple as it was. Brook's angry tirade against Logan's failure to report in, the train wreck, the knowledge that the Pedrozas of the world were winning made everything wrong with his life.

Today the bureau itself seemed a monument to poverty. Ernie's own actions seemed limited to preventing the poor from reaching the gold of America. The Company, as Logan and Wheeler called themselves, were digging holes in the surf, and each wave rapidly filled their efforts. Digging was no longer sufficient, the tide was moving relentlessly against them. He felt he was spitting into

35

the desert to extinguish the heat. It all seemed so suddenly useless. Even his own life was now meaningless and limited, his working expectancy dreadfully shortened.

Ernie remembered his mother and father, their own struggles for a place in America. Relegated to the ghettos of poverty, his parents had capitulated to the system, shorn of hope even for their children. It had been a bitter moment of recognition for him, a staggering ruthless actuality, that his parents had given up hope for any of them. That was when he'd made his escape, abandoning them to their small, constricting world. Today he could understand this determination to run the border and vanish in the faceless crowds of the city. He alone, with the possible exception of Logan, knew what the border represented, that invisible line between parents and children, the distance between hope and despair that separated the strong and daring from the old and weak. A future free of parental poverty, of inherited disappointments, crippling pride.

Yet he had tracked them, turned them away. He saw the hurt in their eyes, the desperation. He also knew he would see them again, that they would be back with their quiet persistence. The lines at the border were long, and someday they would make it. He was standing guard with a net to catch the wind, and it was proving to be futile.

3

The Rio Grande Saloon was so dark they could barely see their drinks. The walls of the establishment were draped with serapes and sombreros, while the horned trophies of long-horned steers pierced the shafts of light, their deadly wide-spaced tips thrust forward to impale the smoke. The rough-hewn walls were patterned with a thousand long-since-forgotten brands.

Ellen complained, "My arm is sunburned from sitting in that damn car!" She held it aloft for all to see, trying to catch it in the glow of their table lamp.

Ernie leaned forward, inspected it closely before kissing it. "Just to make it well," he crooned across the table.

She had mellowed with the first drinks. The surly façade of the desert Ellen was gone, causing Ernie to cuddle close.

Logan had his own leg pressed against Emily's, admiring her scrubbed, glowing face, appreciative of Ellen's sudden sweetness. Emily's breasts were hidden by a thin cotton blouse, but their dampness lingered in his mind. "It's a good thing you didn't get burned somewhere else," he told Ellen, glancing at the front of her sweater

"I once got sunburned in a car," Ernie said, leaning against Ellen as he took a healthy swallow of Jack Daniel's. "One time I was driving from El Paso to San Antonio, five hundred and eighty-two miles of the hottest goddamn driving I ever did see! Had myself this convertible. You remember that, Bob, that sixty-five Cadillac, sweetest damn car you ever did see! Had the top down. Not too smart, right? Had my shirt off. But it was so damn hot I even took off my pants and shorts. There I was, stark naked at one hundred miles an hour. The wind was in my face. I was getting a little of Ol' Sol's rays. Well . . . somewhere between Fort Stockton and Sheffield . . . I got the goddamnedest burn you ever did see! And I don't have to tell you where, do I?" Ernie pointed dramatically to his groin, nodding in appreciation as the girls winced. "Hell! I ain't *never* been burned like that! Never! I put that ol' top back up real quick and it still wouldn't stop stinging! I mean, it was so sore I didn't think I could take it for one more minute! So I pulled into this li'l ol' pump and grocery store, so damn sore I couldn't even get my pants back on!"

The girls had covered their mouths with their hands, their eyes wide in anticipation.

"I wrapped this T-shirt around me, to hide my private parts—so help me God, this is the truth—and I went into the store like that!"

The girls were beginning to laugh and Ernie had to grab Ellen's arm for silence. "This ol' girl was working there. 'Ma'am,' I said, 'I got troubles!' Now, this ol' lady was in her sixties, and there being no other way for me to explain it, I just upped and dropped that T-shirt. 'What can you give me for this?' I said. Well . . . she looks like some ol' hog that's been hit between the eyes. Her mouth fell open and she just stared at it. Then she left and went into the back room, was gone a hell of a long time. I figured she was getting something for it. Then she comes out with this other little ol' lady and says, 'We'll give you seventy dollars and half the store.' "

Logan shook his head in disappointment. He'd allowed himself to be suckered into one of the oldest stories in the world. Despite this, he began to laugh. The girls had tears in their eyes and he knew Ernie was now unstoppable.

Logan's day had begun so badly, yet turned about so quickly that he was still slightly bewildered by the events. He'd completed the bus report, counted all the victims and parts and numbered the plastic sacks before he realized that Ernie had still not returned. Logan trailed the jeep out into the desert to find Ernie sitting alone in his vehicle. Logan rolled to a stop beside his friend, sensing the despair and anger before he spoke. "What's up?"

"Nothing," Ernie replied.

"Oh, I thought maybe you were a little down. . . ."

"I guess I am. . . ."

"The girls are waiting for us tonight in Durbin. . . . We've got a sure thing, Ern."

"Swell." Ernie sighed.

Logan felt the peace and quiet light of day's end on his face. He saw the sun grasping at the horizon as it bathed the sand in orange flames. "You mad 'cause I was gone so long?"

"No. . . ."

"You're mad because I forgot your lunch. . . ."

"It doesn't matter." Ernie shrugged.

"I found some money, Ern," Logan said aloud to the sunset. "I found so damn much money I still can't believe it. . . ."

Unimpressed, Ernie mumbled, "That's nice. . . ."

"There's a body . . . in the Merida wash. It must have been there for years. There was this box of money—tens—twenties—more than I've ever seen in my life. . . ."

Ernie had his head cocked to one side, staring at Logan with sudden interest. "What the hell you talking about?"

"Money." Logan laughed in disbelief. "Money, Ern . . . more goddamn money than you've ever seen. Thousands . . . maybe hundreds of thousands sitting there in the wash. . . . *That's* what took me so long." Logan threw his head back and laughed in a short burst of relief. "There was so damn much of it that I didn't report it . . . I kept it . . . it's hidden in the wash . . . I didn't know what to do, so I buried the body again and hid the jeep . . . I needed time to think."

"You been sipping?" Ernie demanded.

"No!" Logan said indignantly. "I found us a fucking fortune and you ask if I've been drinking?"

"Yes! I think you've been drinking!" Ernie shouted.

He had spent the better part of an hour telling Ernie about his discovery. Speaking quietly, calmly until Ernie was convinced there was something to the story, though he wasn't sure exactly what.

It had lifted Ernie out of his depression at the day's events, whisked them through the evening to the back booth at the Rio Grande Saloon, where Ernie held his hand in the air, demanding the girl's attention.

"Y'know, I was in here one time when this ol' drunk came in. Man, he was really soused, y'know." Ernie waved the laughing girls silent. "The drunk came staggering in, bumping into tables, knocking over drinks until Dick, the bartender, jumped over the bar to give him the old heave-ho. But this drunk says"—Ernie crossed his eyes, screwed his mouth into a drunken scowl—" 'I gotta go to the baffroom!'

"Dick tells the fella, 'You get your ass back there and when you're done, you get the hell outta here!'

"So I'm sitting at the bar, minding my own business, everybody's forgotten about the drunk by now. Then I hear this groan, *'aahhh.'* Everybody looks around, then we hear it again. *'Aaaaahhhh!'* Then we remember the drunk. Dick and I rush back to the john and Dick throws open the door and says, 'What the hell's going on here? I told you to do your business, then get the hell outta here! You're scaring all my customers away!' The old drunk says, 'I'm trying . . . I'm trying . . . but every time I go to flush this thing something crushes my nuts!' 'No wonder, you dumb bastard!' Dick yells. 'You're sitting on the mop bucket!' "

Ellen threw a hand to her mouth. She tried to laugh and

swallow her margarita at the same time. She choked, laughed, coughed, beat at Ernie with her free hand to make him stop. He slid an arm about her and began to pat her back gently.

Emily collapsed against the front of Logan's cowboy shirt. He threw his arm around her shoulders as she roared against his chest. Logan saw that both girls were in their arms and sent a wink of victory across to Ernie.

Ernie laughed. "Isn't this better than sitting out there in some ol' car?"

Emily cried, "Is he always like this?"

Logan looked at Ernie nuzzling Ellen's hair, remembered the bus, the money, and skeleton in the wash. He thought of Ernie sitting alone in the jeep on the desert, of the propping up it had taken to bolster Wheeler's sagging morale. "Yes, ma'am, he's always like this," he replied.

"I won't be able to eat," Ellen wheezed, "if he keeps these stories up," pinching her lips between her teeth to stop the laughter.

"Another time," Ernie shouted above their feeble protests, "another time I was in here and Dick says to me, 'See that fella down the bar? Well, he's been drinking beer since I opened at seven this morning and he hasn't been to the john once.' I looked at my watch and it was after nine at night! So I says to him, 'You've got to be kidding.' 'Nope,' he says, 'hasn't gone one time!'

"So I watch this guy for a couple of hours, and Dick ain't lying! I mean, I watch this guy sockin' them beers away until midnight. Then all of a sudden the guy freezes, a beer at his mouth. He sets the glass down real slow and walks kinda funnylike toward the front door. He opens it, stands there a moment, and then unzips his pants. Dick yells to him. 'You can't pee there!' The old guy looks back at us and says, 'I ain't gonna pee here. I'm gonna pee waaaay over there.' "

Ellen beat weakly against Ernie's chest. "Stop!" she demanded of him as she clutched her breast in helpless laughter.

Emily's body shook against Logan as she cried, "Oh . . . oh," repeatedly only to start laughing uncontrollably all over again.

Logan caught Ernie's bright, drunken grin. He nodded knowingly. The day had taken an abrupt about-face for them, and they understood without saying a word that the evening had just been decided.

"Let's order." Logan smiled.

Logan slept all the way to the checkpoint. He stumbled from the car somewhere between Durbin and Stone Hill, his pained eyes closed against the brilliant morning sun. Ernie set up the portable stop signs for the traffic checkpoint before he took the bureau sedan down the road to post the warning markers. He left Logan clutching a stop sign for support.

Logan never understood how his partner could consume such quantities of liquor and be so fresh the next morning. For Logan each morning was a tortuous struggle to come back to the living. It sometimes took a few hours just to clear his head and shake the evil taste from his mouth. Logan was standing by the side of the road trying to relieve himself when Ernie returned and said they were ready for business.

Ernie took up a position next to Logan and sent his own stream to the dry sand. "Did something happen last night that I don't know about?" Ernie asked.

That was another difference between them. Logan could drink most of the night and never lose consciousness, whereas Ernie fell quick victim to the effects of the alcohol. "Like what?" Logan mumbled as he tried to find the ridges in his teeth with the tip of his tongue.

"I just had a feeling you creeped me last night."

Logan flipped himself inside his trousers. "Would I do a thing like that to you, old sport?"

"I got the distinct impression that I reached out to pat a smooth little ol' tummy and felt your hairy ass instead."

"Imagination, sport, imagination." Logan adjusted the sunglasses on the bridge of his nose. He smiled as the world became a tolerable squint.

"No . . ." Ernie insisted as he patted his green worsted trousers smooth in front. "I remember it distinctly. I opened my eyes at one time and you were humping Ellen."

Logan lifted the hat, held it just high enough to let his hand run through his hair. "Now that you mention it . . . I'm sure that you're right." He saw Emily, her legs drawn up and parted, her head against the pillow as she slept. He saw Ellen, Ernie's dark head against her shoulder as he struggled drunkenly with the words to a song. He remembered Ellen's arm coming up, the hand caressing his own face, her fingers running across his lips as she beckoned him to fill the vacancy between her own legs. Logan had slipped from Emily to Ellen, riding the other girl slowly at first while Ernie incoherently crooned. Then Ernie's hand came to his ass and patted it reassuringly, prompting Logan to batter the smiling girl beneath him. Ellen moaned loudly, squeezing the two male heads to her breast as she bucked up to meet Logan. He remembered hearing Ernie's muffled singing as he lay exhausted on the moaning girl's body.

"Yep," Logan confessed, "I think you're right, old sport." He grinned foolishly as the first car appeared in the distance.

Traffic checkpoints were a familiar sight along the border highways. The Immigration Service sprung them suddenly some sixty to one hundred miles inland of the border to catch those aliens who'd managed to make it across the Rio Grande undetected.

Early-morning traffic consisted of local farmers, tourists making the run to El Paso, and aliens with green work cards hurrying to their assignments. In late afternoon the traffic would change. Vacationing boaters would be leaving the nearby lake; Air Force personnel would be out on liberty.

The patrolmen usually ignored the boats and trailers, waving the blue-uniformed young men through the checkpoint, their eyes keyed for the dark complexion of the wetback.

Logan and Ernie traded off constantly, one taking the passenger side of the vehicle while the other handled the driver. They knew what they were looking for and exactly how to find it. They knew without speaking if an approaching auto was suspect. A quick glance at the weight over the rear tires tipped them to additional trunkloads. A car with six green-carded nationals might also reveal two without papers hidden under the backseat. Two or three Mexicans alone in a car made it suspect, for their autos seldom traveled half loaded.

By noon they'd taken seven illegal aliens. Two had been hidden in trunks, two in false compartments in trunks, one slung underneath the auto in a makeshift sling, one hidden under a rear seat, and another balanced precariously above the engine of a car. A bureau van was dispatched from Del Amo to return them to the border. By then the first of the pleasure boats were working their way down the highway. Fishermen, water-skiers, and power boats were waved quickly through the checkpoint, given just a quick glance as they went past.

While they lunched on roast beef sandwiches picked up from a diner near Durbin, Logan drew the size of the money box on the ground, and they guessed excitedly at the amount hidden inside. Between cars, they returned to their drawing, each man staring silently at the marks on the ground. Each man analyzing over and over again how his share would be spent. An approaching auto dragged them back to reality. The auto dispatched, they would return to the shade of the Chevrolet sedan and count the bills piled within scratched lines measuring three feet by two feet by one foot deep.

They were interrupted by the air brakes of a large tank truck as it slowed, then crawled to the stop signs. Ernie took the driver's side of the rig while Logan crossed in front of the large bumper and worked his way down the shaded side. Logan rapped the shell with his ring, hearing Ernie's answering taps from the far side. They tapped their way to the rear and met at the back bumper. There was talk of a new device that could be attached to any vehicle to measure airwave vibrations, heartbeats, and muscular movements. It would tell agents within fifteen seconds whether a person was hidden aboard the vehicle. Logan and Wheeler didn't have this gadget; few areas did, as it was still experimental. The two patrolmen relied on instinct.

"It doesn't sound right," Logan said. "What do you think?"

Ernie gave him a slight nod of agreement. "Hey, boss!" he called to the driver, waving the man to join them at the rear.

The man emerged slowly, swinging to the ground with practiced ease.

"What do we have here?" Ernie asked the man.

The man shrugged. "Water."

The two patrolmen gave the driver a long moment of silence. Sweat popped out on the man's forehead and he was forced to look away. Ernie went to the large rear valve. "Open it," he ordered.

The driver was all too eager to spin the large handle, sending a stream of water splashing on the hot asphalt. Logan climbed atop the fender, the ring tapping incessantly. He loosened the rear hatch and slipped the flash-

45

light from his belt holder. The cover was thrown back; the beam played inside. Frightened eyes ducked the light. *"La Migra!"* several called in fear. *"La patrulla!"* someone whispered.

"Afuera!" Logan called down as he pulled the magnum from his belt. (Come out of there!)

The splashing of bodies scurrying about in confusion echoed up through the open hatchway. *"Apúrense!"* he called down. (Hurry up!)

A young man in his mid-twenties emerged first, his eyes shut against the bright sunlight.

"Afuera, las manos en la cabeza!" Logan shouted, rapping the butt against the tanker's side. (Come out with your hands on top of your head!) He beat the shell loudly, creating a frightful sound that echoed inside, sending the men scrambling for the hold.

"Vámonos!" Logan announced: (Let's go!)

Slowly they emerged, frightened, pathetic soaking-wet creatures Logan could barely stand to look at. Some were weak, others revived by the fresh air; two fainted dead away once their feet touched solid ground.

"Los veo!" he said, shining his light inside and calling to the remaining aliens. (I see you!) The stench inside the metal canister was unbearable, the heat killing. Logan watched as the last damp man slid to the ground. Logan kept the revolver trained on the twenty-four men while he searched the foul-smelling water for yet another alien. When he was satisfied the tanker was empty, he jumped to the ground.

The men stood in a long erratic line, hands on top of their heads, weaving uncontrollably from the bouncing of the truck. Another man fainted; his companions, too fearful to extend a hand, let him fall face first into the hot sand. Logan waved them to separate. Ernie came forward, his weapon drawn, and began to pat the men down. As each man was frisked, he was seated in the shade of the truck. Logan watched the men carefully, noting that the driver had his hands manacled behind his back and lay face down on the shoulder of the highway.

The aliens were all male, between sixteen and forty-five, wet and hungry, scared silent by the uniforms and weapons, shivering from fright in the 100-degree heat. Logan waved the weapon down the line, ignoring Ernie's methodical search. He realized they had been inside the truck for days; the stench would have been impossible to acquire in just a single day. The water had been chest deep, and he marveled that none of them were dead. But they were a hardy people. People everywhere were hardy, tough people. The Montagnards of Vietnam's central highlands had been hardy people. They, too, had stood shivering with fright during the searches of the villages. Logan remembered that only the clothes were different. Whether it be Rhade tribesmen or villagers outside of Ban Me Thout, they had all stood warily alarmed at what the Green Berets might do with them.

"Cuánto tiempo hace que comieron?" Logan asked the group. (When was the last time you were fed?)

The frightened men looked to one another in surprise. "Two days," one of them volunteered.

Logan pinched his lips together to hide his anger. Ernie responded by jerking the truck driver to his feet. "Transporting illegal aliens is a federal offense, friend. If there was a law against keeping these people in water to their armpits for two days, I'd hit you with that one, too. If there was a law against treating people like animals, you can bet your ass I'd throw that one at you, too!" Ernie sent the man toward the Immigration sedan with his foot. Ernie opened the door, and just as the man was about to duck his head, Ernie slammed the man against the top of the car. Logan could hear the crack of the man's nose from across the highway.

The driver tucked his face against his shoulder, trying

vainly to stem the flow of blood from the crooked nose. Ernie shoved the moaning driver inside, warning, "You'd better not get blood on that upholstery, friend!"

From the trunk of the sedan came a long chain with handcuffs attached, which Ernie brought to the group. Logan held the magnum loosely to the ground as each man was joined by one wrist to the chain.

Following a call to Del Amo, the truck was moved off the highway, the aliens seated comfortably in its shade, stoically awaiting the authorities and the long ride back to the border.

Ernie brought both canteens and two remaining beef sandwiches. He passed the canteens to both ends, looked at the two sandwiches in his hands, and said to Logan, "Where's that guy that does the magic act with the loaves and fishes? We could sure use him now." Ernie shrugged, passing one sandwich to each end. "One bite," he apologized, "there is no more for a while."

"Did you tell them to send us some food?" Logan said.

"Yeah. I told the dispatcher, and Brook came on the line two seconds later and told me we're not running a catering service."

The sandwiches never reached the men in the middle; twenty-four men sharing two sandwiches left over a dozen without a single bite.

"I'm sorry that there isn't more," Logan told the men sitting before him. "How much did you pay that coyote?"

"Two hundred and twenty-five dollars," one of them answered.

"American dollars," said another.

"Where did you cross the border?"

"Quemado."

"When?"

"Three days."

"Why have you been in the truck two days—"

"Three days," one of them interrupted. "Two days for some, three days for others."

"Why three days?" Logan asked. "Quemado is less than a hundred miles from here."

"The truck"—one of the men spat at the vehicle behind him, tossing his long dark hair as he did so—"it break."

"Ah, the truck broke down and you had to stay inside until it was fixed. You couldn't be seen?"

"Yes. . . ."

"How did you cross the border at Quemado?"

No one offered an answer.

"Did you cross in the truck?" Ernie asked, knowing they would never divulge their method. It had been successful once and it would be successful on their next attempt.

"No . . ." one of them replied.

"Was there another man beside this one, the coyote?" Logan asked.

"No. . . ."

"Is this the man you paid?" Ernie asked.

"Yes. . ." one of the older men answered.

"But he has no money," Ernie explained. "What did he do with the money?"

The men shrugged in wonder.

"If he has the money, I would give it back to you," Ernie told them, leaning forward on one knee.

The men only shrugged again.

"That's the worst part of it," Logan whispered in English. "They lose all the way down the line." He shook his head in anger as he shot a look at the driver in the bureau's sedan. "Where were they taking you?" Logan continued.

"Work!" one of them snapped irritably, causing the others to grin slightly.

"Where is this work?" Logan persisted.

One of the men swung his head in the direction of the desert.

Ernie asked the group, "Did they promise you good pay?"

"More than one hundred dollars each week," one of the young men said proudly.

Logan shook his head sadly for the men to see. "That is not true. They will steal your money. The coyote will come back," he told them. "He will ask for more money from you or he will tell *la Migra*. Then what will you do? You will pay him, believe me. They will steal your money. There will be little to send home. The employer will cheat you of your hard-earned wages, and who will you turn to? You cannot call the police! You will pay taxes but you will not be able to claim the benefits. What they tell you is *lies!* They will leave you nothing except the hard work and just a little money."

"That's right," Ernie said in disgust, "tell them how bad it is. Maybe you won't see them again for a whole week. Save your breath."

Logan glanced down the long line of men. They were curiously unafraid now. They stared at him with quiet resignation. They understood all that he had told them but seemed indifferent to their fate. Their lot was to storm the borders, the patrolman's lot, to turn them back. Logan knew they both understood this. There was nothing else for him to say. He let his gaze fall to the ground, snatched up a dried twig, tossed it in his hand before he slowly rose and followed Ernie to the bureau sedan.

The driver's eyes had begun to close and the blood caked his wide mustache. An approaching car interrupted their questioning. Logan checked the auto through quickly, then climbed into the front seat of the bureau sedan. He sorted through the truck's papers as Ernie slid half into the front seat, his body twisted across the cushion facing the bloodied driver.

"Don't I know you?" Ernie demanded of the man.

The frightened driver cried, "No!"

"My friend wants to kick the shit outta you," Ernie explained to the man, a smile breaking across his face. "Can you understand me?"

The man nodded nervously.

"But I told my friend it does no good. You're an animal. You don't give a fuck about your own people. Those people could have been dead in there, and it wouldn't have meant a fuck to you. No one can talk to your kind of garbage because you have no feelings!" Ernie continued to grin; his hand went to the revolver and slipped it from its case. He raised it over the back of the front seat, extending his arm until the magnum was poised against the end of the twisted bloody nose. The driver backed as far away as possible, but the muzzle painfully followed his every move.

"Y'see," Ernie hissed, the smile turning to a savage snarl, "we can't talk to animals. You have to shoot an animal. You understand that, don't you, friend?"

The driver couldn't move his head; the barrel had him pinned painfully in place. He tried to signal with his terror-filled eyes.

"You take their money and you give them *nothing! Nothing!* You help *no one!* You *take!* You give *nothing!* The world will be a better place without you motherfuckers!" Ernie cocked the hammer.

"Ah!" the man screamed, squeezing his eyes shut.

"I'm going to blow your fucking head off!"

Logan saw the tears spring from the man's clenched eyes. "Leave him alone," he said firmly.

Ernie ignored his partner. "I want you to run, motherfucker!"

"No!" the man cried.

"Run!"

"No!"

"Run, you scuzzy bastard, or I'll kill you right here in the car!"

"Leave him alone," Logan insisted. "He won't ever come back."

"He'll be back!" Ernie yelled. "He'll be back tomorrow! They *always* come back!"

"No, he won't," Logan offered. He turned in the seat to face the man. "Will you?" he asked.

"No!" the man cried desperately. "I won't ever come back!"

"We gotta kill him!" Ernie insisted.

Logan shook it off. "I don't think we'll ever see him again."

"You'll never see me again!" the man agreed. "I promise! I give you my word!"

A loud sigh escaped Ernie's lips as the hammer came back slowly into place. The driver blinked his eyes; the Adam's apple bobbed. Ernie slid the weapon back to the front seat. "If I ever see you again, you bastard, I'm going to kill you on the spot. You understand me, friend?"

The man nodded his head gratefully.

Ernie drew the revolver into the holster. He gave Logan a wink, then slipped down low to the seat. "God . . . I want to see that box," he mumbled.

Logan tipped the hat over his eyes as he peered down the deserted highway, a smile breaking across his lips.

4

"Well, no goddamned skeleton drove that jeep down in the wash!" Ernie said that night from the back booth of Alicia's. The Quemado establishment had been their nighttime haunt for the six years they had been partners. The back booth was immediately cleared whenever they entered. The table was hurriedly dressed with a bottle of tequila, salt, quartered limes, and a container of hot sauce that Ernie spooned directly to his mouth. Each spoonful was followed by the stamping of feet, loud gasping cries of delight, and tequila chasers.

"It's been there a while," Logan agreed as he downed his tequila, chasing it with his mouth applied to the salt on the back of his hand. The mariachi band fought the patrons for attention, singing loudly above the noisy airmen and squealing hostesses.

Ernie pursed his lips, blowing the fire of the sauce about the booth as he asked, "How long do you think it's been there?"

Ernie had broached the same question a dozen times since Logan had informed him of his find. In exasperation he said, "Shit, Ern, I don't know! I didn't do an autopsy on the guy! Hell, I didn't even want to touch him!"

Ernie thought for a moment, stirring the contents of the bowl. "You shouldn't have left the money there. . . ."

"What the hell was I *supposed* to do? I couldn't take it to the bus wreck! I wasn't even sure you'd still be at the marker! I couldn't drive around with that damn box on the back of my jeep!"

"You should have hidden it." Ernie pouted, the liquor and fire already reaching his brain.

"I *did* hide it!"

Suddenly frightened, Ernie whispered, "Suppose somebody finds it."

"Nobody's found it yet!"

"Somebody might find it while we're sitting here!"

"Ernie . . . Jesus Christ . . . you're driving me crazy! It's been there for *years!*"

Ernie thought about this as one of Alicia's girls passed the booth dragging a young airman up the stairs by his belt. Ernie smiled at the young Mexican girl, his mind envisioning the sensual delights awaiting the airman. He knew all the girls, had sampled their wares, inspected their bodies, until they all ran together into flashing eyes and teeth and the overpowering smell of lime and hot sauce. He watched them disappear up the stairs, then turned back to Logan to ask, "How big is that box again?"

Logan caught himself measuring it out on the table. He withdrew his hands quickly. "Big enough," he said.

Ernie undertook the ritual of the tequila, with the lime, the liquid, and the salt. He made a wry face, then leaned back, a crooked grin splashing drunkenly across his face. "I ain't never stole nothing before—not really. We should have told the sheriff about it."

"Absolutely," Logan agreed.

"I mean . . . that's his job. . . ."

"Exactly!"

"We could get our ass in a sling if we kept that money. . . ."

"We could get thrown off the patrol."

"A man would be a fool to let a few thousand dollars tempt him like that—"

"Sure . . . what's a few hundred thousand dollars anyway?"

"A guy would be a fool to even consider it," Ernie reasoned aloud.

"You're absolutely right, Ern. That's what I *like* about you, when you're right, you're right."

"I mean—sheeeeeit—throw away a career for a few . . . measly . . . how much do you think?"

"Hundreds of thousands of dollars."

"Throw it all away for a few measly . . . hundreds of thousands of dollars. It doesn't make any sense."

"What would we get out of it anyway? A lifetime of what? So we bring it down here to Mexico, say . . . So we run a small whorehouse like Alicia's here . . . or one in Mulegé or La Paz. . . ."

"Or Mexico City."

"Or Mexico City . . . yes . . . I mean . . . it's stupid to even *think* of it."

"You know, sport," Logan said, leaning close, "I knew you would help me reason this out."

Ernie fell against the table, his face just inches away from Logan's as he asked, "So what are we going to do with all that money?"

Logan enjoyed Ernie when he was like this, a large child who could be easily led. "First?"

"Yeah. . . ." Ernie giggled. "What are we going to do with it first?"

"First we move the money away from the body, someplace where we can reach it whenever we want it. The next thing we do is find out if the money's clean. That's the most important part. Once we know that, we can tell Brook to shove this job up his ass—and his electronic goddamn fence with it."

"Sideways!" Ernie exclaimed excitedly, his dark brown eyes swimming from the tequila, his head nodding rapidly in agreement.

Logan grinned. "Sideways."

"But when do I get to see it?" Ernie abruptly demanded. "I've never seen it, you know."

"Tomorrow we should be back on patrol in section seven. We'll see it tomorrow."

"Tomorrow?" Ernie asked.

"Tomorrow, old sport, tomorrow."

"Oh, Jesus . . ." Ernie whispered in rapture until a sad distant look clouded his gaze. "Did I ever tell you . . . we never had nothing . . . my whole family never had a goddamned thing, Bob. All my life was like that, but I was the oldest. There are no hand-me-downs for the oldest. When this job came along, I was happy for the first time in my life. I was my own boss out there in that jeep—a sign that someone crossed the border was all the excitement I needed. . . . I mean, that's not too much to ask for, is it? Did I ask for so much, Bob? Why did they have to tell me about that goddamned fence? Why did they tell me I'd have to spend the rest of my life in some goddamned room waiting for a red light to come on somewhere?" Ernie rolled pained eyes to the smoke-dark ceiling. "I can't do it!" he cried. "My life don't amount to a hell of a lot—but, damn it, it's mine! I'm at rock bottom and it took me all of my life to get here!"

"I know what you mean, sport," Logan said softly.

"Do you know what that money means to me? To us? I mean . . . this is it! The jackpot! The whiz-bang ending my folks used to dream about! I mean . . . it's ours and nobody can tell us what to do anymore!"

"I feel the same way, sport."

Ernie fastened Logan with a quizzical expression. "You're not lying to me, are you?"

Before Logan could answer, the questioning gaze became a withering stare as Ernie leaned in close. "If you're lying to me about that money, Logan . . . so help me God . . . you're my dearest friend . . . my only friend . . . but so help me God . . . I'll kill you."

56

Logan appraised his partner calmly. "The money's there, old sport."

Ernie closed his eyes gratefully, the air escaping in a quiet hush.

Logan knew little of Ernie's previous life, little of his parents. More than six years before, they'd been assigned as partners. Wheeler had been on patrol in section seven almost two years; it was Logan's first day in the sector. Logan drew an alien in the flat known as Cabazón while Ernie drew two in the rugged Borazo Canyon area. Logan collared his man almost immediately, handcuffed him in the rear of the jeep, and decided to assist Wheeler at Borazo Canyon. He drove north to the mouth of the canyon, where he met the two unsuspecting aliens sweeping up the difficult terrain. Having one pair of handcuffs, he forced his first man to hug Wheeler's suspects before he locked the man's wrists about the waist of his two companions. Logan was calmly smoking a cigarette with the three suspects when Ernie arrived up the canyon an hour later. From that silent moment of confrontation, they'd become friends.

In the six years that followed, the bond grew rapidly. They shared the desert, death, and good times equally. They were two men with no past, no future except the present. Willing to accept each other for what they were. Logan felt it was this ready acceptance that bound them so closely. The aliens, the very nature of the patrol's existence, were faceless men also, with no past or future, only the present. It was an unwritten rule between them, Ask no questions; never question the future of themselves or their quarry.

For Logan, Ernie was closer than any brother he might have had or wished for. It was a closer bond than Logan had found in the service. In Nam there had always been that doubt of someone being snatched unexpectedly away. Here there were dangers, equally shared, tolerated but in control. There were no mines to shatter a friendship, few unseen hazards. Six years of daily companionship and nightly drunken revelry south of the border had married them, more surely than any vow. They'd become so attuned to each other's thinking that the signs they passed between them went unnoticed by others.

The pilot, Ewing, a full-time cynic, part-time criminologist and psychiatrist, once told Logan that the fact that he and Wheeler screwed together, was a further sign of their love for each other. Each time they penetrated a girl, they were penetrating each other. Each amorous adventure was a renewal of their own love. Logan's answer to this was to laugh as loud and as hard as possible. Later he wondered if it were possibly true.

The mariachi band had moved to their table. Rodolfo, the leader of the group, led the musicians into "El Rancho Grande," Ernie's favorite number. The black-outfitted, silver-trimmed minstrels bowed gratefully when Ernie stuck a bill into the belt hidden by each portly stomach. They laughed loudly when he 'sang *"aiiii yiiii"* at all the breaks, repeating the number half a dozen times before other Americans crowded to the booth to join Ernie's drunken chorus. Alicia herself slid next to Logan as all the attention of the club centered on the two drunken patrolmen.

Ewing's early-morning flight cut a sign, a single pair of prints, near the Sierra wash of section seven.

"Jesus H. Christ!" Ernie screamed when they were alone. "I ain't *never* gonna see that money!"

"Let's find the guy," Logan said, "and get Brook off our backs. Then we can double back and pick up the money."

Ernie slammed the jeep into low, cried, "Sheeeit!" as he disappeared in the dust.

Logan lit a cigarette, waiting for the cloud to settle

before he followed. They'd crossed into Texas at six that morning, going straight to the squad room, where they showered, shaved, and slipped into clean uniforms. The temperature was already in the eighties and it was still several hours until the brunt of the sun would be felt. Weather reports predicted an unusually warm day.

Logan poured himself a cup of coffee as he watched Ernie's dust cloud race across the desert floor. His partner had driven them to the border singing "If I Were a Rich Man" while Logan tried vainly to pull all his faculties together for the morning meeting. Logan stuck the stainless-steel thermos between the seats, let out the clutch smoothly as he balanced the cup and cigarette with one hand. The area along the drag road was smooth and soft. To the south he could see the trees lining the Rio Grande, some seven miles away. To the north, the rising faces of the different mesas, split occasionally by a large wash that carried rainwater south.

The area was clear of brush of any kind. One had to drive north for several miles before any chaparral, squawbush, or scrubs appeared. Twenty miles to the west, in the direction they were headed, one could see sotol groupings and squawbush or creosote. The area in between was arid and hot as a griddle by noon.

Section seven was by far the most desolate sector under the bureau's jurisdiction. Older patrolmen avoided it, passing its control to junior members of the service. It had been Ernie's first assignment out of the Del Amo office. Logan had been the fifth partner Wheeler had broken in in just two years. Ernie's infectious enthusiasm for the assignment communicated itself. Soon Logan could see the advantage of manning the remote outpost. The Del Amo office was so surprised to find two men who relished the detail that they pampered them in order to keep them there. Regulations were eased; morning roll calls were not mandatory. Brook even looked the other way at their drunken escapades below the border. The other patrolmen were so delighted to find two men who liked the section that they did their best to see that Logan and Wheeler were freed of the mundane details the others had to put up with. The patrolmen seldom left section seven, except to work on occasional traffic check. The other activities of the bureau were now almost foreign to them. This dedication was reaffirmed three years back when first Wheeler, then Logan, declined promotion to immigrant investigator in order to remain together in section seven. They were rewarded by being chosen for occasional loan-outs to county or state authorities in search of lost or missing people, an assignment they both enjoyed.

Ernie cut the first sign an hour later. It was a heavy footprint—a man of considerable weight. Both men sat near the sign, casually sipping their coffee as the sun climbed higher and higher. They extinguished their cigarettes, snapped off the transistor.

"I'll take it." Logan sighed. Ernie gave a brief nod, tapped the wide brim down low over his eyes as he wordlessly sent the jeep off to the north. The men had a proven system. One would track the signs from his jeep while the other would speed ahead four or five miles to intercept the track. If the point man made contact, he would radio the man to the rear. The tail tracker would leave the sign and whip ahead beyond the point man, leap-frogging another four or five miles.

If no sign was found by the new point man, then they knew their quarry was somewhere between them. The point man would then work toward the rear until they had their prey. It enabled them to cover large areas of ground in a short amount of time while the slower, moving man afoot struggled forward.

Thirty minutes later Logan received Ernie's brief "I cut a sign," telling him that his partner had found the trail far ahead. Logan swung his jeep north, found the point where Ernie had picked up the trail, and, speeding past it, continued for another three miles before he turned toward the logical path of the alien's travel.

A few minutes later Logan cut a sign and relayed this to the rear, and the men once again switched positions. Twenty-five minutes later Ernie called to the rear, "I've got him up here," and Logan went forward to serve as point man.

For forty minutes Logan crossed and recrossed the area now dotted with chaparral. When he was convinced their man had not come this far, he radioed back, "I can't find him up here."

"I've still got it," Ernie called.

"Working my way back," Logan answered. He drove slowly in a large snakelike pattern, weaving across the desert, dodging chaparral, eyes glued to the ground for any sign at all.

"Logan?"

"Yeah?"

"It's a doubleheader—our man's carrying a kid. I've just picked up two sets of tracks. . . ."

"Coming in."

Ernie was waiting by the side of his vehicle. He pointed silently to the tracks, which had begun to turn westward.

Logan bent to the ground. He'd been working the area too far to the north. "The big one's hurting," he said with grim realization. He noticed his own dark black shadow. The heat of the day was now on them.

Ernie moved a few feet ahead. "The kid's got a bum leg." His hand palmed the tiny print, his fingers feeling the short right instep. "I'll take the kid," he announced suddenly.

They kept both sets of tracks between them as they drove through the spotted brush. When the child's tracks veered suddenly away from the adult's, Ernie left his

61

jeep and ran forward on foot, his body bent toward the ground.

Logan climbed from the jeep; he found the hand marks where the man had fallen, saw the telltale signs of his struggling erect with great effort. The two sets of prints were mixed, the boy helping the adult now, the child's impressions deep in the sand, as if he were supporting the adult. A few feet away he could see the outline of the man on the ground. He could smell the fear of the boy as the child veered off to try to get help.

Logan saw Ernie's tracks on the heel of the boy; he watched Ernie's back in the distance as the patrolman zigzagged through the brush. Logan traced the drag marks of the adult as the man moved off alone into the thicket. The man was searching for shade, the child searching for help. Logan left his jeep and went into the shoulder-high chapparal. He followed the handprints and deep, stumbling knee pockets. He himself was running now, the brush slapping at his cheeks as he held his arms in front of his face for protection.

The man was almost hidden, just the legs visible from the brush pulled carefully about his head. Logan had hoped they would have been smart enough to bring water. He tumbled the brush away and pulled the dehydrated man to a sitting position. He noticed that there was no water container near the man's hands. He unslung the canteen from his shoulder, uncapped it, and sent the liquid to the dry, dust-covered lips. For a second there was no response, then the hands came alive, snatching at the container, spilling more water down the throat.

"Take it easy," Logan said as he wrested the container away.

"La patrulla . . ." the man moaned.

Logan took a deep breath and let it out slowly. "You bet your sweet ass, pal, *la patrulla.* Have I ever let one of you bastards die on me? Not on your life." Logan knew the man didn't understand a word being said, so he smiled warmly and tipped the canteen to the man's lips. "You're damn right, *la patrulla*," he whispered as the man fought frantically for each precious drop. "Your ass would be mud if it wasn't for *la patrulla*."

Logan shaded the man's face with his body as life came back to the man's eyes. "Ruiz . . ." the man cried suddenly, the dry lips trembling in horror.

"Take it easy," Logan whispered. In Spanish he said, "The patrol's going after Ruiz." In English he said to himself, *And one of the best trackers that kid's ever seen.*

Ernie was moving southward, almost sprinting now. The child was lost and swinging back toward the Rio Grande in its confusion. Ernie cursed the stupidity of child and adult for trying to negotiate the desert in the heat of the day. Three hours in the sun after the long trek across the Rio Grande invited calamity. He only hoped they'd been smart enough to bring water.

The child was lying on its chest, its cheek white with the fine desert dust, its legs spread in sleep. Ernie noted the right foot was smaller than its counterpart. Frantically he threw himself to the ground, spreading his dark shadow over the boy's upper torso. With one quick move he flipped the boy onto his back, unslung the canteen, and had the tiny neck in the palm of his hand. He dribbled water to the cracked, parched lips, watched helplessly as it ran away unnoticed, washing little wet creeks in the dusty chin. He tried once again, tipping the head back and pouring a thin stream of water directly into the mouth. The liquid ran down the corners of the lips, past the ears, and into the sand. "C'mon, Pepito . . . c'mon," he urged as he poured yet a third time. When the boy failed to respond, Ernie shook the tiny neck angrily. "Damn you, drink!" He shook the boy once again, then applied the canteen to the tiny lips. Even when it occurred to him that the boy might already be dead, Ernie refused to believe it. "God damn it!" he screamed in helpless rage as he shook the boy violently, whipping the tiny neck about. "You die on me, you little bastard, and I'll *kill* you!"

Ernie dropped the lifeless head to the sand, clasped the canteen between his knees, and began to slap the boy's face with both hands. "What the hell's a kid like you doing out here anyway?" He massaged the boy's chest with his hands, rubbing and pumping at the same time, not really sure what he was doing but demanding some sign of life. The chest was small; he could span the protruding ribs with both hands. He grabbed the skinny neck with two fingers and lifted it aloft. The other hand brought the canteen to the tiny pale lips. "You'd better drink this!" he shouted in frustration. "Drink! God damn it, drink!" He shook the head and was rewarded with a small moan. Ernie felt his own breath catch in his throat, heard his own stifled whimper as he brought the canteen urgently forward. The tiny mouth began to suck at the moisture; the small white tongue came into play. Ernie blinked rapidly to keep the swimming from his eyes. The mouth was sucking noisily at the small amounts of water being rationed out.

"You little bastard." Ernie sniffed, unexpectedly wishing he could blow his nose.

The boy's eyes opened slowly, the dust-covered lids raising in a flutter of uncertainty. The brown eyes focused on Ernie Wheeler and he saw the fear creep into them. He smiled his crooked smile as he said, "Scared shitless, aren't you, boy? . . . Well, you should be. 'Cause I'm the mean son of a bitch that's going to send you back. You got me, boy?"

The boy looked around in panic as he searched wildly for the older man. Ernie forced the child's attention back to the canteen, plying the mouth with cool water.

"Gonna take turns carrying each other across that desert, huh? Well, that's a big ol' son of a bitch out there.

Hell, you gotta be *twice* your size before you try something like that. You gotta wait at least four or five more years. . . ." Ernie abruptly realized that, should the boy try it again when he was older, he and Logan would not be there to save him. It was a disconcerting thought.

Ernie placed the boy's hands firmly around the canteen as he lifted the lad in his arms and began to follow his own tracks back to the jeep. The boy looked to be ten or eleven, small, wiry, the large brown eyes alive in the white, dusty face.

"You're a skinny little shit, you know that?" he said as he smiled down at the boy in his arms.

Logan had the man in the shade of the jeep. The man wailed continuously for the boy, Ruiz. He was the boy's father, he explained; they were all that was left of a once fairly large family. The sons and daughters had married and moved away. The man interrupted his thoughts continually to cry, "Ruiz," and gaze tearfully around the desert. Logan left the shade of the vehicle to search for Ernie; his partner had been gone far too long and he now began to fear for the boy himself. He couldn't bear to tell the man his worst thoughts, he couldn't bear to hear the man's story. The man continued to explain about the Benavides, that his name was Jorge, his son, Ruiz. That Ruiz was all he had left in the world, that there was a sister in California. Logan had to walk away a few more paces as he scouted the horizon, had to put more distance between himself and the old man's pitiful story.

When Ernie finally appeared, it was as a small speck in the distance. Logan could see the bundle in his arms and fired the jeep to meet him. The reunion between the old man and his son rendered both patrolmen pathetically helpless. There was much clutching and kissing as the old man wrapped his arms around the boy and rocked him repeatedly.

Logan had to turn away from the encounter. He went

to his jeep, withdrew two meat loaf sandwiches, and silently passed one to each of the Benavides. He watched them devour the sandwiches between wondrous caresses and praise of their good fortune.

"They're on their way to San Diego," Logan explained haltingly. "The old man has a sister who works there. . . . She has some sort of job . . . in a hospital there . . . her insurance and all. . . . She sort of promised to see that the boy has this . . . operation. . . ."

Ernie turned away abruptly. "I don't want to know. . . ."

"The boy's mother died from the flu . . . some sort of epidemic last year. . . ."

"Aw, shit," Ernie whispered.

"It's just him and the old man . . . the others are all gone. . . ."

Ernie shouted over his shoulder, "I don't want to *hear* about it!"

"Ernesto?" the boy called in Spanish. "How far is California?"

Ernie avoided the boy's eyes, throwing a hand out to the northwest as he replied, "It's a long way, Pepito. . . ."

"Ruiz," the boy corrected.

Ernie nodded, mouthing "Ruiz" silently. When he looked back to Logan, his partner was kneeling in the sand, squinting up at Ernie, his face solemn.

"You're going to take 'em to the highway," Ernie stated after a long moment of silence.

Logan dipped his head twice in confirmation.

"They'll probably get picked up in El Paso."

"I know." Logan lit a cigarette as he watched the two Mexicans. "Last night we were talking about how much the money meant to us—the chance we were getting— how lucky we were to be getting an out to all our problems. What it meant to have a new start. I couldn't help but think what a new start might mean for the boy—and his father. . . ."

Ernie glanced at the Benavides, the old man with the very young son. The old man with a quiet strength about him. A man with nothing, yet respected and loved by his son. He wished it had been the same in his family. Ernie reached into his pocket and withdrew his wallet. He passed several bills to Logan. "If they can flag down a bus, they just might make it." Logan took the money between two fingers; he looked at Ernie for a long moment, nodded, and added a few bills of his own to the pile. These he folded carefully and stuffed in the elder Benavides' shirt pocket.

"What the hell's a few bucks," Ernie reasoned aloud. "Hell, we're rich, ain't we?"

"California?" the old man asked in disbelief.

Logan shook his head. "No. San Diego," he corrected him.

"And I'm damn tired of you giving our lunch away!" Ernie shouted as the Benavideses were loaded in the jeep.

"San Diego!" Ruiz cried, hugging his father.

5

The jeep was just as Logan had left it. Sand covered the bottom half of the vehicle; cut brush hid the driver, windshield, and rear. The sun cut through a cleft in the wash, raking the dark shady area with a bolt of bright white light.

"Jesus, it's spooky," Ernie whispered as he climbed from his jeep.

"Bring your shovel," Logan called quietly as he went forward, taking a deep breath before throwing the brush aside. The partially buried skeleton was still bent over the wheel embedded in its chest; one arm extended through the broken windshield, a silent testimony to the force of impact.

Logan cleared the brush away and turned his attention to the metal money box buried in the side of the wash. He noticed that Ernie was transfixed by the skeleton, staring numbly at the white bright patch of sunlight striking the skull. "Give me a hand," he whispered as he dragged the box loose from its new home.

Ernie backed to the container, reaching blindly for the box, his attention locked to the fleshless driver with the grinning skull. "Jesus," he murmured.

Logan dragged the container to his jeep, Ernie stumbling behind the box, his wide eyes trying to take in the canyon, the jeep, and the grinning occupant.

Logan threw the money container to the hood of his vehicle. He, too, sensed the strangeness of the gully. The canyon walls were darker than he remembered, save for that blinding slash of sunlight. He had the feeling the wash had slipped to the bowels of the earth, that they were standing in an immense underground cavern far beyond the reach of sunlight. Logan thought of *King Solomon's Mines* and the film made in the mid-twenties of poor Floyd Collins buried alive in a Kentucky cave. For a brief, horrifying instant he felt as if the skull were laughing at them. That the skull knew some curse that would keep them from ever enjoying the money. That already some spell was in progress to render them as impotent as the former owner of the treasure.

Logan shook the gothic horrors clear of his head as he pried the lid free and spun Ernie to face the container. "Was I lying?"

Ernie gave an involuntary jerk before pressing close to the bills. His legs were rubbery and he tried to whistle his astonishment several times, but his lips had gone dry and no sound came forth.

Logan scooped the loose bills up in both hands and deposited them on the hood near the windshield. Then he began removing the packets of banded money. All the twenties were set on one side of the hood, all the tens piled in front of Ernie. "How many bills in a package?" he asked softly.

Ernie shook his head in dismay; he'd never dealt with money in bundles.

"Then you'd better start counting one of those packages," Logan advised him.

Ernie was extremely nervous. Several times he lost count and each time he cast a quick glance over his shoulder at the skeleton, as if he half expected the corpse to criticize his clumsiness.

In frustration, Logan told him to count the loose tens that lay on the hood while Logan counted the twenties. Several minutes later they agreed that there were one hundred bills to a package.

Ernie was beside himself. "One hundred ten-dollar bills," he mumbled repeatedly.

"One hundred twenty-dollar bills," Logan added.

Frantically they began to stack the bundles in their respective denominations. Ernie carefully stored his tens in stacks of ten until he'd accumulated thirty rows. Logan set out ten rows of two hundred and fifty bundles. Then both men hurriedly added their piles. Ernie got so flustered by the zeros that his first figure was twenty-five thousand dollars. Logan insisted that was wrong and readded Ernie's pile, arriving at two hundred and fifty thousand dollars. As Ernie watched, Logan quickly calculated the worth of the twenties. Dramatically he took the pencil from his blouse and wrote "six hundred thousand dollars" on the inside lid of the box. Both men stood there staring at all the zeros until Logan remembered the tens and reached forward to write beneath it "two hundred and fifty thousand dollars." He drew a long line below the numbers and began to add, bringing the zeros down with a snap of the wrist. Ernie counted each zero out loud. Together they whispered, "Eight hundred and fifty thousand dollars. . . ."

Ernie gasped. "Eight hundred and fifty *thousand!*"

Logan echoed, "Eight *hundred . . . thousand.*"

"I don't believe it!" Ernie cried.

Logan asked softly, "What the hell was he *doing* with all that money?"

"Who cares!" Ernie shouted as he caressed his pile.

Logan picked up a packet of tens, flipping them slowly under his thumb. "These numbers are consecutive. . . ."

"So what!"

Logan dropped the tens and reached for the twenties. He went through several of the bills before stating with conviction, "These came straight from some bank. . . ."

"Who gives a shit?" Ernie said as he began to kiss the bundles. "Love you, love you, love you. . . ."

The excitement of the zeros was rapidly waning as Logan tried to understand the meaning of the consecutive serial numbers. "Maybe somebody's looking for them. . . ."

Ernie was still enraptured by the simple existence of the money. He held a packet of bills under each eye. "Am I awake? Is this for real?"

"We have to make sure we can spend it," Logan thought aloud. "We have to be sure. . . ."

"Hell, that's simple!" Ernie explained. "We just take a few bills into town and see if they pass!"

"And if they don't?" Logan asked sharply, unexpectedly upset by Ernie's denseness. "The whole damn thing may be counterfeit! Then we'll have the Feds on us!"

"No!" Ernie cried in horror. "Don't ever say that!"

"Let's face it, sport, this may be funny money. Either way, we could be in a hell of a lot of trouble!" Logan began to restack the money in the container. "We'll keep a couple of the loose ones and run some kind of check on them."

"Hey," Ernie announced, suddenly suspicious of the packets in his hands. "How come these tens say 'silver certificate' on them but the twenties say 'Federal Reserve'?"

Logan began to thumb through the tens, going from one packet to another. "They all say that. . . . What the hell's a silver certificate?" Ernie asked fearfully. "Maybe they're no good?"

Logan shrugged helplessly. "We'll take one of each with us . . . and find out . . . if we can. . . ."

Logan stored one of each denomination in his wallet. The rest of the bills were rapidly stacked inside the container. Logan swung the metal box to the rear of his own vehicle. "Let's see if there's anything else aboard the wreck, anything to identify the guy. . . ."

71

Logan went to the skeleton, took a moment to gather his nerves before digging the rest of the torso clear.

Ernie whispered, "What are you doing?"

"We have to find out who this son of a bitch is and what he's doing here!"

Ernie looked at the shaft of sunlight raking the grinning skull. "I'm not touching him," he decided.

"I'll do it," Logan said bravely. "You check out the glove compartment and see what's in there."

Ernie bent several times toward the interior of the vehicle; each time he straightened up warily. "He's watching me. . . ."

"Dig, God damn it!"

Logan managed to clear the interior in front of the driver, using his hands to scoop the hard-packed dirt away from the ignition and instrument panel. "The headlight switch is still on," he whispered across to Ernie. "The guy must have been driving at night."

Ernie finally uncovered the glove compartment and forced the door with a large buck knife. He withdrew a vehicle registration, two parking tickets from a metered lot, a gas receipt for Uvalde, Texas, paper towels, a pair of old cotton gloves, and a map of Texas open to the Del Amo sector.

"We'll take those with us," Logan said.

The key ring in the ignition was of the round metal wire type, consisting of two keys. One of them was still inserted in the ignition itself, while the other hung loose beside a crusted, oddly shaped medallion. Logan debated taking the keys, then decided against it. If the vehicle were ever found, the missing ignition key might be an important factor.

The medallion on the key ring was unusual. When brushed clean, it contained a cross embossed on one side and a crest on the other. The cross was circled and the lettering too timeworn to be read clearly. Logan left it on the ring and turned his attention to the area under the seat.

In clearing away the rear section of the jeep, Ernie uncovered yet another metal box. This metal container was longer than its companion and only seven inches wide. Forcing the lid, he discovered two rusted fishing poles with reels attached and an old Mauser-type rifle. The clip was rusted tight and the scope hung loose of its mounts.

"We'll take the whole thing, box and all," Logan decided.

Logan managed to free the sandy waist of the skeleton and probed in the sand until he unearthed the victim's wallet. Both men examined it carefully, until Ernie reasoned that a thorough investigation of it would be better handled at their apartment.

"Do you think it'll be missed?" he asked Logan.

"It could have been washed out of the jeep during the rains or thrown loose on impact and then washed away."

Ernie accepted this and went back to digging the rear of the jeep free. Logan envisioned the accident itself. He followed the imaginary path of a vehicle, driving at night, unaware of the deep wash ahead. Leaving the ledge above them at high speed, it would have nosed into the far bank with terrific force, enough impact to collapse the overhanging bank on top of the vehicle, burying it almost immediately from the eyes of Ewing and the others who flew the area daily. Sand from subsequent rains would have built up around the jeep, piling it deeper with each succeeding rainfall, until even a man on foot might just walk right on by it. Logan reenacted the crash several times until he was completely satisfied with his explanation.

"Texas . . . MS . . . star . . . sixty-four . . . seventy-four . . . 1963," Ernie mumbled as he copied the license number from the rear bumper Logan joined him to examine the plate. It had once been white with black letters, "Texas" stamped above the number, "1963" below.

Logan sighed. "At least it gives us a year to begin with."

"You think he's been here since 'sixty-three?"

"Could have been. I can't read the driver's license in the wallet, but my guess is it must be at least ten years old. . . ."

Ernie straightened up. "Well, what do we do now? Do we have to dig him out and bury him?"

"No, let's bury the jeep and get out of here before Ewing does his afternoon flyover."

"What do we do with the money and fishing gear?"

"Let's stash it near the old Kaufman chimney; it's as safe there as anywhere."

"Suppose somebody finds it," Ernie complained.

"We can't take it back to our apartment," Logan reasoned. "It's too risky."

Ernie made a fist as he said, "If somebody touches that money. . . ."

"I know." Logan grinned. "You'll kill him."

"Damn right!" Ernie announced. He began digging with his shovel, throwing large scoops of earth over the rear of the vehicle. "Do we have to cover the guy, too?"

"Hell, yes!"

"I can't!"

"Why?"

"I can't stand throwing dirt in the guy's eyes and stuff—*eeech!*"

"You cover the jeep, I'll cover the guy."

"You know this stuff won't stay if we get a big rain," Ernie cautioned.

"Maybe it will. . . ."

"Do we care?" Ernie questioned.

"I think the longer it stays buried, the better for us."

"You remember that song 'The Worms Crawl In, the Worms Crawl Out'? That's what this reminds me of. Reminds me of those old Karloff movies where Igor and his

74

assistant dig up bodies for experiments. *Eeech!* I don't know how people can work with stiffs all the time. It's spooky."

"Keep digging." Logan laughed.

They swept the area clear of all tracks, driving to the Kaufman chimney dragging brush behind their vehicles to eliminate any sign of their having been in the wash.

Each item found in the wallet was carefully laid out on the dinette table in the small apartment. Logan examined the wallet while Ernie studied the contents of the glove compartment. The radio in the background played the latest country and western hits. Paintings of naked women, brown, big-busted, smiled down on them from their black velour backgrounds. They were Ernie's women, just as the apartment had once been Ernie Wheeler's apartment. Logan had been invited five years before, and the Durbin apartment was now home to both of them.

A dozen of Ernie's women decorated the place, each beckoning the patrolmen to climb atop their sensual bodies and luxuriate in enveloping blackness. They were all different, yet somehow the same. Each had full pointed breasts, dark liquid eyes. Each had a knee raised to hide her secret treasure.

Logan carefully slit away the plastic window of the wallet, freeing the driver's license. It was a 1963 issue, the color faded from the center, leaving just a faint pink border. It identified the driver as Michael Curtis, dark hair, five feet nine, one hundred and forty pounds, blue eyes, date of birth: July 18, 1938. A resident of San Antonio, Texas, 113 Blythe Street, apartment D.

The other plastic windows of the wallet were empty. There were no credit cards, but there was one hundred and sixteen dollars in bills. Logan discovered, tucked in a small key pocket of the wallet, two phone numbers, a realty card belonging to Dunhill, San Antonio, and two air-mail stamps in a small cardboard folder.

Logan took the telephone numbers to the phone. Each dialing was followed by a recording stating that the numbers were no longer in service.

Ernie asked, "What's up?"

"Two phone numbers, both disconnected." Logan withdrew his own wallet; he flipped through his identification cards, credit cards and called to Ernie, "Let me see your wallet." Wheeler slid it across the counter and Logan flicked through it to find an ample supply of identification.

"What are you looking for?" Ernie questioned.

"The guy's got nothing in his wallet. Just a driver's license and a business card for a realty outfit . . . a few stamps . . . phone numbers and a hundred and sixteen dollars in cash. . . . Where the hell are his credit cards? His auto club? Insurance company?"

"How come we didn't find a tackle box or hunting gear?" Ernie added. "That bothers the shit outta me. Who takes off with fishing poles and no tackle box? Did he have a hunting or fishing license?"

"Neither one . . . just the driver's license issued in 'sixty-three that was never renewed in 'sixty-four. You make anything out of that stuff from the glove compartment?"

"Not really . . . usual shit . . . a map opened to Fort Worth showing the border and Del Amo . . . a couple of punched parking tickets from Dallas and Fort Worth. . . . The only thing that can be read is the punch itself." Ernie slid the parking tickets across to Logan, who held them up to the light. "They look like Twin City parking stubs, but there must be a couple of hundred lots in each of those cities . . . the gas receipt from Uvalde is almost impossible to read. The only thing that can be seen on it is the name of the station. The cotton gloves are so old it's impossible to tell if they were new or used . . . paper towels . . . standard service-station stuff used in cleaning windshields."

"We don't have a hell of a lot." Logan sighed.

"We have eight hundred and fifty thousand dollars," Ernie reminded him.

Logan nodded. "All we have to do is find out if we can spend it."

Ernie went to the refrigerator, popped two beers, and brought them back to the table. He balanced the two empties atop the already overflowing plastic container of empty beer cans. There would be a maid to clean up the following morning, a Mexican woman named Geneva, who changed the sheets and overhauled the apartment three times a week. They did little except sleep and change clothes there, seldom made anything more ambitious than coffee. Five years before, when Logan first moved in, they tried rotating cooking chores. But Logan's meals consisted mainly of ham and eggs, and after numerous battles with eggshells, Ernie decided Logan's cooking left a lot to be desired. Ernie's specialty was chili. Twice a year he'd spend his day off whipping up an eye-watering pot of fiery chili. It was followed with foot stamping and uncontrolled wheezing on Logan's part, while Ernie downed bowlfuls without emotion.

"We sure as hell ought to be able to make something out of all this," Ernie said.

Logan threw up his hands in frustration. "But there's *nothing* here that spells money! He sure as hell didn't rob a bank with those fishing poles or an old bolt-action rifle! And that damn box just fits that money exactly! It's almost as if it were *made* for it!"

Ernie shrugged in exasperation. "Maybe it's counterfeit."

77

"But who in the hell can we trust to ask about it? We can't just walk into a bank and ask if this is counterfeit; they might be looking for the numbers or something."

They began thinking through their long list of acquaintances in the various border towns. The only sounds in the room were Loretta Lynn on the radio and the beer cans tapping absently against the Formica tabletop.

Logan picked up Curtis' wallet and turned it over in his hand. It was a small container, the type carried by men who didn't want to be burdened by a full-sized wallet. Closed, Logan noted, it measured just half the size of his own billfold.

"Maybe he was a bag man for the mobs," Ernie suggested.

"Maybe he was making a buy on some shit from across the border," Logan countered.

"Nobody rides around with that kind of money. He'd have had ten guys with him just to see he didn't get ripped off. Eight hundred and fifty thousand is pretty damn tempting. Besides, say he was alone in it, which is goddamned foolish. What the hell would he do with the stuff once he had it? He had an open jeep, remember? He couldn't drive around with a ton of grass on the ass end!"

"Maybe he *was* a bag man," Logan said, beginning to agree with Ernie's first suggestion. As soon as he said it, he realized it wouldn't be possible. "That's no good . . . bag men are little old ladies or well-dressed, distinguished-looking elderly businessmen. A bag man wouldn't be riding around the desert with that kind of money. He had to have stolen it from a bank or been given it by a bank. That's the only thing that would account for those damn serial numbers!"

"He could have ripped off a bank."

"Or a client," Logan added.

"Either way," Ernie probed, "the guy had dough, taken

78

from somewhere, or someone, which means there must be others who know he had it. . . ."

"Which means," Logan continued, "as soon as the guy's found, somebody is going to know that the money isn't there and whoever gave it to him—or had it taken—will start looking for it. . . ."

Ernie toasted Logan with his can of Pearl beer. "The longer the guy's hidden, the better it'll be for us."

"When are we off this week?"

"Tuesday."

"Then Tuesday we'll go to San Antonio and see what we can find out about Michael Curtis of 1113 Blythe Street."

6

Number 1113 Blythe Street proved to be a run-down series of connected bungalows. Corporate plans for the property were outlined on a curbside billboard, showing an architect's drawing of high-rise condominiums that would soon be occupying the premises. Demolition of the bungalows was only months away.

The present occupant of apartment D was a retired Navy chief, who proceeded to tell them he was widowed, had been a resident in good standing since 1969, and had seen the rent raised three times in the last year. He was obviously quite drunk for that early hour of the morning.

Logan and Wheeler had approached the man on the pretext of looking for an old Army buddy named Benson, who they thought had occupied apartment D.

The chief's answer was to rail at the corporate ownership of the property, the total lack of repairs, the rent increases, and the quality of the other tenants. They left him at the curb, his suspenders hanging to his knees as he cursed the billboard and all those corporations that conspired against the nation's armed forces.

They traced the realty card to a florist shop on Fifth Avenue, overlooking the river. Ernie gave the young man behind the counter a sad tale of his long-lost uncle, a former real estate broker named Benson, whose only address had been with Dunhill Realty.

The young man shook his head; his parents had occupied the premises since June, 1964. The building had been empty when they acquired the property. Ernie thanked the boy and went outside to meet Logan.

They took their coffee at a small restaurant along the

river walk. Logan had failed to uncover a Dunhill Realty with the local telephone operator. The men exchanged reports and sipped their coffee quietly. Of the two leads they had, both had aborted rapidly.

"I think we're going to have to resort to newspapers," Logan said. "The telephone operator thought the library might have old editions on microfilm. We could divide them up and check 'sixty-three and 'sixty-four for robberies of eight hundred and fifty thousand. Maybe we'll come up with something. . . ."

"Jesus," Ernie swore, "that's going to be a lot of work!"

"You have a better idea?"

The San Antonio *Express* began the new year of 1964 with extensive coverage of the Dallas assassination of John F. Kennedy. It recapped that November with photos of the parade route, the Texas School Book Depository, Lee Harvey Oswald in custody, Jack Ruby's shooting of the alleged assassin, the Dallas police holding the rifle aloft, Ruby awaiting trial for murder, Earl Warren, wounded Texas Governor John Connally, and pictures of the slain officer Tippit.

Logan tried to skip past the assassination highlights, but he was drawn back to it and found himself rereading the whole calendar of events, beginning with the presidential motorcade.

Logan could remember the day as if it were yesterday. He could even recall the words and smells around him. It was a day he would never have forgotten. Others he had talked with remembered it in quite the same way, going into minute details that had little bearing on the news flashing across the world.

Logan had been in Vietnam. With his Vietnamese strikers, he tried to reach the security of the outer perimeter before dawn. It was imperative he get his men back inside the compound before the VC caught them in the open glare of daylight.

The wire had been deserted. Three times Logan called the password and received no reply. The terrible fear that the base camp had been overrun was foremost in his mind as he crawled through the wire. Instead his American companions were gathered about the radio as the dread news of that Dallas day was relayed thousands of miles to the front command posts.

"President John F. Kennedy"—the Saigon correspondent choked emotionally—"the thirty-fifth President of the United States . . . die . . . died . . . at approximately one p.m. Central Standard Time . . . of a gunshot to the brain. . . . The presidential motorcade. . . ."

The words from Saigon struck the American A Team with the deadly ferocity of a VC mortar. Some cried openly; others brushed back tears from their tired faces. Logan remembered squatting on the floor, his face hidden by the arms wrapped about his weapon as he sobbed in disbelief.

"The President's day began with a breakfast reception. . . ." Logan withdrew his head from the microfilm machine. He glanced across at Ernie working his way through the latter half of 1963. What had Ernie been doing on that day? he wondered. Did his partner remember it as vividly as Logan himself? Did anyone remember it as well as he? He could even recall the last message of the President as Kennedy apologized to the crowd for Jackie's tardiness. "Mrs. Kennedy is organizing herself," he told them. "It takes longer, but, of course, she looks better than we do when she does it." Logan recalled the laughter of the crowd, but there was no joy in the Green Berets gathered in that little radio dugout. The words only punished them further as they realized the broad Boston accent had been silenced forever.

Logan had total recall of all the words; he'd sat through the endless torture of repetition as tape after tape of the familiar voice was played and replayed. Each man in the dugout had been subject to repeated painful reports of the violation of their President. It was a personal loss even though many miles separated them. "He talked sense," one said. "I just liked the guy," said another.

Looking at the microfilm gave him an extraordinary sense of power. He alone seemed to know the outcome. He alone knew that Jack Ruby would be dead in just a few years, that others would die. Many of those only remotely connected with the shooting would succumb of natural causes. He felt the power of some great seer, a Merlin, a prophet, able to see that there was no future for any of these people. Earl Warren would die in the summer of 1974. The dressmaker, Zapruder, who filmed the shooting, would be dead. Wounded Governor Connally would be involved with the Nixon debacle and would fall from grace. Johnson would die shortly after his announcement that he would not be a candidate for reelection. The Kennedy mantle, which passed in Air Force One to Lyndon Johnson, would in turn be worn by Richard Nixon. Nixon would drag it through one term and seek reelection in a manner that would topple his government. Like Humpty-Dumpty, many of the Nixon men would be tumbled from office, leaving a long line of officials await-ing their turn at the bar of justice. Logan knew none of these men could possibly foresee the advancing dangers. He wished he could warn them of what the future held. But it was history now, bound by nature to repeat itself, upping the cost each time it did.

Logan turned the crank, speeding his attention into the new year, trying to concentrate on the purpose of his visit. Pope Paul VI flew to the Holy Land, the first pontiff to travel by air, the first Roman leader to leave Italy in one hundred and fifty years. Logan searched slowly through the pages, finding several robberies and murders but none whose hauls equaled the sum they held in their possession.

His body demanded a cigarette and he went by Ernie's

machine, to find Ernie deeply involved with the first woman in space, a Russian junior lieutenant. Logan passed on by with a chuckle; Ernie was as caught up with history as Logan had been, reading articles somehow missed years before, knowing they had no bearing on the money that had brought them there.

By the end of the day Logan had reached February 1 and Ernie had reached June 17, the day the Supreme Court ruled eight to one that required reading of the Lord's Prayer or Bible verses in schools was unconstitutional.

Ernie bubbled over with information on the way back to Durbin, reeling off items concerning Major Gordon Cooper's twenty-two space orbits in May of 1963, followed by a Russian's eighty-one, then a Russian woman's forty-eight orbits.

Logan mentioned his recapping of the new year, the shooting in Dallas, the workings of the Warren Commission. He expressed his own doubts about its findings. To which Ernie replied, "C'mon, Logan, you don't believe that conspiracy bullshit?"

"Part of me does. . . ."

"Hell!" Ernie scoffed. "There were too many people involved in the investigation! If there'd been a conspiracy, how would you keep all those people quiet all these years? Shit, somebody would have come forward if there had been anything to it."

"What about all those people who died afterward?" Logan asked.

"So what! People die all the time!"

"But almost forty of them, Ern!"

"So tell me. How do you keep the FBI quiet, the CIA, the Secret Service, the Dallas police—I even knew a guy from the Texas Department of Public Safety, an undercover agent who was working on the case! How in the name of hell do you keep all those people quiet?"

"I don't know," Logan admitted, "but somebody sure did."

Ernie dismissed this with a loud "Impossible!"

"Ernie," Logan cried in anger, "how can you say that after all the shit that's come out about Watergate and the CIA and the FBI and the assassination plots over the world? How can you still say that?"

"That's exactly what I mean!" Ernie said swiftly, turning to face Logan in the seat, a finger under his nose as he pointed out. "It all came out, didn't it?"

"You don't believe there was a guy on the grassy knoll?"

"No!"

"Oswald acted alone."

"Yes."

"I don't believe you."

"You missed the boat, pal." Ernie grinned. "Every time there's a shooting these conspiracy guys come out of the woodwork. The same thing happened with Bobby Kennedy in L.A. People refuse to believe one guy can do something like that and get away with it. But that's the only reason it works—one guy does it." Ernie tipped his hat down low over his eyes, ending the discussion. Reaching for the dashboard of his Lincoln, he snapped the radio on, hearing Tammy Wynette sing tearfully about the man that done her wrong.

After the song ended, Logan asked softly, "Do you remember what you were doing on that day, Ern?"

"Yeah . . ." Ernie answered without moving from his low position in the seat. "I was getting my car serviced. It was supposed to be ready by noon. I was really pissed when I went there and the wheels were still off it. Everybody was listening to the news—nobody knew if he was dead or what . . . just the report that shots had been fired. I stayed there till three listening to all the reports coming in. . . . When I left, my car still wasn't ready,

85

but I remember I didn't really care anymore. . . . Yeah, I remember."

They passed through an electric eye as they entered the sheriff's office. The deputy looked up at the sound of the buzzer, swiveled in his chair as the two men entered.

"Bob Logan and Ernie Wheeler, Immigration," Logan announced. "Somebody phoned our office in Del Amo to report night flights into Stone Hill mesa?"

"That would be the sheriff; he's on the phone right now. Have a seat." The deputy waved to the chairs against the wall of the crowded office. "There's coffee if you want a cup."

"Do you have milk?" Logan asked.

"We have that dry cream stuff in the jar."

Ernie took a cup, but Logan waved it off. "It gives me a sour stomach," he told the deputy.

Moments later the interior door to the sheriff's office opened and a weathered giant of a man filled the doorway. The two patrolmen got to their feet in awe. The sheriff wore a light tan stetson with the front edges curled to a point. The hair tumbling out from the stetson was snow white and curled at the massive shoulders. A large bulbous nose shadowed the drooping gray mustache. One crooked thumb hooked over the gun belt disappearing under the wide expanse of shirt and leather vest. The weapons, a pair of well-worn Colt .45s with pearl handles.

Logan heard his breath catch in his throat, heard Ernie's choked surprise. They stared at the man, who squinted in their direction. The man appeared to be left over from a turn-of-the-century Remington illustration.

Logan went forward to offer his hand. Closer inspection revealed the man to be in his middle seventies, with the brute strength of a much younger man who had lost the battle of the waistline.

Logan said simply, "You must be Jim Wells."

"Name's on the door," the sheriff replied, unimpressed, dropping Logan's hand to reach for Ernie's extended one. "I'm Bob Logan, and this is my partner, Ernie Wheeler."

"Logan?" Wells asked as he drew them into his office, his wrinkled hand pulling Ernie forward. "Bob Logan's kid?"

Logan nodded in surprise.

"I'll be a son of a bitch!" Wells exploded, taking Logan's hand once again and pumping it furiously in his meaty grip. He dragged Logan to a picture on the wall, shoving the patrolman's face within inches of a faded photo of two dozen mustachioed young men trying their best to look sternly at the photographer. Wells jammed a thick thumb against the glass. "Now, is that your old man, or is that your old man?" he boomed.

Logan saw his father's face, saw a man much younger than he ever remembered. He felt a warm flush creep over his body. "That's him, all right," he said in wonder.

The thumb went down the line of men, stopping at the man on the end with a rifle across his chest. "Now, you tell me, boy, is that your sheriff or not?"

"That's you, all right," Logan agreed. He sent his attention back down the line of men, back to his father, with some ridiculous holster hanging between his legs. He wondered whatever became of his father's belongings.

"You're damn right!" Wells shouted in his ear, pounding a fist to Logan's back.

Ernie had his head between the men as he studied the picture. "Texas Rangers? I thought they were disbanded a long time ago."

"In 1935," Wells said sadly. "They call them the Department of Public Safety now, but it's not the same thing. That's one of the last pictures ever taken—El Paso, 1934. We were just kids," Wells said absently. "Just a bunch of hot dogs . . . had no idea it would someday end. Hell, we thought it would go on forever." The deep voice trailed away as Wells looked at his youth in the dusty glass.

"So you became a sheriff?" Logan laughed.

"Twice," Wells answered, his attention coming back to the two young men in his office. "I retired from one place up north. Retirement. . . . Shit! Lasted all of four months. Then I heard about an opening at Stone Hill and wound up here running for sheriff. That was a little over a year ago."

Ernie offered, "Pretty soon you'll have two pensions."

The mass of white curls swung Ernie's way, the eyes hard and unforgiving. "A pension means you're a dead man. I got no use for one. What the hell do I do with two?"

Ernie slipped quietly into a chair before the desk, trying to make himself as inconspicuous as possible.

Wells shook the shoulder-length white locks and shoved Logan to a chair. "Tell me about your old man," he demanded.

"Not much to say." Logan shrugged. "He died in 'fifty-two. I was just a kid."

"What about your mother?"

"They split up years before that. I used to see him all the time, but she couldn't tie him down."

Wells chuckled, leaned across to Ernie, and said, "That's his old man, all right. The same ornery son of a bitch I knew."

"He came by to see me a couple of times a month—we were living in Austin then. They had him writing tickets near Highway two-ninety. He said he liked it."

Wells shook his head angrily. "Couldn't of! Had to hate it. You can't put people like Logan and me out there writing tickets. That's an insult to people like us. That's rookie stuff!"

"It was just a small funeral," Logan continued, "just me and my mom and a few friends."

"Damn shame," Wells said.

"Anyway"—Logan shrugged away the thought of the small headstone in Austin—"we were sent here to talk to you about that report you filed with our office."

"The airplane?" Wells nodded as he remembered the report. "Sure. A couple of desert bums reported it, harmless old coots. Didn't pay Toots any mind until Amarillo came in and reported the exact same thing. Then I called Immigration in Del Amo, talked to a Brook, thought it might be something you boys would be interested in. Old Toots is a drifter, moves about a lot, never stays in one place too long. Lives with a couple of dogs in abandoned sheds and mines. He wanders around the washes looking for gold or something. I've only seen him twice since I became sheriff. You know the kind, talks to himself a lot, probably mad at the world. Always stays in Hadley County, never wanders that far away.

"Amarillo lives up the road out of town, about forty miles from here, up on the mesa. Pretty smart old boy, lives in a camper on the back of a pickup truck. Lives off some sort of pension with a couple of wild burros he's adopted. Comes into town once a month to get his check and buy groceries. Says he's heard that plane for a week now, regular as clockwork. He figures there's a runway up there by him somewhere. Knows the plane is a Cessna and it comes in real low."

Wells struggled up from the chair and went to the plastic-covered map behind his desk. Hadley County was marked in a bright green border. Wells took a red marker from his desk and placed a dot at Amarillo's camp on the mesa. "The old man is here . . . and Toots reported it further south and a little east." Wells drew a straight line between the two places and continued it south, drawing a red line across the Rio Grande through section seven into Mexico. The red marker led them on a straight line to Ciudad Bravo, just two hundred miles below Quemado.

Wells turned to face the two patrolmen. "My guess is that it's flying something in from Ciudad Bravo and leaving it on the mesa, then getting the hell back out again. But that's just my guess. That's why I thought you boys might be interested." He flashed them a quick grin that raised the handlebar mustache on his face.

"We'll check it out," Logan agreed.

The old town of Stone Hill was elevated on boardwalks against the seasonal torrents that washed the main street twice a year. A new shopping center had been built off the highway, drawing the tourist dollar, forsaking the old part of the town, abandoning the wooden structures to decay.

Wells waved them off from the front door of his office. "You, the Logan boy, come back again so we can chat!"

"Will do, Jim," Logan called as he sent the jeep out onto the dirt road leading through the old part of town.

"I'd sure hate to have that old buck pissed at me," Ernie exclaimed. "I have the feeling he could still give a guy a pretty bad time of it."

"I'd make sure I had a baseball bat or something." Logan laughed.

They were leaving the last of the old wood-framed business dwellings when Logan sent the jeep into a wide U-turn.

"What are you doing?" Ernie screamed as he hung precariously to the side of the vehicle.

"Didn't you see that sign?" Logan whipped the jeep to a halt in front of an unpainted wooden structure with the word "coin" peeling off its dirty front window.

The store offered stamps, coins, and biblical quotes, all presented in a dusty window display. The door creaked in weathered agony as they went inside. The two occupants never looked up from their books. One bent over a tired Bible while the other man, wearing a cracked plastic visor, offered them a moment's attention. Beneath the green shade Logan could see the gray stubble of beard, the red-rimmed eyes of a drinking man.

"Need a little information, sir," Logan said to them.

The man with the visor rose with a great effort, went behind the almost empty counter, adjusted the visor to make it all official, and sighed, "All right."

"I was wondering if you could tell me anything about this?" Logan asked as he passed the man the ten-dollar silver certificate. "I won it in a poker game the other night, and my friend and I were wondering if it was genuine."

"Silver certificate," the man mumbled as he withdrew a large magnifying glass from beneath the counter and began to scan the bill. The other old man was leaning against an unlit potbellied stove, forming the words he read with his toothless mouth.

"It's in good shape. . . . I'll give you twelve and a half dollars for it."

"Then it's real?" Ernie asked quickly. "It isn't a phony?"

"Counterfeit?" the man said in surprise. He bent to the bill once again, the two patrolmen leaning in tight until the man placed a stale unlit cigar between his teeth, forcing them to give him a little more room.

"Good background . . . nice lacing behind the numbers . . . looks real good."

Logan pressed the man persistently. "Are you sure? There's no mistake?"

"Well. . . ." The bill was flipped gently. "The paper's real . . . has good red and blue threads . . . numbers evenly spaced . . . lines firm and complete . . ." The hands turned the bill again. "The points on the seal are sharp and even . . . a Smith-Dillon signature . . . blue seal . . . six twenty-five B . . . New York issue . . . 1953 B printing . . . might go as high as thirteen and a half."

Logan let the air escape him slowly. "Then it's good."

"Wouldn't give you thirteen and a half if it wasn't," the man said derisively.

Ernie shoved one of the twenties under the man's nose. "What about this one?"

The man looked up impatiently, gave a slight whimper of annoyance before bending to the new bill. "Sixty-three A. . . green seal series. . . . 'In God We Trust' is on the back side again . . . that's good . . . Granahan and Fowler signature . . . that's good . . . it's an eight sixty-nine K . . . that makes it a Dallas bill."

"You're sure?" Ernie demanded.

The man replied irritably, "Of course I'm sure. If it had been issued at the next printing, it would have had to have a 'sixty-nine issue and would have had Elston and Kennedy's name on it. Why do you ask my advice if you're going to say, 'Are you sure?' "

"I'm sorry," Ernie apologized.

"And it's a good bill?" Logan insisted.

"Yes!" the man snapped impatiently. "Look behind the face of Jackson. Isn't that a beautiful engraving? If it was counterfeit, the lines would not be so detailed, so finely etched. That fine screen would be gone. This is fine workmanship! The best!"

Logan retrieved the two bills and replaced them with a ten from his wallet. "You can keep this for your troubles. We really appreciate this, thank you."

"I'll go as high as fourteen for the silver certificate, but that's my final offer."

Ernie asked, "Why so much money for a ten-dollar bill?"

"They don't make them anymore!" the man stated, clearly shocked by their stupidity. "The last ones printed were the 'fifty-three B series, just like that one there. The government discontinued them in 1963."

"So . . ." Logan thought aloud, "if a guy had a couple

of ten-dollar silver certificates, they might be worth more than ten dollars each."

"Maybe fifty percent more," the man explained. "It would depend on the condition."

The two patrolmen were already at the door when Logan called, "Thank you for your time. We really appreciate this."

"Fourteen's as high as I'll go!"

"Maybe some other time." Ernie smiled, closing the door behind him.

They climbed down the broken wooden steps to the street, both men struggling to remain silent. Logan slid behind the wheel, headed the jeep in a wide arc to the east without even a glance in Ernie's direction. They were well out on the highway when Ernie pulled himself up to the windshield and yelled to the sheep grazing at the side of the road. It was a loud, long scream of joy, which he followed with a beating of his hands on the windshield.

7

Amarillo's camper was a wood-framed home built on the rear of a 1949 Chevy pickup truck. The roof and sides were cedar-shingled, with a small pointed metal smoke-stack twisting skyward from its peaked roof. Small windows with screens were cut into the sides for ventilation, and a pair of steps led from the desert floor to the rear entry. It resembled something out of Al Capp's *Li'l Abner* Dogpatch community. Its construction was imaginative, revealing a great deal of workmanship, hardly the home of a vagrant. The Chevy body was covered with a fine layer of dust, but outside of that it looked as if it had just been driven from some showroom floor.

Logan sounded the horn of his jeep, sending several long blasts across the desert air. Ernie bent to the ground, checking the tracks until he was satisfied that all the prints had been made by one man. They were sitting in the shade of the camper, smoking cigarettes, excitedly calculating that the money they'd found had unexpectedly increased its worth by another one hundred and twenty-five thousand dollars in silver certificates, when Amarillo appeared on the horizon. He was a small man, apparently in his late sixties, preceded by a large brown-and-white hunting dog. Amarillo walked with the aid of a large staff, the six-and-a-half-foot pole advancing in front of him, an ancient apparition floating above the heat rising from the desert.

The ghostly figure came silently forward, the dog trotting a few steps before waiting for his master to reach him with the staff. Behind the man and his dog followed

94

a small dust cloud, moving relentlessly forward, a fine powdered shadow that pursued them slowly.

A large loose-brimmed hat hid the old man's face in shade. It was removed in an elaborate ceremony some one hundred feet from the patrolmen. The staff was tucked under one arm; the dog took this as a cue to flop down before Amarillo's feet, picking his spot carefully to attain maximum shade. The interior brim of the hat was given a careful drying as the man studied his two visitors. The bald pate received a slow wipe of the cloth before the material was stuffed deep into a rear pocket of the bibbed overalls. Then the hat was replaced on the head, the dog made it to its feet, and the staff moved forward.

The dust cloud to the rear dissipated, leaving the patrolmen staring at five wild burros of various sizes.

Ernie whistled. "Look at that!"

"If he's Noah, there has to be an ark around here somewhere."

"How do?" Ernie called.

The man nodded as he approached, taking in the blue shoulder patches and uniforms as he went past them to the shaded rear of the camper.

"Sheriff Wells told us where to find you," Logan said as the dog came over and smelled his legs. It was an old dog with watery eyes, and every effort it made seemed herculean. It moved off to Ernie's legs and sniffed both feet while the man unlocked the rear of the camper.

They could see that Amarillo was not ready to discuss business. The man poured water from a gas can into a large pan. The burros and dog gathered around it and sucked noisily at its contents.

Ernie spoke over the clatter of the man's efforts. "The sheriff told us about the airplane and we wanted to talk to you about it."

"Don't you believe me?" the man asked as he picked stray twigs from the largest burro's coat.

"Oh, we believe you," Ernie answered quickly.

"How low was it?" Logan asked.

The man looked at Logan for a moment, decided to cooperate. "Seventy-five . . . a hundred feet."

"That low?" Logan questioned.

Amarillo met his questioning gaze and said firmly, "That low."

Ernie asked, "Do the planes land around here?"

"Plane," Amarillo corrected him. "A Cessna one eighty-two. Been coming over at eleven each night for the past week."

Logan smiled at the man. "How do you know it's a Cessna?"

"Spent thirty years with Convair in California, had to learn something about planes."

"Did you ever hear it land?" Ernie asked.

"No. . . ."

Logan asked the man, "Then how do you know it *does* land?"

"Don't have to know a lot about planes to know that when they cut back on the throttle like that and come in with flaps and rudder working at seventy-five or a hundred feet, they're not thinking about dusting crops."

"Any idea of where the landing might be taking place?" Logan asked.

"Educated guess . . . I would say the far side of the mesa. There's a gully that runs through the middle of this thing dividing it in two. The Mexicans called it Alianza mesa; the white folks call it Stone Hill mesa— Alianza has something to do with two parts or something like that. . . . But the far side gives them more runway— no brush except along the banks."

"Have you heard anything else?" Ernie asked. "Any cars, trucks, anything like that?"

"Saw a jeep," the man offered after a moment's thought.

"When?"

"Last week sometime."

"Did you hear the jeep at night? Before or after the plane comes in?"

"Nope . . . too far away."

Logan lit himself a cigarette and then threw the pack of Marlboros to Amarillo. The old man shook one out, weighed the pack in his hand before he slipped it into his bib pocket.

Ernie stifled a laugh as he asked, "Anything else you can tell us about the jeep?"

Amarillo snipped the filter off his cigarette with a long yellow thumbnail, broke the remaining portion of the unfiltered cigarette in half, sending the unused butt into Logan's box, which was immediately replaced in the pocket of his overalls. "Just one man . . . no other occupants."

"Where did you see him?" Logan asked in annoyance, realizing the man had just hit him up for his only pack of Marlboros.

"Up on the flat."

"No problem landing up there?" Ernie asked.

"Not for a Cessna. You couldn't put a Super Connie down there, but a Cessna will make it just fine. . . ."

"You didn't see the license number of the jeep?" Logan asked, the germ of an idea creeping over his anger.

"Nope. . . ."

"Could it have been . . . MS-6474?" Logan asked quickly.

Amarillo held the match steady and leaned into the flame with the butt of the cigarette. "Could have been. . . ."

Ernie and Logan exchanged quick silent glances. A smile crossed Ernie's face as Logan went to the jeep and called in to the Immigration dispatcher at Del Amo. He reported his position as Alianza mesa, the name given it on the map, described the plane to Brook as a Cessna 182 that appeared to be landing at night on the north end of the mesa.

Brook's reply was to have the patrolmen maintain surveillance of the mesa while the Del Amo office checked the information with the Customs and Federal Drug Enforcement agents.

Logan signed off, took a deep breath as he dialed in the sheriff's frequency for Stone Hill.

"Wells? Logan here at Alianza mesa. Everything checks out with your man Amarillo. He reported a jeep in the area. Can you run a check for me on a jeep with the license number Michael Sierra . . . six . . . fower . . . seven . . . fower. It may just be one of the local rabbit hunters and might not mean a damn thing."

"I'll get on it right away," Wells responded. "I'll be in touch."

"Thanks, Jim. . . ten-four."

Ernie gave him a knowing nod. "That's damn beautiful, pal."

"Maybe Wells can find out something," Logan whispered. "Maybe there's an old warrant on the guy for bank robbery or something."

There was nothing the patrolmen could do but wait for Del Amo's final instructions. Ernie busied himself with the burros, trying to pet the animals even though they shied away from him. The larger animals were skittish, but the youngsters weren't above having their long ears and noses rubbed. "How did you come by them?" he asked the man.

"They're mine!" Amarillo shot back defensively. "I don't think there were any left in these parts."

"It took over a year before they'd trust me. I'm their

98

friend now." Fear sprung to his eyes as he asked the men, "You're not going to send them away?"

"No," Logan answered calmly, trying to reassure the man that the bureau had no interest at all in his pets. "We just don't see many of them anymore."

"There are lots of them," Amarillo whispered secretively. "You just have to know where to look." He clicked his tongue and the burros drifted to the rear of the truck for a good rubbing. The old man began with the heavy male. "People shoot them for dog food. . . . What a waste. . . ."

"Fine-looking animals," Logan announced.

"Beautiful," Ernie agreed. "They really like you."

"They've been my friends for two years now . . . don't cause me any trouble at all. . . ."

"That's real nice," Ernie said, grinning broadly to ease the man's worries.

"I was going to spend my winters in Mexico," Amarillo explained as the burros nuzzled him for attention, "but that was two years ago. I came across these poor dumb burros and we sort of adopted each other. I've been up here on the mesa ever since . . . love these damn things. . . ."

"You have any trouble making ends meet?" Logan asked as he searched for a cigarette. Then he remembered that his Marlboros were in the top pocket of the man's overalls. He held his hand out to Ernie.

Amarillo watched as the package of cigarettes changed hands. He watched hopefully, but none was offered. "I get a small pension from Convair," he said wistfully as the cigarettes went back to Ernie. "I sold my home, couldn't afford the taxes anymore. I live in the camper now. I planned to do a lot of fishing, winters in Mexico, summers on the rivers up north . . . till I met these . . . creatures. Been stuck here ever since. Things are so expensive these days. I don't know how people make it on Social Security. I have a little portable TV that I watch sometimes—like the nature programs the best—but there's that man on those commercials that tells us we need six months' savings . . . he makes me sick. People are out of work and he tells them to put six months' savings in the bank! It's crazy! I just stay up here with my burros now . . . don't care if I ever get to fish up north."

"Why don't you just let them go?" Logan asked.

"Who'd look out for them?" Amarillo shot back. "The local hunters would just shoot 'em!"

"I see," Logan said, nodding as if he understood. In the distance he could hear the *whump* of an approaching helicopter. It appeared as a tiny speck in the blue sky, the sound increasing as the image grew larger.

"Jesus H. Christ!" Ernie swore. "I'll bet a dollar to a doughnut it's Brook."

"Who else would come in like the Marines?"

The chopper was one of two assigned the patrol, but they were seldom used for cutting signs. Aerial coverage was handled by Ewing in the Cessna, leaving the choppers for the busier highways and farm regions. Everyone in the bureau knew the farmers' timetables for planting and harvesting. Each crop had its picking time, a height of activity during which the bureau would swoop down with its investigators and patrolmen, catching many of the wetbacks in the fields, the choppers hovering overhead directing agents to the fleeing workers. These were assignments Logan and Ernie seldom took part in. Ernie had been on two raids in six years, whereas Logan had managed to avoid them all.

Of the two choppers assigned to Del Amo, one had been removed from service and assigned to Brook for "special assignments." It served as a personal ferry service for Brook and visiting VIP's in the area. Often it was loaned to Customs or one of the arms of the Justice Department, leading many to believe that Brook's career was to be paved at their expense. Many of the men resented the time spent on loan-out to one of the federal agencies, a habit of Brook's that was causing increased hostility among the men. Smugglers of grass, heroin, coke, and pills were brought to ground by Border Patrolmen and Immigration investigators. Then they stood helplessly by while Customs and federal Drug Enforcement agents were called to the scene and given credit for the arrest, a bust they hadn't taken part in at all. Brook was given accolades for his ingenuity, receiving the respect of his superiors in Washington, while his own men slunk back to their assignments, cursing the government's lack of understanding.

At a time when funds for the bureau were lowest, the collars in the narcotics traffic were desperately needed to justify salary increases and more equipment. Instead Customs and Drug Enforcement went on record as having made the busts, and were rewarded by Congress with healthy budget increases, letting the Immigration Service go begging.

The men blamed Brook for this, and rightly so, for it was Brook who saw to it that the other agencies were informed of every bust made and with sufficient notice to guarantee their involvement.

The chopper kicked up a large dust storm that sent the burros racing for cover and forced the patrolmen to nail down their stiff-brimmed hats with both hands. Brook scurried from under the blades, his quick sweep of the terrain seeking some unknown assassin.

"The general's arrived," Logan shouted as the first supply bundle was thrown from the chopper.

"We're spending the night," Ernie moaned as another bundle hit the ground.

Brook raced up to the men and placed a hand on each

of their shoulders. "I've been in touch with the federal people on this; they think we're on to something."

The two patrolmen nodded wisely to each other.

"You men will remain here to confirm tonight's flight. Establish definite contact with the smugglers and report to the office as soon as anything develops. Everyone will be standing by. There are food and supplies here to help you through the night. There's also a portable radio linking you directly with the federal narcs. You men are to make no move on your own, is that understood?"

"No move on our own," Logan repeated. He let it sink in slowly for Brook to see, then nodded agreeably. "Got it."

"This could be something big," Brook whispered, avoiding the old man in the background. "I can't tell you the full implications right now, but . . . it's big. You have my word on that."

"Big," Ernie repeated, his face looking very serious.

"We pull this off and it will be a real feather in our caps." Brook glanced back over his shoulder as the last of the supplies hit the ground. "Food, water, gasoline, radio, everything you'll need for a successful stakeout. Everything you'll need for a two- or three-day stay."

Logan stuffed his hands deep in his pockets, suddenly fed up with the game. "And we're not to do anything?"

"That's the plan," Brook snapped. "You're to do nothing that will endanger a successful bust. When this goes down, the federal narcotics boys want plenty of men here to make sure nothing gets . . . gets. . . ."

"Fucked up?" Ernie offered.

"Exactly!" Brook gave them a brief nod, squinted in the direction of the north section of mesa, and shouted, "Good hunting!"

They watched as their boss ducked under the blades and disappeared into the plastic bubble. The blades whipped up to speed, the craft rose, spun rapidly about on its axis, and left them choking dust.

"Sheeeit!" Ernie screamed. "Ain't that the cat's ass!"

The patrolmen ate an early supper, sharing their meal with the old man and his dog. The fire in the small butane stove was extinguished well before sunset, eliminating any chance of its being seen from the distance.

All the supplies were packed in the rear of the jeep before Logan took it into the wash to hide it from the air.

He called Stone Hill. "Is the sheriff there?"

"Wells is gone for the night."

"This is Bob Logan, Immigration. He was going to run a license number for me. Did he leave me any message about that?"

"Oh, yeah, that license! He's having a rough time with that. San Antonio's going to have to go through their Department of Taxes files for the whole county. It must be a real old plate. He said to try him in the morning."

"Right." Logan sighed. "Thanks a million. Ten-four."

Logan cut brush from the nearby banks with his shovel, removed the federal band radio from the vehicle before covering the jeep with greasewood plants. When he was satisfied no metal or glass could be seen from the air, he went back to the camper.

Ernie was bundled into one of the winter coats flown in for them. Logan shook away the chill and pulled on his own parka. He gave the area a quick once-over, making sure no lights were burning, no reflections danced about to give their position away. He hung the binoculars around his neck as he joined the two men at the rear of the camper.

The old man said to the sky, "Gonna rain soon."

"Tomorrow?" Ernie baited him.

Logan looked up at the moon; it was still clearly visible, but the stars seemed to be missing from the sky.

The old man ignored the taunt. "Just watch the burros. If you see them head for shelter, then it'll be raining in a couple of hours. That's all the notice they give me."

"Let's just hope it doesn't rain," Logan shot across to his partner. "I sure wouldn't want an unexpected rain running down through section seven."

Ernie nodded, remembering the jeep and the skeleton in the wash, the loose sand piled around the remains—sand that would wash away easily now that it had been unpacked and broken down.

"I'm with you." Ernie frowned, then he turned back to the old man to ask, "So finish telling me about this fellow Toots."

"A bum," Amarillo cursed from beneath the blanket around his shoulders, "just a bum. I caught him in my water about three weeks ago."

Logan asked, "Know where we can find him?"

"Just a bum," Amarillo insisted, "liable to be anywhere. Felt sorry for him at first—seems like an educated man. But he's crazy! Talks to himself all the time. Has these two dogs with him. Two months ago I shared my camp with him for two days . . . was stepping in dog shit for a week. Then he came back and stole some of my water. He's just a bum!"

"Does he cover any special territory?" Ernie asked.

"Been in the county for thirty years—won't tell me what he does, afraid I'll cheat him out of it!" Amarillo snored in disgust. "He picks up bottles and cans from along the highway and sells them to make a few bucks . . . spends it on wine most of the time . . . sad, sad." Amarillo shook his head several times, pulling the blanket tight around his face as a sudden chill wind swept the mesa. He mumbled "good night" to the men, rose, and went inside the camper. The door closed with a loud click, then opened to admit the dog.

Ernie slid deeper into the jacket until only his eyes were exposed. "I ain't never going to be cold again. That's what I always say, and one of these times I'm going to mean it. Once we take off with that dough, I'm going somewhere that's always warm."

"We'll hire a couple of live-in maids to keep us warm." Logan chuckled.

"All my life I've been cold." Ernie shivered. "When I was a kid and we lived in Chicago, all I remembered was the cold. Damnedest winters I ever saw. I was sixteen when I took off and joined the Marine Corps. They turned around and sent me to Korea; now *that's* cold, brother!"

"I've never been there. . . ."

"No, you had the warm one in Nam. I can't begin to tell you how cold it was. We sat in a line of foxholes for four days without moving. Nobody moved . . . freezing our asses off . . . listening for those goddamned bugles . . . listening for any sound at all. . . . I was scared shitless. We were sitting in water to the waist . . . then the cold set in. . . . Water froze at our waists . . . our legs were numb . . . they didn't sound the bugles . . . they just crept up close, then began to throw grenades into our position. . . . One landed right in my hole. I couldn't move! My legs wouldn't work! I stared at that damn thing, knowing it was going to kill me any second, and I couldn't move! I guess I scooped it out of the hole and threw it out in front of me. It started to roll back real slow, just an inch at a time, then I ducked. . . ." Ernie looked at Logan, blinking several times as he tried to shake it away. "That's the way they caught us . . . frozen in position like a bunch of sitting ducks. We were firing our weapons like crazy because we couldn't get up on our knees and fight properly. They gave us medals and sent us off to the

Osaka Army Hospital. We fought because we couldn't run . . . I decided right there and then, I'm never going to be cold again, never."

"Gimme a smoke," Logan whispered. He took the pack, lit one between cupped fingers, and passed the pack back to Ernie.

"You're one of those guys that's never been cold."

"That's it." Logan grinned above the parka.

"I knew it," Ernie grumbled, "you can always tell."

Logan wanted to tell Ernie about Vietnam and the heat, the oppressive heat that wilted your clothing, and the smell that accompanied the heat, the rotting odor of decay and mold gathering on your possessions. The bugs, the insects, the mosquitoes that filled your eyes, ears, and nostrils while you sucked frantically for fresh clean air. He wanted to tell Ernie about the jungles and swamps and the thousands of leeches that crawled inside your shirt and trousers. Of a war in which everyone smoked something so that the lit ends of their cigarettes could be used to burn the sucking leeches off arms, legs, chest, back, and buttocks.

He wanted to tell Ernie about the booby-trapped bodies of his companions, boys his own age, feared even in death. Or the dust-offs and firefights or the deadly ambushes.

He wanted to tell Ernie of the villagers, maimed, burned, scared, scarred, and homeless, whom he helped make into refugees. Peasants caught between two warring ideologies, understanding little except that what had once been their father's or their father's father's was now gone. Two warring factions that successfully rid a small country of its heritage of young people.

He wanted to tell Ernie that he had been one of many that had created the history of the Vietnam War. He only regretted he had not left it with a future.

Logan wanted to tell Ernie about all of this, but the men never played one-upmanship with each other. There had never been a moment between them when one man's confession acted as catalyst to the other of a similar burden. Ernie had used the chilling night to speak of something that had been bothering him. Someday Logan would speak of the delta and its nightmares.

'You're right, sport," Logan whispered. "But pretty soon there'll be no more cold for us, no more stakeouts. No more of Brook and his petty shit. I wonder where we'll be when the gadgets are installed."

"Somewhere warm." Ernie's teeth chattered.

"Two weeks away from cutting a sign and you'll be going bananas."

Ernie smiled. "Hey, that was the best part of this whole fucking thing! You know how many people can do what we do? You know what it means to finally find something you can do better than anybody in the whole damn world? I hear these guys talk about hunting bears . . . and elephants and lions . . . sheeit! You know what I say?"

"No, what do you say, Ern?"

"I shut 'em up pretty damn quick. I say to them, 'You ever track a man? You ever get down on your hands and knees to smell human shit and try to guess how old it is?' And that shuts them up pretty damn quick! Them and their guides and high-powered rifles are all bullshit! Until they track a man, they have no idea what it's all about!"

"Everybody knows that's how ol' Ern gets his jollies."

"That's right! When I see a man's track, I get a hard-on! And if he's easy . . . leaves a lot of signs . . . then I really get pissed."

"Ol' Ern likes 'em tough."

"The tougher, the better," Ernie announced.

Logan could see the excitement in Ernie's eyes; the shadowed moon reflected off the large dark pupils, giving the face an intense, almost diabolical gleam.

Logan knew Ernie had inherited the dark hair, eyes,

and complexion from his mother, a Mexican girl who crossed the border in the early 1900s, when the term "wetback" had yet to be coined. Ernie had spoken of her only once, and then in a drunken stupor, torn by liquor and pride. His parents had married late in life, two failures—a domestic and an itinerant postman grasping at some final claim to posterity. She had entered the United States by paying a fee of three cents at the crossing station. Raised seven children, doing her best to see that they were properly schooled, though she herself would never become a citizen, would never learn to read or write.

"There cents," Ernie would often repeat when he was drunk. It made little sense to anyone around them, but Logan knew exactly where Wheeler's attention lay at that moment.

"The reason you track so well," Logan explained, "is all that Mexican blood in you. Only the Mescalero Apache and the Mexicans can track like that."

"A couple of the best cowhands in the Texas Panhandle spent years teaching me that. It wasn't easy for a kid from Chicago. By the time I was twenty-one I could read a sign with the best of them. Did I ever tell you about that guy I tracked near Marfa?"

"Yeah. . . ."

"Six days! *Six days* I tracked that son of a bitch. It was my first year on patrol. They were going to send in a chopper to help me out. I told them I'd shoot that motherfucker from the sky if he even came close! Oh, man, it was beautiful! This guy was fantastic! He walked all the way from Nueva Rosita just to get to the border! That son of a bitch had already walked over a hundred and fifty miles before I came upon his track!"

"You told me already. . . ."

"All he had left were a few *frijoles* and a little water in an old Purex bottle. I mean, he wasn't even pooped. He took me over the rocks, boulders, even climbed walls and backtracked on me! He was like a cat, covering his jobs in sand, making me dig for it to be sure. I never saw a guy like that! I must have lost his trail a hundred times! But I always got back on it. Ran him to ground just a thousand yards short of the highway. If that son of a bitch ever reached the road and threw out his thumb, I'd have been done for. But I beat him to it. One tough SOB all right."

Logan closed his eyes sleepily and replied, "A year later you caught the same guy again and this time you let him go."

"Who told you that?" Ernie demanded. "You weren't even there!"

"You told me the story before; this time I put two and two together and I realized you probably let him go."

"Yeah . . ." Ernie said in surprise. "I did catch the guy again, just a year later. You can't forget a guy like that. He ran me over the same damn ground. But I knew where he was headed and I was waiting for him this time. He knew me right away . . . he wasn't scared . . . matter of fact, he smiled—I don't know what the hell came over me—I saw that look in his eye. He knew I was going to send him back. I knew he was going to try it again, so I said, 'Get the hell outta here, you bastard!' He was really surprised . . . I was really surprised."

"Well," Logan mumbled sleepily, "we won't be doing much more of that. It's just a question of time, old sport— just a question of time. . . ."

Logan dozed in the parka, his feet thrust out in front of him, hands stuffed warmly in deep pockets. He dreamed of his mother in Austin, tending her small yard, visiting his father's grave on Sundays. He made a note to send her some money—from his share, of course—to take care of the peeling paint of their home. He wanted to do something to atone for the long months between visits. Yes, he decided, he'd send her a thousand dollars. No one would be suspicious of a thousand dollars. It would make her happy, he thought.

He woke to Ernie shaking him lightly. Opening his eyes, he heard the engine in the distance. Logan scrambled to his feet stiffly and peeked around the corner of th camper. The plane was flying without lights. Ernie had it marked with an index finger, tracking it in the darkness. The plane was approaching rapidly, one hundred feet above the mesa and slightly to the east of them.

The burros spun about in a group before racing off to the south; they turned after several yards and, in confusion, swung wildly to the west and disappeared in the wash.

The plane's throttle was eased back as it passed abreast of them, the running lights now suddenly flashing on the wing and tail.

"Didn't I tell you it was a Cessna one eighty-two?" Amarillo called from the doorway of the camper.

"He's too far out," Ernie said over the binoculars, "can't make out the serial number."

"Probably a rental anyway." Logan yawned as he followed the plane's trajectory with his own field glasses. He eased himself up the camper steps, going on tiptoes to attain the maximum height advantage.

"Touching down," he called to Ernie, "seven, maybe eight miles out. There's brush in the way and I can't see, damn it!"

"Hey, old-timer," Ernie shouted, "what chance do we have out there driving without lights?"

"Not without lights," the old man warned them.

Ernie called to Logan, "You see anything?"

"The brush is in the way."

"He'll be leaving in just a few minutes," Amarillo said calmly.

Logan climbed down the steps, fumbling the two-way radio to his mouth. "Hello, blue boy, Immigration calling!"

Logan threw the switch to hear their reply. "Hello, blue boy," he repeated, "come in, blue boy!"

"Where in hell are they?" Ernie shouted.

"Maybe they don't work after ten," Logan answered.

"Hello, blue boy . . . Immigration calling . . ."

"I'll try Del Amo!" Ernie cursed, hurrying into the wash for the jeep radio.

"Don't tip it!" Logan warned. "The plane may be tuned to our frequency!"

From the darkness of the brush, Logan heard Ernie's call. "Hello, Del Amo . . . seven four here!"

"This is Del Amo. Go ahead, seven four."

"We're unable to raise blue boy on our two-way. Check that out for us, please, we'll stand by."

"Roger, seven four, please stand by."

Ernie rapped the mike against his leg as he impatiently awaited their answer.

"Seven four? This is Del Amo. . . ."

"We read you. . . ."

"Blue boy does not receive you, seven four."

"Fuck!" Ernie screamed.

"Repeat, seven four."

"I said. . . . Hell! Tell blue boy we have the groceries, unable to transmit."

"Roger, seven four, please stand by."

Logan saw the lights of the plane lifting in the air. The aircraft went dark as it swung across the face of the clouded moon, heading southeast. "They're leaving," he called to Ernie in the wash.

"Blue boy understands, affirmative, seven four."

"The groceries have been paid for, they're on their way home."

"Roger. Please stand by, seven four."

Logan came down into the wash, patting Ernie's parka until he found the package of cigarettes. "What's up?"

"That fucking radio Brook brought us doesn't work!

111

The damn thing was probably never checked out in the first place. I have to go through Del Amo."

"Christ," Logan murmured wearily.

"Seven four, this is Del Amo. Brook says to wrap it for the night."

"Shall we come in?" Ernie asked.

"Stand by, seven four."

Ernie threw the mike into the front seat. "Sheeit! This is getting to be like the Mickey Mouse Club!"

Logan crooned, "M-I-C, K-E-Y, M-O-U-S-Eeee. . . ."

"Seven four, this is Del Amo. Orders are, stay on the mesa. Federal narcotics agents will meet with you at oh eight hundred."

"Swell," Logan grunted. "If the plane was listening, they've heard it all now."

"Roger, Del Amo. You do mean blue boy, don't you?"

"Sorry . . . seven four. . . ."

"Seven four clear."

Ernie dropped the mike into the cradle. "Well, pal, where do you want to sleep?"

Logan kicked the brush aside and slid into the passenger seat. "This is as good as anything."

Ernie wailed, "You're not going to give me the goddamn steering wheel!"

"One of us has to take it, old sport." Logan had his feet thrust out, his head tucked protectively inside the coat.

"Aw, Christ," Ernie moaned as he slid behind the wheel. Only the glowing end of Logan's cigarette showed from the passenger seat. "We should have moved inside with the old man."

"The dog probably has a million fleas."

"Only Brook would bring us a radio that didn't work. . . ."

Logan mumbled, "We should have asked for cigarettes. . . ."

112

The brush crackled as the burros went by them and stood protectively under an overhanging ledge.

Logan looked across to his partner. "What did he tell us about the burros?"

"He said they would seek shelter if it was going to rain."

"Would you call that shelter, or am I crazy?" Logan asked.

"I don't think that you can call that ledge shelter. If it was going to rain, would they stand in the wash?"

"We're in the wash. . . ."

"We're not burros."

"Thank God," Logan sighed as he stubbed the butt out against the bottom of his boot. "See you in the morning, sport."

"That old guy's a little squirrelly if you ask me."

Logan woke to the plunking of raindrops bouncing off the brim of the wide, stiff stetson. He opened one eye slowly, closed it in disbelief, then opened it once again. The windshield before him was dotted with water spots that began to connect themselves as they raced to the hood. Large wet drops stabbed his worsted trousers, disappearing instantly in a spreading damp spot. The jeep announced its own predicament by playing the plinking of the hood against the hollow drumming of rain striking the roll bar and canvas tarp covering their supplies. The hood of the engine plinking in three-quarter time while the canvas behind them struck some strange forgotten Gold Coast tempo that Logan took to be seven-eighths time. The brim of his hat joined the rhythm section with its own bass of two-four time.

Logan was swept along by the pulsating meter until he managed to open both eyes, the burros watching him from the protection of the overhang. Between the jeep and the burros, Logan could see a small trickle of water beginning its run down the wash.

The sky was gray; the wind came up to send the rain

slanting across the wash. He elbowed Ernie's side, calling, "Ernieeee."

"Ummm," the bundled figure moaned.

"Guess what, Ern?"

"Uuummm?"

"It's raining. . . ."

Logan reached across to the dash with one hand. He snapped the radio on, took the mike, and cuddled it beneath his chin. When he was sure the equipment had warmed up, he said sleepily, "Hello, Del Amo. Come in, Del Amo. Hello, nerve center, God damn it!"

"This is Del Amo."

"Do you have a weather report for the area?"

"Is that you, Logan?"

"Yeah, Willy, do you have anything from San Antonio or Houston?"

"You mean weatherwise?"

"That's exactly what I mean! You see—where I'm at, sleeping out here in the wide-open spaces, where the deer and the buffalo roam, it's goddamn raining! Is this going to break, or is it going to hang with us awhile?"

Ernie opened two tiny slits and said in shock, "It's raining!"

"No shit," Logan swore as the rain drummed demandingly on their open vehicle.

"Logan? Houston reports rain. A real front's blowing in; they expect it could last two to three days."

"Thanks a million, Willy. Tell Brook we're coming in!"

"Roger."

Ernie bolted upright. "It's raining, Bob!"

"That's good, Ern, real good." Logan saw that the burros now appeared to be laughing at them. "Let's get the hell outta here. . . ."

Ernie rubbed his eyes with one hand while the other flailed for the ignition. The jeep came to life instantly and Ernie sent it climbing to the top of the mesa. Amarillo was standing in the doorway of the camper as they went past, a broad smile on his weathered face.

Logan waved a hand at the man and said under his breath, "Don't get your asses wet," as Ernie raced for town.

8

There were twenty-four of them assembled in the tiny Stone Hill Motel room. Twenty-four men of various Justice Department agencies, notably, Drug Enforcement, Customs, and Immigration and Naturalization Service. The cramped quarters had rapidly filled with cigarette smoke. The windows had been opened to catch the fresh air; the rain outside could be heard beating on the parked autos of the various agencies present.

Bob Logan and Ernie Wheeler occupied the small toilet area, stepping into the shower stall when anyone squeezed through the open doorway to relieve themselves or flip a butt into the commode.

Federal Narcotics Chief George Fleming tried to hold the group's attention to the county map, to the large circled area known as Alianza mesa. At Fleming's side stood Brook, beaming knowingly in the direction of the men leaning against the walls or crowded on the double bed. Opposite Brook, Customs Investigator Ramsey Byner watched Fleming with interest.

"Chances are," Fleming was telling the group, "the actual signs of the runway and the pickup vehicle will be washed away before the storm breaks. But with the help of Brook and his patrolmen, we can relocate the area and establish a pretty good stakeout. The patrolmen know the area well and they'll lead in two groups, one from the west to establish a perimeter along this portion of the mesa, and another from the east to secure this area. Our concern is with the northern half of the hill. That's correct, isn't it, Brook?"

"Yes," Brook replied, clearing his throat. " *'Alianza'*

is a Spanish word meaning 'alliance.' The Mexicans called it that—"

"We are concerned only with the northern sector," Fleming interrupted.

"Yes . . . that is correct." Brook coughed nervously. "Patrolman Wheeler will lead in the group from the east and Patrolman Logan will bring in the group from the west. Logan? Wheeler? Identify yourselves, please."

Two hands waved from the bathroom over the shoulder of an agent relieving himself. The man crouched to give them more room in the crowded doorway.

"All units will be in position by noon," Fleming continued. "It gives us a long wait, I know, but I'd like us in position in plenty of time, just in case the drop comes down earlier than planned.

"Ramsey Byner's Customs investigators will be split up among the two groups, as will my boys from the Drug force. A small ground-control unit from the Air Force will be set up in the brush just west of the runway. He'll warn us of the plane's approach, hopefully picking it up on radar while it's still some distance away. Two immigration helicopters will sit out of sight on both sides of the mesa, ready to be airborne at a moment's notice. There'll be plenty of radios provided to tie us together into one network with our own wavelength.

"Nothing's been overlooked. Vehicles will be waiting for transport, there'll be plenty of flak vests, shotguns, radios, portable quartz lights, and four-wheeled vehicles. We'll set up an effective crossfire between the two perimeters, trying to keep in mind we don't want to be caught in each other's line of fire. My boys will handle that end of it, seeing that everyone's properly positioned."

Ernie whispered to Logan, "It's going to be a goddamn circus out there!"

"Yeah," Logan agreed. He dropped his cigarette in the

toilet and squeezed into the doorway. "Can I ask a question?" he called to Fleming.

Fleming flashed his professional smile. "Be our guest."

Logan held the frame awkwardly as he leaned into the room. Several men gave way that he might stand erect in the doorway. "Y'know . . . this might not go down so good . . . there's too many guys. . . . Do you know what I mean?"

Logan could see that Fleming wasn't accustomed to having his plans challenged.

Fleming said slowly, "I'm not exactly sure I know what you mean."

"Well . . . there are too many guys in there. I mean, if I were one of the smugglers, and it rained real hard for a couple of days on my runway, I'd want to take a look up there and make sure it was still in good shape. I wouldn't want that pilot of mine coming in in the dark and then finding out that the rain's chewed up the mesa. I'd probably go up there early myself and check it out. That way I'd have time to divert the flight someplace else."

Fleming said briskly, "I've considered that."

"Maybe there'll be a flyover by one of the guy's buddies. Either way, they're bound to catch us out there setting up our radar and portable lights. . . . It'll look like a damn circle jerk." Logan ignored the angry flash from Brook, the slight threatening gesture of his boss taking a small step in Logan's direction. "What's the guy in the jeep going to think when he drives by and sees us setting up one of them big radar trucks? He's bound to see our tracks going in. I mean, hell, we can't hide thirty guys!"

Byner, the Customs investigator, came to Logan's rescue. "Do you have a better plan?"

Logan scratched his head uncomfortably; he hadn't had this much attention since Vietnam. Avoiding Brook's intent stare, he replied, "I think we ought to keep it simple, real simple. Just send a couple of guys up there. I mean, what the hell do we get if this comes off? We get a plane . . . maybe a jeep full of shit . . . which is okay, I guess." Logan floated a hand about the room. "But they're bound to make us with all these guys!"

Byner added quickly, "You have other thoughts on this?"

"Sort of. First thing is, we don't know for sure that they'll come back right away after the rain lets up. They may wait a day or two. Secondly, if we grab the jeep and the plane, we don't know where they came from or where they're taking the stuff. We might be able to sweat it out of them, but chances are they won't know too much anyway."

A burly thick-chested man sitting on the corner of the bed replied, "Keeping it off the street isn't enough for you?"

"Sure," Logan snapped, "that's one answer, but my suggestion is this: We use just a couple of men to stake out the runway area. After the plane's unloaded, we try for the aircraft before he can leave the ground. We make sure the pickup vehicle is away from the mesa with the shit before we try for the plane. If we miss the aircraft, it's no big deal, because he's empty anyway. The rest of the guys stake out the highway and wait for the pickup vehicle to leave. Maybe, just maybe, he'll lead us to something bigger."

"Suppose we lose him," the man on the bed said.

This man was beginning to annoy Logan. He began to wonder who this man was who talked for Fleming, Byner, and Brook. He directed his irritation at him. "He has to come out somewhere! He has to go in and come out. He has to be able to signal the pilot in some way that it's okay to land. If we don't spot him going in, we have another chance to nab him on the way out. Whoever's on the runway will know which direction the jeep's

119

entered from, probably the north, since it's the most accessible. All they have to do is say that their man is leaving and if all else fails, we use the choppers to scan the highway. It ought to be real easy at night to spot him. He has to use some sort of driving light—I don't give a shit how well he knows the area. And he can't go on the highway without lights, that's too damn risky. From there we just tail him home."

"I like it!" Byner announced. "I like the idea of knowing where the stuff's headed. This way we have a chance to get the pickup man and possibly his contact or his stash. I like it!" Byner nodded enthusiastically to Brook and Fleming. "Let's not kid ourselves, in two days they'll have another operation going. I'm for hurting them bad, as bad as possible. I'll take a chance on tailing that vehicle anytime."

Logan saw the man on the bed give Fleming an imperceptible nod. Fleming broke into a grin. "All right! The two border patrolmen will stake out the runway with just a couple of my men. The rest of us will concentrate our efforts on locating the pickup vehicle going in or out of the area."

Logan looked over his shoulder to Ernie; he hadn't planned on their being included in the stakeout. He gave him a helpless shrug.

Ernie touched his temple with an index finger. "Smart, Bob, real smart."

"Gentlemen," Fleming addressed the room, "assignments will be posted. Relax until the weather breaks. It may be forty-eight hours, so let someone know where you are at all times. That'll be all."

"Jesus," Logan whispered as he stared at the massive amounts of water running beneath Highway 90. It belched out from two eight-foot flood-control cement pipes in a

120

large forked muddy torrent before joining immediately to race down the Merida wash.

"Jesus is right," Ernie groaned, his face pressed against the glass of the enclosed sedan as huge boulders were torn from the safety of the bank and slipped beneath the raging water.

Sixteen miles away lay the hidden vehicle and Michael Curtis. Both men knew the jeep and its occupant would be no match for the angry river tearing away at its hiding place. The hastily shoveled camouflage would be rinsed free of its prize as the rapidly sweeping river gathered its tributaries, growing to massive proportions in its race south. They watched the wash, powerless to stop its ripping, reckless rush to their discovery.

Logan slipped the car into drive, suddenly eager to be as far away from the wash as possible.

Given forty-eight hours of unexpected time, the two patrolmen changed into civilian clothes and hurried to the nearest major city to continue their urgent search of the records. With Stone Hill inundated with Justice Department investigators they chose Odessa, hoping its library would provide them with the answer to the money's origin.

They drove the eighty miles in the rain, ran the distance from the parking lot to the oil city's library, and settled down with their respective machines, both men sensing the critical importance of discovering some hint to the money's source.

Ernie uncovered the largest robbery to date, bringing Logan quickly to his machine. It was a mail-train heist in England of some $7,000,000, or 2,500,000 British pounds. Logan tried desperately to connect the August 8 robbery to the money in the wash. But the 1963 English theft had been in pounds and appeared too farfetched for even the remotest speculation.

It was still pouring when they left the library. Neither

had managed to turn up a single clue to a robbery, murder, kidnapping, or extortion plan whose loot would equal the sum they'd buried beneath the Kaufman chimney. Ernie demanded a drink, selecting a bar, with a neon oil derrick spouting a continuous red gusher, named the Dry Hole.

The music of Buck Owens escorted them to the dark bar. They were pleasantly surprised to find the room filled with brightly chattering young women. The patrolmen pulled themselves atop a pair of empty stools, ordering Jack Daniel's on the rocks as they waited for their eyes to adjust to the dimly lit, promising atmosphere.

Ernie asked the bartender, "Where did all the women come from?"

"Shift change, telephone company."

Ernie gave Logan a smile as he rubbed his hands impishly. "Looks like we struck it rich, pal."

Logan had progressed beyond that point; he was remembering the two telephone numbers hidden in his wallet, numbers he'd tried unsuccessfully to call from San Antonio, numbers long since taken out of service. He tipped the cowboy hat to the rear of his head, allowing the blond curls to slide forward as he began his slow sweep of the room. He knew he'd need to meet a special type of girl, one who'd take the numbers without question and produce a quick reply without demanding a searching explanation.

The booths were crowded with women, huddling conspiratorially over their drinks, breaking the hushed silence with a brief, abandoned laugh. Logan gave each face careful attention, looking for some sign, a moment of recognition that would sound its alarm: She can be trusted.

Sonny James began his ballad as Logan connected. He wasn't sure whether she found him or he had found her. He was conscious of a pair of eyes waiting for him, drawing him to the next booth, where she waited his scrutiny. Her drink was held against her mouth. She set it down slowly, sending a pink tip to snake out between the lips and snatch at the moisture. She stared at him, ordering his consideration. Satisfied she was acceptable, she tossed the pale blond ponytail into place. Logan felt his stomach flutter as the signs were passed between them. The toss of the hair was provocative, almost a challenge. Logan grinned; the girl did not smile, her sober countenance altering slightly as she shifted her tongue in her mouth and let her eyes narrow.

She drew him from the stool, pulling him toward her and her companion as Logan absently adjusted his shirtfront and carried his drink and windbreaker to her booth.

She was incredible, he thought. She refused to be intimidated by his intent staring, but gave back in kind. Even when his legs were against the table, she continued to appraise him through smoky green eyes.

"Bob Logan," he said softly, ignoring the bespectacled girl chatting foolishly to her indifferent companion.

"Julie." She breathed her response.

"Julie," he repeated, his mouth acutely dry, his fingers beginning to tremble with excitement.

The girl refused to look away, her pale sparkling eyes traveling rapidly over his face. He said simply, "You're a beautiful girl, Julie. . . ."

"I know," she whispered, her lower lip moving provocatively against the music. "I think *you're* beautiful. . . ." She slid to the center of the cushion, inviting him closer.

Logan was extremely warm as he coasted into the seat and felt their arms touch momentarily. She had him thoroughly uncomfortable and obviously relished it. He took a sip of his drink, his gaze locking with hers. He sent his glance drifting eagerly to her mouth, inspecting the soft wide lips and the tongue working excitedly within. He tried to think of something witty, but the eyes had defeated

123

him. He bought time for his numbed brain by bringing the glass to his lips.

She recognized the act for what it was and sighed. "I've never seen you in here before."

"The one major regret of my life," he explained. Then he tested her with "I'm just passing through for a few days. . . ."

Her mouth drooped in disappointment. "That's too bad."

"But I'm nearby. . . ."

"That *is* nice." She smiled again. The glass came up in her hand, the tip of the tongue locating the rim before she sipped.

Logan knew that each move was a sensual reassertion of her hold over him.

"I'm Ernie Wheeler," his partner said as he joined them in the booth. "You girls just get off work?"

"We work across the street," the girl with glasses replied. "For the phone company. My name's Shirley." Ernie distinctly heard her say "fow-n company."

"I knew I'd heard your voice somewhere." Logan grinned, ignoring the other occupants of the booth.

Julie answered softly, "You sounded familiar, too."

"Married?" he asked.

"Divorced," she replied.

"Children?"

"Not yet. . . ."

"Engaged?"

"Not at the moment. . . ."

"Nasty weather!" Ernie interjected.

"Great day for a roaring fire," Logan offered, "and a little wine. . . ."

"I have the fire." She breathed sensually on his face as she leaned into his shoulder.

"I know you do, darlin'," Logan choked. He cupped his

124

chin in one hand, giving himself up to her pale green eyes. "What have you been doing with your life?"

"Waiting . . ." she grieved, "waiting for some big cowboy to come along and sweep me off my feet."

Logan ran his tongue over his parched lips.

"Are you a cowboy?" she asked softly.

"I could be," he said, surrendering completely.

"You're beautiful. . . ."

"Girls are beautiful . . . not boys. . . ."

"You're not a girl. . . . How do you know what I think?"

"I don't . . ." He retreated.

"We look at men the same way they look at us. . . ."

"Are you a leg woman?" He laughed, uncertain where she was leading him, but powerless to stop her.

She shook her head slowly. "I'm big in the ass department."

"Ass?" he said, louder than he wanted.

She nodded. "It's the first thing I notice about a man. It's the first thing I noticed when you came in."

"You have me at a disadvantage." He swallowed noisily.

"I know," she agreed.

The music from the ornate box filled the room, binding him to the girl with the pale green eyes. He didn't know how long she held him captive or why. "What are we doing for supper?" he asked.

"No plans—not till you came in."

"How about . . . steak? Lobster? Baked potato with sour cream and butter?"

She nodded a quiet "yes."

"And wine? Red wine? White wine?"

"With coffee . . . after."

"After? Yes, most certainly, coffee after."

"Most certainly. . . ."

"Do you know such a place in Odessa?" he asked.

"There's a wonderful place about a mile from here. . . ."

"I bet there is."

"It's called the 'Sixty-niners.' "

"I know that place!" Ernie interrupted. "We used to call it the Head Over Heels in Love Dinette."

"The Eighteen Sixty-niner!" the girl with glasses answered.

Ernie grinned. "I was just dreaming."

"Do you smoke?" she asked him when they were alone in her apartment.

"What?" he mumbled into her hair.

"I have some very good grass from Mexico. . . ."

"Sure," he said against her skin.

From a kitchen drawer she brought the makings of a roll-your-own kit. Julie eased him down on the long-haired sofa, stacked the record player with Neil Diamond, Elton John, Stevie Wonder, and Joe Cocker. She rolled the first one professionally, shaking the grass from a large salt shaker. Within seconds she had the tailor-made between his lips and a match lighting the end of it.

Logan wanted to taste the fingers holding the match, wanted to lift the sweater or kiss the wide soft lips, but he inhaled deeply, holding it inside his chest as she watched eagerly for his reaction.

"Good," he said, exhaling. She held one finger aloft and disappeared inside the bathroom. He heard the water running, the toilet flush. He wondered how Ernie was doing with the girl with the glasses. Julie had given Ernie the phone number where Logan could be reached, had seen to it that Ernie knew where to pick him up the following morning, leaving all the occupants of the car absolutely certain that Logan would be spending the night at Julie's apartment. Logan sensed that he had no control of the situation; the girl took everything upon herself, leaving Logan little to do except follow her lead.

She emerged in her robe, her hair down about her face in soft feathery fingers. She took the butt from the ashtray, placed it in a small round stone, and puffed it back to life.

Logan could see she had shed her bra as the center of the robe parted slightly to show him the soft white breast. He sent a hand along her stomach, the tips of his fingers searching stealthily for the union in the robe. Finding it, he sent his hand inside, touched the soft nakedness that burned his palm.

She ignored his hand; bending to the table, she rolled a fresh cigarette in the holder, lit it, and pressed it to his mouth. He took a deep drag, sipping air, while his hand played inside her robe.

She eased him back to the cushions, telling him, "Relax. It's my turn." She placed the tip of her tongue in the corner of her mouth, unbuttoning the front of his shirt, pulling it wide to expose his matted chest. Her nails cruised through the hair before they settled on his nipples. She tweaked them erect, bending close to watch their growth. "You like that," she whispered.

Logan wanted to say "no." He wanted to tell her that he seldom enjoyed being touched except in the groin area. But these fingers were different; he was enjoying what they were doing to him. "Yes . . ." he confessed. He sent one hand out to hold her breast, but she elbowed it aside. He drew his arms back above his head as he puffed the joint deliciously. He gave her plenty of room, watching with excitement as her mouth enveloped the tiny peaks and held them with her teeth.

"You like that. . . ." He moaned his answer, feeling the room charge with electricity. He no longer knew if it was her mouth, or the cigarettes, or her hands, or the crooning words that excited him.

"You like this?"

"Yes. . . ."

"You would not want me to stop. . . ."

"No . . . please. . . ."

"We like the same things, Robert," she whispered against his chest. "Let me . . ." she coaxed, her hands pulling the large buckle free.

Logan clutched the pillow to shut out the loud pounding in his head, but it refused to go away. He withdrew his head from beneath the pillow, tasted the dry aftertaste of the grass as he looked about her room. He saw her robe lying across the chair, heard the persistent pounding. He looked for his clothes, but they were nowhere about. He crawled from the covers, tracking the steadfast rapping sounds to the front door. His clothing lay in a bundle at the foot of the couch; he pulled the boxer shorts past his legs, snapping them at the waist.

Opening the door a crack revealed Ernie storming in the hall. "What the hell are you doing?"

Ernie shoved his way inside, his eyes red from lack of sleep, the stubble dark on his chin. "I slept in the car last night!" he yelled. "That's what the hell I'm doing!"

"Why did you sleep in the car?"

"Two nights in a row I had to sleep in a goddamn car!"

"Why did you sleep in the car?" Logan repeated as he stumbled into the kitchen in search of coffee.

Ernie took a note from the electric coffeepot and passed it to Logan. "What a lousy night!" he shouted as he threw open the cabinets, searching for a cup.

"What the hell happened?"

"I took her home," he said, pouring himself a mugful of steaming coffee, "and we were getting ready to get it on, you know. She went into the bedroom and I took off for the john. I mean, I had to take a crap real bad. Wow! Like it was a real award winner, you know what I mean? Well, I flushed the toilet and the damn thing backed up on me. The damn thing wouldn't stop! Toilet paper, crap, everything pumping out on the carpet! The damn thing wouldn't shut itself off!"

"So what did you do?" Logan demanded.

Ernie angrily flew into the living room with his coffee. "She came to the door and asked, 'Is everything all right?' What the hell was I going to tell her? That I took an award winner and it was lying on the carpet? I tried to shut off the water! But there was no valve under the crapper! I mean, I'm down on my hands and knees and water's running out from under the door! And she keeps saying, 'Is there anything wrong?' Finally I just threw open the door and when she came in, I went out! I slept in the car. . . ."

"Why did you run?"

"I didn't know what *else* to do!"

"You left that poor girl with her toilet backing up like that?"

"What the hell am I supposed to do?" Ernie wailed. "Call a plumber at midnight?"

"Ernie. . . ." Logan shook his head in disappointment as he trudged wearily back to the kitchen for coffee. "Ernie, you've got no class!" He poured himself a cup and took half-and-half from the refrigerator to add to the coffee. He leaned against the sink and read the note she'd left him: "I don't know who you are, but I love you!" She'd signed it "Julie," adding a dozen X's across the bottom.

"I telephoned Fleming already," Ernie called from the next room. "It's still pouring. Houston says it will be clear by tomorrow, as planned. So everything's being held for another twenty-four hours."

"Did you check in with Brook?"

"Yeah. He says we're to wait for Fleming to give us the word. Until the mesa bust goes down, we're to stay close to the Feds."

Logan took his coffee into the bathroom. "Looks like we have another day off."

Logan lifted the lid to relieve himself, saw the note Scotch-taped to the mirror, and pulled it loose. "There's a new toothbrush on the sink. I'll call you the first chance I get. Please . . . don't leave before we talk. I love you." There were many X's, but no signature.

Next to the toothbrush lay a Gillette razor and a tube of shaving cream. Logan flushed the toilet and ran his hand over the day's growth of beard. "You want to shower and shave?" he called.

"I need something," Ernie answered.

Logan opened the shower door and turned on the water. He dropped his shorts as Ernie asked wistfully. "I guess everything went all right with you."

"It went all right. . . ."

"Yeah, you had the best-looking one. . . ."

"Yours wasn't so bad, Ern."

"I shouldn't have run out like that, but when I saw that big turd come out, I lost my head. . . ."

"That wasn't too smart," Logan called through the shower door.

They spent the day at the Odessa library, heads stuck into microfilm machines as they scoured the local papers for any news within the country. On November 1, 1963, the South Vietnamese government of President Ngo Dinh Diem was overthrown. The President and his brother were killed in a military coup. Logan read the news over Ernie's shoulder. He'd been in Nam that day and remembered thinking he wasn't at all unhappy with the turn of events. The coup against the Diem brothers had begun at one in the afternoon. The special forces had watched the revolt with interest. They weren't at all surprised when government troops stormed the palace the following morning and executed the Diem brothers. The action brought the pro-American Major General Duong

"Big Mink" Van to power. Logan realized he'd condoned the action at the time.

Logan closed out the day at his own machine with the news of three civil rights workers missing in June, 1964. They had now covered most of the period in question. They'd scoured the newspapers from June of 1963 to June of 1964 and hadn't uncovered enough robberies in the nation to account for *half* the money they had in their possession. They left the library in the evening to meet the girls at the Dry Hole, an encounter Ernie reluctantly agreed to under considerable pressure.

Ernie secured a booth while Logan went to the pay phone near the rest room and placed a call to Sheriff Wells.

"Are you putting me on?" Wells asked him.

"No, why?" Logan asked in surprise.

"Hell, that license number you gave me was issued in 1963! It's been missing since 1964! There hasn't been a trace of it until you boys came up with that number!"

"Amarillo was probably mistaken. Maybe it's been up there on one of those sheep farms," Logan explained.

"For over ten years?" Wells shot back. "I asked San Antonio to give me what they had on it, but the lines are down somewhere between here and there. I'll let you know if I can trace it, but I think you boys are on a bum steer."

"I guess you're right," Logan replied. "Thanks anyway."

"Nothing," he remarked to Ernie as he rejoined the group in the booth. Julie had two surprises; she had traced the numbers given her by Logan and she planned to cook supper for the four of them.

Logan tried his best to hide the excitement created by the phone numbers. He had told her they were old listings of a former buddy missing since early 1964 or late 1963. He passed it off lightly, saying, "I really appreciate that. I'll get them from you later."

The girls were in the kitchen cooking when Julie brought him the slip of paper held between two damp fingers. Ernie moved down the couch to read the listings.

"These came from line cards in Dallas and Fort Worth," she explained. "I couldn't find a thing on them, so I called a friend of mine in Fort Worth and he had to go to the tubs to get them."

"Tubs?" Ernie asked.

"Each phone number is listed numerically in a 'tub.' The number itself is called a line card. It has all the service information listed and the name of the person or business occupying that listing. When the number is changed, the name's erased and a new one written in on the line card when it's been reassigned. They usually do that sixty days after it's been disconnected; that's to keep people from getting the old number when they call."

"So you were able to trace the old listing for these numbers?" Logan asked as he began to realize how complicated the system had become.

"They write it in pencil; matter of fact, they use number two lead just so they can erase the names. I had to have both line cards pulled, in both cities, and ask if they could read the old listings. Sometimes it's almost impossible. The Fort Worth number was listed to a pay phone in the Texas Hotel and the Dallas number was listed to the police department. So I think you have the wrong numbers."

"The garlic bread!" Shirley shrieked from the kitchen.

"I think you must have made a mistake," Julie shouted as she raced away.

"I think you're right," Logan called after her.

Ernie shook his head in disbelief. "What the hell would the guy have been doing with the phone number to the Dallas police?" he whispered.

"Maybe . . . he was a cop," Logan said softly as he stared at the two numbers.

"A cop with eight hundred and fifty thousand?"

"Maybe he was making a big buy. . . ."

"Without escorts? Or wires? Or microphones? No chance. They just wouldn't let him go off alone with all that money."

"Maybe they didn't know it," Logan guessed. "Maybe the money was scheduled for a buy and he decided to take off with the department's payroll . . . just like *we're* planning on doing. . . ."

Ernie agreed. "He could have had a friend on the force to finger it for him . . . it wouldn't be the first time it's happened. . . ."

"I don't know. . . ." Logan sighed. He hadn't been prepared for this. He hadn't been at all prepared for a Dallas police listing. The consecutive order of the bills now seemed ominous. He kept his voice low as he said, "Maybe it was some sort of payoff . . . maybe they wanted to be able to trace the bills . . . shit! I don't know!"

"They wouldn't have to be marked if all the numbers ran consecutively like they do," Ernie responded. "All the banks have to do is look for a twenty between two sets of numbers and we're screwed!"

Logan crumbled the paper, rolling it into a tiny ball, and burned it in the ashtray. "Does that mean that this guy was in it with someone else? If so . . . was his half of the loot eight hundred and fifty thousand? Or was that to be split with someone else?"

"If his share was eight hundred and fifty *thou*"— Ernie whistled under his breath as he added rapidly— "then the two of them scored for a million . . . seven hundred . . . *thousand*—"

"Sshh!" Logan stopped him. "Jesus, that's a hell of a lot of dough!" He whispered cautiously.

Ernie hissed angrily, "I'd just like to know what the hell we have here!"

"I can't help but think there's something in everything

133

we've seen and learned so far. Some other piece of information that we took from him . . . something important is slipping right by us. . . ."

"We've looked through everything! We can't run a tracer on the guy!"

Shirley entered with a pair of highballs to end the discussion. "You're going to really like supper." She glowed in Ernie's direction.

9

Logan's assignment on the mesa was to be shared with a federal narcotics agent, a burly Easterner named Lou Grillo. It had been Grillo's questions from the bed at the motel meeting that riled Logan; now he found himself sharing the stakeout of the mesa with this curious man.

Grillo arrived for the assignment in low-topped shoes, a thin worn sports jacket, and the trousers from a discarded suit. He showed an intense dislike for Texas, its surroundings, the two-day delay, and the Border Patrol's participation in a government smuggling bust. Logan sensed the hostility and needled him. "Is that your idea of outdoor clothing?"

"Just drive the fucking jeep," the agent growled.

Logan entered the area from the south, keeping his vehicle in the brush, leaving as few tracks as possible as he swung in a wide arc through the most inaccessible territory possible. Emerging to the west of Amarillo's camper, the four-wheel drive kept to the damp wash as it approached Alianza mesa. Logan reached his position by eleven thirty, a half hour before a federal air-surveillance plane, a twin Beech, flew over the area and radioed all units that the mesa appeared to be in good condition.

"Why don't you bust some of these plane-rental outfits?" Logan demanded of Lou Grillo as the agent watched him covering the jeep with brush. "That's where all the big shit's coming in from!"

Grillo kept his hands to his pockets, leaning out of the cigarette smoke curling past his face. "As long as they file a flight plan with either the FAA or the Mexican

135

government and meet all the plane-rental requirements, what the hell are we to do?"

"Bust those flying services!" Logan insisted.

"Look, friend," Grillo fumed, "you stick to the beaners and leave the big stuff to guys who know what the hell they're doing."

Logan went about furiously hacking brush, throwing the greasewood out of his way until he was satisfied the jeep was well covered. He didn't like being treated like an unruly child. He hated the prejudicial scorn Grillo had for the patrolmen, the derisive rivalry that existed between bureaus.

Seething with anger, he climbed the wash to the mesa, his arms loaded with coffee, binoculars, and the two-way radio. Logan kicked a shelf clear of rubble, set the thermos in a stable spot, removed the field glasses from their case, and set the radio within easy grasp.

Knowing the agent had brought nothing with him, Logan set about pouring himself a cup of hot coffee, lit a Marlboro, and enjoyed both in a noisy war of attrition.

Grillo cursed the steep bank as he slipped and slid, crawled and clawed his way to the mesa lip. The agent settled down uncomfortably on the face of the gully, the coffee and cigarettes within arm's reach.

Logan searched the mesa with field glasses, scanning the steaming soil, the sun climbing the sky, drying everything in its reach. He kept one eye on Grillo, waiting, praying the man would attempt to reach for Logan's coffee or cigarettes. Grillo disappointed him, preoccupied with maintaining a perch on the steep wall.

Ernie reported that he was in position on the eastern edge of the plateau and Logan acknowledged the call. Other units radioed in their positions alongside the highways. Fleming had agents dressed as linemen atop the telephone poles, a small flood-control crew worked the culverts, a paint truck marked the center line with two extra crew members. At a small airport in Madera a border-patrol helicopter awaited instructions. Men dressed as sheepherders guarded a flock along the highway's western boundary.

The expected pickup unit never materialized.

At dusk the road crews packed it in, returning to Stone Hill for a change of clothing and vehicles. One by one the units returned to take up secondary stations along the highway, radio receivers close at hand.

Logan finished the last of his sandwiches. He knew there was now a better-than-average chance the drop had been canceled. The air began to chill rapidly as the sun set behind them. Grillo dozed in his sports jacket, his arms wrapped around himself for warmth. They had not exchanged a dozen words all day.

Logan was grateful he had dressed in old Western boots, a heavy mackinaw for the night, and faded blue jeans. He was thankful he hadn't worn his worsted uniform for lying around in the dirt. He could see Ernie across the way chatting with his federal companion. It helped to have someone along for the long hours of waiting, especially someone to talk to. He gave Grillo another glance, shaking his head in disgust. His had been the most unfortunate draw of all.

The night was fresh and clean, laundered by the rain; it hung a bright white moon for him to contemplate. Logan's attention went back to the Kaufman chimney and the stacks of tens and twenties buried there. He wanted to shake Grillo awake and tell the man that he didn't need this, that he was a rich man and didn't need this at all. He wanted to announce over the radio that he and Ernie Wheeler were leaving; the risk was not worth their sudden new wealth. He wanted to tell someone he and his partner were wealthy men and the bureau had no right to subject them to undue hazards.

"Red-and-white Bronco," the radio crackled at his elbow, "four-wheel drive . . . license number . . . Alfa Bravo . . . one . . . thuh-ree . . . fi-yiv . . . niner. Repeat . . . license number . . . Alfa Bravo . . . one . . . thuh-ree . . . fi-yiv . . . niner. Vehicle blew past twice at power-line repair road . . . Highway seven-niner . . . Vehicle entering area at repair road . . . over."

"All units are advised," Fleming answered.

"It's going down," Grillo grunted, suddenly awake.

Logan wondered which of the men in the motel room had made the call. The voice was that of a military man, familiar with combat jargon, someone accustomed to using a field phone, possibly an artillery spotter or A Team leader. Logan wondered if he could pick out the man among the many from that crowded room. What would he say if he did meet him? When were you in the country? If the man answered with "Early sixties," then Logan would know a lot more, would know how to proceed with the rest of the meeting.

"How much time do we have before he gets here?" Grillo asked.

"Almost an hour."

"What do you do if you have to take a crap out here?"

"You find a friendly bush and take a crap."

Grillo tried to stand, but his loafered feet went out from under him and he hit heavily on his side, rolling uncontrollably to the bottom.

Logan restrained a laugh until Grillo managed to get to his feet, holding an elbow. It was no longer funny and Logan felt guilty but couldn't force himself to ask the cursing agent if he were all right. Instead he said, "You have any shit paper?"

"No," the agent grunted in pain.

"In the glove compartment."

"Thanks. . . ."

The patrolman took in the pants with the dirty shiny seat, the scuffed loafers, the sports jacket with the elbows

138

ready to shred, and he began to chuckle. "Don't crap next to the jeep. We're liable to step in it if we're in a hurry."

Grillo ignored the taunt. With a bundle of paper clutched to his chest he moved cautiously off into the brush.

"Don't use all that paper." Logan laughed. It was permissible to laugh now that it appeared Grillo was unhurt.

"Fuck you!" Grillo snarled as he walked hesitantly into the dark brush.

Logan gave the man a few minutes, then called, "Look out for snakes! I had a partner bit on the balls by a diamondback rattler! The guy was taking a crap and the snake went for the heat!"

The brush exploded with Grillo's charge. The federal agent rushed off to the south in his confusion, crashing through the desert willows with one hand held across his face while the other held the pants aloft. The agent reached the wash, toilet paper gripped between his teeth, looking frantically around for the jeep. He relaxed visibly when he saw the covered vehicle.

"He begged me to suck the poison out," Logan continued.

The hand covering the face came down slowly to take the paper from the mouth. "What happened to him?" Grillo asked in terror.

"He died." Logan grinned.

It took the agent only a second to realize he'd been had. "You bastard!" he screamed.

Logan could see that Grillo was tossed between charging the wash to take him or pulling up his pants. Grillo wavered undecidedly before the pants won out. "You guys are fruitcakes," he screamed. "Only a nut would work out here!"

"That we are," Logan agreed.

"Get me back to the city, Lord!" Grillo prayed as he zipped his pants.

Logan waited till Grillo reached the lip of the mesa and settled into his familiar burrow before he said, "You can shove the city. You can shove the smog, the traffic, the bullshit. I wouldn't have it for twice the salary."

"Fuckin' fruitcakes! You guys are all short on one leg from standing on hills, for Christ's sake! Don't you guys ever wait anyplace level?"

"We leave all that level shit and glory crap to you boys. We don't want you to do anything hard."

"Fruitcakes," Grillo repeated.

"Standing on a hill beats the hell out of busting some kid for carrying a joint, then throwing all the forces of justice against him to see he gets at least ten to twenty for it."

"You'd rather collar beaners?" Grillo asked in surprise.

"There's no bullshit out here, Lou. We turn 'em back seven days a week, rain or shine."

"Chasin' down greasers isn't my idea of a good time."

"But there's no favoritism!" Logan snapped, getting angry at the man near his elbow.

"Don't give me that!" Grillo laughed sarcastically. "There's been plenty of you guys on the take!"

"You don't have guys on the take!" Logan spat back, turning to face Grillo, setting his feet under him in preparation. "Don't give me that crap! Every time there's a big bust that just starts to lead somewhere, somebody up there in Washington pulls the plug because they don't want some favorite son embarrassed!"

"And Brook doesn't phone the manufacturers ahead of time to tell them you guys are going to be around and run one of your green-card checks? Why do you think there's nobody there when you try to bust these large businesses? And when they're successful, how many of them carry union cards with the garment workers and suddenly we

140

find ourselves with another nonunion plant? You live under a rock, pal?"

Logan was stunned by Grillo's angry words. That same rumor had been circulating among the Immigration investigators. Three times in the past year investigators had uncovered companies hiring illegal aliens. Three times the Immigration officials had raided the plants only to find the premises almost deserted.

"There's a lot of juice in Washington!" Grillo continued. "Senators and Congressmen don't want their campaign contributors embarrassed! If illegal aliens are going to embarrass someone, it's squelched! If somebody's son is mixed up in smack, it's squelched! That's the way it's been and that's the way it'll stay!"

"Brook?" Logan asked numbly.

"Yeah, Brook," Grillo answered, the anger rapidly diminishing. "What I've said is off the record . . . Brook has no choice in it . . . he's like every other mother's son. He does what he's told and he moves up the ladder like a good boy. You'll do the same when it's time for your promotion."

"Juice," Logan whispered, recalling that another man he knew used that same word frequently. Ewing, the pilot, the cynic, a clinically observant man some ten years older than Logan but endowed with a bitter wisdom and philosophy he'd shared with the young patrolman the day Logan had flown as spotter.

Ewing had shown the patrolman how he used the sun to read the ground signs zipping below them. How he used the sun's rays striking obliquely to the ground to detect impressions in the earth, adding with a weary sigh, "But if it wasn't for the wetbacks, we'd have no jobs. Supply and demand, Bob—the great American way. We need the wetbacks. Don't you see that? We need them to storm our borders and flood through the gates; otherwise we can't justify our big budget requests to Congress every

141

year. We're losing the battle of the borders!" he cried in amusement. "The brown horde is sweeping the country-side!"

And Logan had said in confusion, "But they are!"

"Yes. . . ." Ewing smiled as he banked the Cessna over on one wing. "Convenient, isn't it? We ask for a lot of money each year, that gives us juice with the Congress."

"That doesn't make any sense," Logan protested.

"Sure it does!" Ewing exclaimed confidently. "Where would the FBI be without subversives? Where would the Army be without wars? Where would the CIA be without the Russians? It's all relative, Bob, all relative. We need more Russian spies! We need more subversion! We can't afford to lose our juice! Where would Henry have been without the Arabs and the Jews? Supply and demand, Bob, supply and demand! If the supply is lacking, we have to create it. We create demands for our services and we do our job so damn well that Congress insists we double our efforts. Democracy in action. Juice, my boy, juice. Thank God for little things, for subversion, for bright college kids who question our authority. Thank God for the Black Panthers and the Brown Panthers, the Minute-men and the SLA. Thank God for drugs, murder, and wetbacks; otherwise we'd all be pumping gas for the Arabs."

"I can't buy that."

"I know," Ewing said, exhaling loudly, "all men are created equal . . . liberty and justice for all . . . espe-cially for the privileged few. Justice has many corridors, one for the red man, one for the black, one for the brown, the weak, the old, the indigent. But you're a young man, Logan, a veteran, I assume?"

"Vietnam." Logan frowned.

"Ah, the last of the great wars. Democracy in action once again. The juice of America against the rind of Communism. That's what we need, Bob, another good war with plenty of bad guys we can hate, something to take our minds off the internal problems of democracy. Maybe we can kick this Arab thing into a full-scale blowup. What do you think of that?"

Before Logan could answer, Ewing had gone on, carried away by some angry bitterness that took control of him, squeezing the words out in rapid succession. "The problem we have with that is those damn Jews! I mean, who ever heard of a six-day war! Nobody fights a war and wins it in six days! Nobody! My guess is, that's what old Henry told them. 'You boys have to learn that a war, to be effective for all concerned, has to last at *least* three to five years! Anything longer and the people begin to question your motives and goals!' You think Henry told them that? I'm sure the Jews have screwed up everybody's plans. I mean, *two* short wars! They should be ashamed of themselves! I guess we can blame the Arabs in part, lousy soldiers! Always were! But we'll train them a little better this time, give them some of them new weapons, tell them a few of the Jewish secrets, maybe slip them the recipe for matzo balls, maybe even sneak them a little closer next time. If we could get them closer to Tel Aviv, then it's land they wouldn't have to fight for. What do you think of that, Bob? You think we can negotiate the Arabs a little closer to Tel Aviv? It's going to be hard. . . ."

"I think you're full of shit."

"You're probably right, Bob," Ewing said sadly. "Congress will use its juice to limit the use of firearms in the good old States and vote arms to the Arabs the same day. We don't want our own people killed with guns, but we'll help any other nation kill its enemy. Just tell us how many you want."

Logan refused to comment; he turned his attention to the ground below them, watching the shadow of the Cessna keeping abreast of them as they skipped across the desert.

Ewing announced, "Class is over for the day. . . ."

Logan asked the window, "How can you stay with it if you hate it so much?"

"Is that what you think? That I hate it? Maybe I do. I had a son—a little younger than you. I always thought he'd grow up and we'd have each other to bounce things off. We don't even speak anymore. He tried to tell me during the Vietnam thing that it was all wrong—that the Justice Department and all eight of its families were full of crap—but I wouldn't listen to him. He said that any government that creates H. Rap Browns, Black Muslims, and Brown Berets had to be wrong. That we're responsible for creating the SLA and the Minutemen. We're responsible for the bombs they plant and the hate they feel. I didn't believe him until it was too late, until I was visited by the government, looking for my son. Did I tell you he was almost your age? He went underground—whatever the hell that is. Now he's one of the ones who plant the bombs. He's one of the haters. They have a file on me, too, now—like son, like father, I guess. One of these days I'll land and they'll give me my walking papers."

"How long ago was that?" Logan asked.

"Last year."

"But nothing's been done to you."

"No, not yet, but they don't have my son yet. He's on their list. I don't know whose list—or why—I don't even know where he's at. I know that they read my mail. I know now that he was telling me the truth—he's the only one who has told me the truth. They have a file on me—somewhere. I can't stop them. I can't even complain! They won't hear any explanation; Brook knows about it, but nobody will tell me what they have—what they want from me. Someday someone will decide I'm an embarrassment to them and they'll dump me, and there's nothing I can do about it. I lack the juice. . . ."

"Nothing will happen," Logan reassured him. "You do a damn good job!"

"You think so?" Ewing asked.

It seemed so important to the man that Logan nodded "yes" before turning away in discomfort.

Logan shook the memory of Ewing away, pausing to look in Grillo's direction. He scanned the man carefully, from the worn button-down collar to the tired old loafers. He remembered Grillo's posture in the motel room, the confident manner, the questions, the slight nod Grillo slipped Fleming. Grillo, so conspicuously out of place with his New York, big-city Eastern manner and clothes, whereas Fleming was so obviously a native Texan. He suddenly wondered, which man was boss? Did Fleming assign Lou to the mesa, or did Grillo assign himself the post? And if so, why? Why was it so important for Grillo to be near the drugs?

"What are you doing here, Lou," Logan asked evenly, "protecting somebody's investment?"

"I don't know what you're talking about," Grillo said firmly.

"Sure you do, Lou." Logan laughed to hide the bitter anger welling up. "Fleming's supposed to be running the show, but you're the one who's really pulling the strings, isn't that it? You're here to see that everybody stays in line, right, Lou?"

"You're *outta* line, buddy!" Grillo whispered, his voice dipping low and threatening. "Your head's been out in the sun too long."

"What's your job, Lou? Are you here to make sure that one of our South American OAS neighbors isn't shamed by a drug bust from their country? What is it, Lou? Hell, we're all part of the big eight in the Justice Department, aren't we? We're all going to toe the line when the time comes, isn't that right?"

"Fuck off, Logan, you don't know what the hell you're talking about!"

Ernie's voice abruptly ended the matter as the radio proclaimed, "He's here on my side! Shutting down. . . ."

"What's he shutting down for?" Grillo demanded.

Logan answered into the radio, "Our man's on the mesa, shutting down."

"What the hell did you do that for?" Grillo repeated.

"So the damn thing doesn't pick up a call! All we need is Fleming to start yelling into that thing and we'll blow the whole enchilada! You can hear a sound for miles around here."

The red-and-white Bronco came over the rise onto the mesa, just a few hundred feet from Ernie's position. Logan dropped his head instinctively. The driver cut the engine; the parking lamps were snapped off. The vehicle sat in darkness until a flame flashed in the cab. Grillo whispered, "He's lighting a steamer."

The Bronco was a good hundred yards from Logan's position, silhouetted against the sky; the men could see the glows from the interior as each drag was taken. Minutes later the cigarette arced out into space and the mesa was quiet, the only sound the tense breathing of Lou Grillo. Forty minutes later the interior light flashed on and the driver could be seen checking his watch. Logan dropped the binocular and checked his own watch. The interior light went off, then on again as the driver opened the door, slammed it loudly, plunging the vehicle into darkness. Logan followed the man as he went to the far side of the Bronco. "Make a note for your report," he told Grillo. "At ten thirty the suspect took a leak."

The passenger door opened and a red light blinked brightly on. Logan watched it sway about, took it to be some sort of flashlight with a red gelatin or cellophane placed over the lens. The object was placed on the ground, the red eye staring out at their position. Then another flashlight snapped on. It was carried away from the vehicle and set on the ground.

"He's marking out the runway," Logan mumbled as other lights were added, indicating the northern perimeter of the landing strip. The red markers were placed fifty feet apart, with two or three of them outlining each sideline. The driver climbed back into the vehicle and drove toward them. "Shit," Grillo complained as he ducked quickly.

The Bronco went to the far southern end of the mesa, stopped, swung a U-turn, and faced north. The man got out once again, placed the lights carefully on the ground as he outlined the far extremities of the runway. This done, the man climbed back into the cab, lit another cigarette, and waited.

"When the plane lands," Logan said, "I'll move down the gully to the loading area. I want to be as close to it as possible. Once the stuff's loaded in the Bronco, it'll get the hell outta here. We may have only a few seconds before the pilot lifts off, so we'll have to be on his ass and really rip out of here."

Grillo grunted approvingly, then complained, "My legs are killing me!"

"A couple more of these and you'll be an old trouper."

"I feel like I'm on the goddamn moon or something." Grillo shivered, pulling the thin jacket close around him. "There's no women, no nothing out here!"

"All the horses are stump broke." Logan grinned. "The only trouble is it's a damn long reach to kiss 'em."

The first sound of the plane's engine came in from the southeast, faintly at first but rapidly growing louder. The headlights of the Bronco snapped on, illuminating the mesa. Logan clicked the radio on when he was sure the sound would not be heard above the plane. "It's going down!" he announced several times. "It's going down!" Then he slipped the switch to the off position as the plane

147

threw on its running lights and the Bronco killed its head-lights. Logan knew it was a further signal between the two men, identifying both air and ground units. A missed response on the part of the Bronco and the pilot would have flown off. It was a very clever signal, he thought as the driver raced down the line, gathering up the lights as the plane's wheels touched down.

"It's a one eighty-five Skywagon!" Grillo shouted above the prop.

Logan read the numbers off the side of the plane as it roared past. "N . . . thirteen . . . twenty-four . . . U!"

"Must be a one eighty-five!" Grillo argued with him-self. "The engine's too big for a one eighty!"

The Bronco had already gathered his lights and was racing behind the plane to the mesa's northern end. The plane taxied to a slow walk and spun itself around in a wide turn facing south. Before the door of the aircraft opened, the landing lights went off and the jeep had whipped down the line, gathering up all the red flash-lights. The unloading began within seconds. Cartons were passed from the far side of the aircraft to the rear com-partment of the jeep.

"Let's go!" Logan whispered to his partner. He could hear Grillo behind him as they scrambled along the steep bank, moving north toward the plane. He could hear Grillo stumbling and slipping in the smooth-soled loafers as the agent tried to negotiate the side of the gully.

The smugglers were still unloading when Logan dropped into position abreast of the wing. Grillo arrived a full minute later, his breath loud and hoarse from the exertion. "They have the rear seats out!" he gasped. "It's all cargo!"

It was almost impossible for Logan to see the loading of the jeep; the aircraft blocked his line of vision and he had to content himself with peering intently at the driver's feet beneath the body of the ship as the man moved back and forth. The pilot reappeared in the cockpit, and Logan yelled, "Get out of there!" to the driver. On command, the Bronco spun to the rear, cranked a hard right, and disappeared into the far brush.

"Tell them what's happening," Logan shouted, stuffing the radio into Grillo's arms. Bolting from the wash, Logan scrambled over the lip of earth and sprinted the sixty yards toward the plane. Ernie popped from cover at the same instant, racing Logan to the unwary man at the controls. Ernie had the magnum pistol high in the air, his legs pumping. Logan knew he could not beat Ernie to the aircraft; the distance was twice as far. He felt his heart leaping in his chest as he fumbled with his weapon and managed to jerk it from the holster without losing it.

The pilot sat in the glow of the instrument lights, giving a last momentary check to his dashboard, the prop whipping the air. He looked up, saw Ernie rushing toward him, and sent the prop into a high-pitched roar.

"Damn it!" Logan screamed as a slight depression caught at his ankle, sending a sharp pain racing up his leg. The plane was just beginning to roll forward when Ernie's body suddenly appeared in the cockpit.

The Cessna 185 Skywagon was a high-winged aircraft, the thirty-five-foot wing mounted atop the cockpit with a support strut angling from the wing to the nose of the fuselage. Logan painfully hurried toward this strut as the plane began to taxi forward. But the distance was far too great and the strut began pulling slowly away from his reach. Logan turned his attention to the rear of the plane, hoping somehow to secure a handhold on the horizontal stabilizer near the tiny rear wheel and, in this way, stop the forward motion of the aircraft.

The pilot fought Ernie to get the throttle forward. They passed Logan by, leaving him with the rapidly advancing tail coming up on his left. Logan timed his run to grab the tail as it went by. It was a gesture that succeeded only in dreams, a human hand snatching a 300-horsepower engine to a standstill. The edge of the plane slapped securely into his palm; the arm was jerked tight by the thrust, whipping him off-balance and flinging him to the rear. He tried to secure a second handhold, balancing the weapon, trying to get an extra finger in place. The ground speed was increasing as Logan tried to set his feet. But it pulled him along in contempt, the edges cutting his hands, his feet flying uncontrollably beneath him. He looked up to see Ernie's upper torso inside the aircraft as he wrestled with the pilot.

My God, Logan thought, *he's going to kill us all!* The tail pulled free of his grasp, leaving him running painfully behind it. The momentum carried him forward until he threw up his hands to catch at the ground racing up in the darkness to meet him. He sprawled face down in the dust as the tail came up and Ernie's feet left the ground. Logan gathered the weapon in front of him, aimed at the dark shape attached to the cockpit, swung his sight to the dark torso of the aircraft, which now began to weave erratically. He forced himself to hold his fire as the target swung back and forth in front of him.

"Jump!" he yelled to Ernie. "Jump! God damn it!" The plane was starting to lift off, but the added weight hanging from the cockpit kept the wheel on that side glued tenaciously to the ground.

"Oh, Jesus," Logan cried as he stumbled to his feet and began to chase after his partner. "Get off," he whispered helplessly. "We're rich, Ern—we don't have to do this anymore."

The end of the plateau was just ahead, sloping rapidly downhill toward the small wash separating this mesa from its sister. The right wing rose in agony—for a brief instant the craft appeared to be airborne. When the left wingtip caught the ground, the tail snapped skyward. The plane froze in midair, pulling a cry from Logan's throat. The craft bounced from the left wingtip to the right, cartwheeling across the mesa, exploding on the fourth somersault as it rose in a shuddering ball of flame that dropped from view into the wash only to reappear as two separate flaming sections. Even as Logan watched, the two became three, the three, four. Disintegrating before his eyes as the Cessna shook itself to death.

Logan staggered to a halt, his breath rasping as he fought for air, the pyrotechnic display startling in its ferocity. A smaller explosion sounded, racing beneath his feet, stabbing painfully into his chest, then another, and still he couldn't move. His arms hung heavily at his sides, his eyes began to tear. The wetness ran all the colors together into an orange canvas and he had to bite his lips to keep from crying out.

The two federal agents skidded to a stop at his side. "Holy Christ!" Grillo said. "What happened to the other guy?"

Logan tried to raise his hand to indicate the flaming wash, but his arm wouldn't respond. His legs began to draw him to the heat, away from the agents to a place where he could be alone with his thoughts, free to sort out the incredible scenario.

"Where's the other guy?" Grillo persisted.

"Fuck you guys," Logan cried. "Fuck all you guys. . . ."

There was no way Logan could explain Ernie to anyone. He could not begin to tell the men that it had been for nothing, that they were rich beyond anyone's wildest dreams. Rich in companionship as well as money. Rich in understanding and affection. Rich in a way few find in their lifetime. Too rich to have taken foolish chances on an operation that was really none of their concern. He knew that if Brook were suddenly to appear, he'd have no qualms about emptying his revolver into the ambitious official.

A head appeared against the flames. It climbed upward

out of the wash, revealing first the shoulders and then the limping figure of a man.

Logan caught his breath and stared in wonder at the swimming orange figure before him. The man stopped to look back into the flames.

"Ernie?" he cried aloud. "Ernie!" he shouted, walking rapidly forward, then running toward the man staring into the flames.

Ernie gave him the familiar lopsided grin, the flames playing off the perspiration and dirt-splashed face.

"You bastard," Logan said, choking, "you bastard . . . bastard. . . ."

"Screwed up your plans for spending all that money by your lonesome old self, didn't I?"

"That's right." Logan sighed in relief as he hid a sniff and passed the arm of his coat across his eyes.

"I couldn't get him out," Ernie said to the fire. "I tried, but I just couldn't reach him. . . ."

Pounding feet brought the two federal agents to a halt beside them. Grillo stabbed a stubby pistol back into the armpit holster beneath the thin sports jacket. "What the hell were you doing on there?" he asked Ernie.

"I was telling the guy that this is a thirty-five-mile zone and I wanted to see his license. He said he wasn't speeding, but I said, 'I'll have to give you a ticket anyway—' "

Grillo snorted, "You fuckin' guys are fruitcakes!"

Logan shook his head at Ernie. "You crazy bastard. . . ."

"Fruitcakes!" Grillo repeated as he and his partner went into the wash to examine the burning debris.

Ernie began to limp back toward his jeep. Logan ignored his own pained ankle and slipped Ernie's arm around his shoulder. "Why the hell didn't you jump?" Logan admonished him.

"I don't know. . . ." Ernie shrugged, grimacing as he put his weight on the painful leg. "I never thought the guy would actually try to take it up. When I realized he was going to try to fly that friggin' thing, we were going too fast to jump! Besides, my arm was stuck inside and my feet were off the ground. He didn't let go of me until we ran out of Astro Turf. We must have hit something . . . 'cause I was sent flying through the air. I saw that strut coming, but I couldn't grab it—it hit my knee—so help me, I didn't jump. I don't know what happened exactly, but it sure screwed up my knee. . . ."

"Crazy bastard . . ." Logan repeated as he guided Ernie back to the jeep.

Federal agents trailed the red-and-white Bronco to the unpainted structure of a long-abandoned sheep farm. Three dozen Drug Enforcement, Customs, and Immigration personnel surrounded the farm immediately after the Bronco entered. Logan, Wheeler, Brook, and Lou Grillo were the last to arrive at the scene. Logan noted that no one made a move until Grillo's appearance, then the agent was briefly informed by Fleming of the plan of action. Grillo nodded his approval and saw that Logan noticed this passing of the command. Grillo fixed Logan with a hard, silent stare. The patrolman threw a knowing wink in reply.

Logan and Wheeler were mere spectators to this final chapter of the bust. It had been only at Brook's insistence that they were even at the scene. There had barely been time to wrap Ernie's swiftly swelling knee before they joined the tag end of the procession to the farmhouse.

Fleming took his own signal to wave the men forward. To the rear, across the field, Logan could see figures moving through the trees to take a position at the rear of the house. Grillo and Fleming took the narrow creek bed that led along the long driveway. The attacking forces left Logan and Ernie alone on the highway, watching the scene with amusement.

Grillo walked up to the front door, complied with regulations by knocking and then identifying himself. Another federal agent, to the rear, cupped his hands over his mouth and shouted, "Come in!" and the door gave way to Grillo's large number elevens.

It was over in seconds, without a shot being fired. Logan and Wheeler went up the driveway, casually strolling to the house, arriving in time to see Grillo with his knee on the suspect's neck, the cuffs being snapped in place. So many men crowded the tiny farmhouse that they barely had room to move.

There was a small cot in one corner, a tiny butane stove with the makings of several days' garbage scattered around. One of the empty bedrooms held eight hundred kilos of grass, twenty kilos of coke, and sixty kilos of heroin, the result of several successful flights.

"Where's the horse coming from?" Fleming asked, jerking the man to his feet.

The driver, a young man in his late twenties, said, "I don't know anything."

A native Texan drawled, "Looks like some of the stuff we've been getting lately from Costa Rica."

Grillo hurried from the other room when he heard this, pulling Fleming to one side and whispering savagely in his ear. Fleming started to protest, resorted to a final angry, helpless stare before announcing, "Book him!"

Grillo directed a warning look at Logan. The patrolman laughed and limped out to the porch.

The agents filed out of the house with the suspect. Cars were quickly loaded with drugs and agents. When Grillo emerged, Logan leaned forward to whisper to him, "Have to cover for your Costa Rican connection, huh, Lou?"

Grillo exploded; his forearm moved up, swiftly pinning Logan's throat to the building. For a long second he held the patrolman in position while the surprised Brook scrambled around both men. Logan kept the smile on his lips, even though the hard forearm was pressed tight against his windpipe. He gave Lou a shove with the magnum pressed against the man's belly. Grillo looked down in astonishment at the barrel thrust deep into his shirtfront. He had never seen the hand move, had never felt the jerk of the weapon from the holster.

"Take it easy!" Fleming announced as he broke them apart.

Lou warned, "You'd better tell this wise ass to shut his fucking mouth!" The hand fell away as Lou shrugged the coat into place and backed uneasily off the porch.

"What the hell was *that* all about?" Brook demanded of Logan.

Logan shrugged, the smile fixed on his face for the departing Lou Grillo to see. "Our friend there is the fixer. It's his job to see that these busts don't embarrass somebody in Washington. Lou knows there's someone up there who wouldn't be too happy to read that we busted a Costa Rican connection. Who's in Costa Rica? Only God and Lou Grillo know."

"Shut your mouth!" Grillo snarled from the waiting auto. In reply, Logan flashed him a two-finger victory sign.

Brook started to protest, "That has nothing to do with our job in this—"

"Oh shit," Ernie moaned, grabbing his knee.

"I'd better get him to a doctor." Logan had Ernie's arm over his shoulder, helping him down off the porch. "You bailed me out," he whispered softly.

"What the hell was *that* all about?" Ernie asked as they navigated the dusty road.

"It's Grillo—he's some sort of public relations man for the government. It took me a while to figure out he was the guy calling all the shots. His job is to see that none of this bounces back and taints somebody in Washington."

"The government's running drugs?"

"No, but there are people who make sizable campaign contributions with money they make off these flights from Guaymas, Hermosillo, Culiacán, and even Costa Rica. It's Grillo's job to see that it stays a local operation, that all the credit for horse and coke is given to the Mexicans."

"Brook knows about it?"

"God only knows. He's so far up their asses that if any of them stopped real quick, he'd break his goddamn neck!"

10

Few people in Texas knew the vagrant known as Toots, though many passed him each day along the highway, collecting aluminum cans and bottles with two mongrels at his heels. Fewer yet knew the name Henry Totelman, his given name.

But he had been among them all the time, his burlap bag over his shoulder, as they sped past him on the highway. In thirty years he'd covered the great canyons in search of the elusive metatarsal print. For over thirty years he persisted in his theory that the brontosaurs once roamed the canyons of Stone Hill and Durbin, Texas. But his quarry was an evasive one, a shallow depression preserved in stone that filled easily with sand, the first concavity to vanish with the wind of early morning or late evening.

He found it was best to look immediately after the rain, when the water had washed the stray sand from the rocky canyon bottom, leaving a hard, clean stone surface beneath his feet. Each succeeding day decreased considerably his chances of finding a clean rock flooring.

The rain had stopped sometime during the night, awakening him instantly with its thunderous silence. He opened the door to the tin shed a crack, glanced at the sky, decided within seconds that opportunity was at hand. He hurriedly gathered his sack and stick, hoping to make the Merida wash by daybreak. The dogs stretched in protest before joining him outside. He moved rapidly for a man in his seventies, his back hunched from years of peering down.

The Merida arroyo ran for forty miles to the Rio

Grande. Toots stored his sack beneath the highway, praying the wind would hear his prayers and hold her breezes until he completed his inspection of the area. There would be few opportunities during the year; he had to take what destiny provided, for a poor man without equipment had little chance of uncovering valuable data. He was just an old man with a stick, poking and probing for the hint of revelation.

The dogs ran on ahead, leaving him feeling for impressions of the great three-toed foot or the telltale sign of a dragging tail.

It was almost sunset when he found the vehicle. The dogs discovered it first and were sniffing excitedly at the driver's remains. It lay on one side, sand piled against its bottom, forming a small coffer dam of damp earth. He gave the tires a brief glance as they hung limply in the air. Toots chased the dogs away with his stick and bent to examine the bleached bones and tattered cloth gathered around the waist. The jeep lay on the driver's side, the skeleton on the hard canyon floor. His trembling fingers followed the fracture of the skull, tracing its path above the eyes in the frontal bone to the place where it leaped to the parietal bone. The teeth were those of a young man in his late twenties or early thirties. The mandible and maxilla bones of the jaw were cracked, the nasal bone fractured. He reasoned that the young man died from severe damage to the head. The chest was crushed, the sternum and rib cage penetrated by the impact of the steering column. The cause of death could be attributed to the massive chest injuries. *The head or the chest?* he wondered. It was impossible to tell without the proper tools. An outflung arm showed fractures in both the ulna and radius, with multiple fractures of the phalanges of the hand.

Toots removed the West Point ring, studied it for a moment, debated its value, then threaded it back on the skinless clenched finger. He stepped around the body to examine the oddly shaped medallion in the ignition. He slipped it from the key ring, buffed it against his leg, and correctly identified the clipped-edged piece as a coin, a Spanish piece of eight, or eight reals, as the Spanish had named it. It had little value, for it took no fool to see it was a simple brass imitation. Toots pocketed it, thinking it might provide him with a trade for something of real value. Satisfied that there was nothing left for him, he gave the scene a last profound look and called the dogs.

"I hear you boys did a hell of a job up there," Hudson told him on the phone.

"We did okay," Logan told the chief patrol inspector. "I'm still at Del Amo Emergency."

"How's Wheeler's knee? Anything serious?"

"They don't think anything's broken, but he may have to be off it for a few days. They just sent him back in for more X rays. He must be all right, he tried to date the nurse."

"Ernie would screw a gopher hole." Hudson laughed. "Oh, Ewing found a body in your section this morning. I hear it's been there quite a while."

Logan tried to sound uninterested. "Oh?" he asked.

"I sent Roget and Lombasino to check it out. They found prints in and out of the area and they're tracking him now. We dumped the body on Kirkland's lap. It belongs to the sheriff anyway."

"No kidding," Logan managed.

"And Fleming told the department the drug bust is in the neighborhood of seventy-five million dollars—maybe more on the street."

"Not bad," Logan said softly. "I need some sleep, Stan. I'm really whacked out."

"Sure. Let me know how Ernie's doing. Catch up on your sleep and I'll call you at the apartment."

"Right. . . ."

"And Logan?"

"Yeah. . . ."

"You did a hell of a job, buddy."

"Thanks, Stan." Logan dropped the receiver on the cradle. Through the glass of the phone booth he could see the patients awaiting treatment. A child with a nose running mucus onto its upper lip began to cry, and the pregnant mother rocked it lovingly in her arms.

The waiting room was crowded with Mexicans; most were American citizens, accounting for seventy percent of the population of Del Amo, just as they did in many other border towns. Logan saw their tired, worried faces and he was overcome with the long night's ordeal. He found he could barely keep his eyes open. Hudson's information rattled around in his head. He wondered about the tracks in and out of the area. He wondered about Roget and Lombasino and who they were tracking. He wondered if he should have told Hudson that Brook was tipping off employers prior to their raids. The weariness engulfing him made it impossible to think clearly. He used the door of the booth to pull himself erect. He slid it open and was greeted with the wailing child. The cries followed him down the hall and into the treatment room. He collapsed in the chair and slid the dirty stetson over his eyes. *The body's no longer a secret,* he thought. Even now somebody was being notified of the discovery, somebody who would realize that the money was missing. It was all out of their hands now. They simply had to sit back and let things take care of themselves. He wondered if he should tell Ernie. He fell asleep debating it.

Logan and Wheeler returned to section seven the following day, but they were not prepared for the young men with rifles barring their way to the Merida wash.

"What do you mean we *can't* go down there?" Logan demanded of the young soldier.

The private apologized nervously. "Orders, sir."

Ernie insisted, "Whose orders?"

The boy shrugged, the rifle held across his chest, sweat pouring from under the fatigue cap. "Army orders, sir. . . ."

Logan thumbed the blue-and-gold-enameled badge above the left shirt pocket. "You know what this is?"

"Yes, sir," the boy stammered, "but no one's allowed in the wash, sir. I'm sorry. . . ."

Ernie adjusted his leg in the sling hanging from the windshield. He sent the boy a disarming grin. "Must be some kind of military secret."

"I guess so." The boy smiled awkardly before pleading, "I have my orders, sir. . . ."

"Course you do," Ernie apologized as two other young guards drifted over to their jeep.

Logan wrapped the wheel in his arms and smiled at the boys. "I hear they found a body down there?"

"Yes, sir," the private replied.

"What's the Army going to do with it?"

"You got me!" The boy laughed.

Another soldier offered, "I hear they're going to bring in a rig and lift that jeep right out of here."

Logan shook his head in disbelief. "Seems like a lot of trouble for an old jeep."

"Sure do!"

"Has the sheriff been around? Sheriff Kirkland?" Logan asked as he lit himself a cigarette.

"Big guy?" one of them asked.

Before Logan could answer, the boy on duty replied, "He was here this morning, real early. But we had to turn him back."

Ernie took Logan's cigarette. "You mean the sheriff of Moss County ain't allowed down there either?"

"That's right, sir."

Ernie whistled impressively. "You boys must be sitting on an atom bomb or something."

"Yes, sir," they piped in unison.

Logan threw them a wave. "Thanks, boys, we'll see you later." He clutched the jeep into gear and swung a large circle, heading south to the drag road. When they were far from the wash, he shut off the ignition and cruised to a halt. "What do you think?"

"Sounds pretty damn big, if you ask me."

"You figure he was an Army man?"

"Hell!" Ernie swore. "He could have been *anything!* If the sheriff can't go down there, and we can't go down there . . . then something big's really going down. . . ."

The next day, the patrolmen found the area in and around the wash undergoing a massive excavation. Soldiers, stripped to the waist in the hot sun, shoveled fifty yards in either direction of the jeep site. Young plainclothes officers circulated among the half-naked workmen, checking each shovelful of dirt moved out of the wash.

"CID," Ernie remarked from their vantage point on the hill. "Army investigators."

Logan pointed to the heavy tracks that tore up the area. "It must have been one of them tank cranes."

"They wanted that jeep pretty damn bad."

"Looks like it."

"Hey!" Ernie shouted, slapping the dash. "Maybe the guy stole a federal payroll! One of them Army payrolls! That's why we couldn't find it in the papers! He ripped off the Army for eight hundred and fifty thousand big ones and they hushed up the whole friggin' thing! That's why they want him so damn bad! They know he had the money with him!"

Logan felt the smile creep across his face as he quickly sorted through the logic of it. "Damn you, Ern! That's it! It has to be!"

"Wouldn't that explain the federal notes? The money in consecutive order?"

"An Army payroll! *That's* why they're digging, because they know it's there!"

"It has to be!" Ernie beat on the dash, emitting a wild, joyous shout, "Oh, God, ain't it beautiful!"

An approaching dust cloud skirted the north end of the digging site. The vehicle slowed, the dust drifted past the Moss County desert vehicle, a modified dune buggy with enormous tires and wire stretcher frames hanging from both sides.

"Kirkland," Logan said softly.

The sheriff saw them sitting on the hill and flung a hand above the roll bar in their direction. Logan honked his response.

The dune buggy left the civilian investigators in a cloud of dust as Kirkland sent the buggy roaring up the hill to their position.

Logan called across the two vehicles, "What the hell you doing, Paul?"

"Slumming," the sheriff replied as he stepped from his vehicle and moved to Ernie's side. "What's this I hear about you taking flying lessons?"

Ernie rubbed the knee. "I solo next month."

Kirkland was even bigger than Wells of Stone Hill. A younger man, Ernie and Logan's own age, with quick eyes that took in everything instantaneously and a brown, weathered face that resembled an old apple core. Two massive hands were raised to rest on the butts of matched magnum pistols. "What are you boys up to?" he asked, reaching into their jeep for Ernie's canteen.

"Been sweeping the drag roads," Logan replied.

Ernie tilted the canteen suddenly, sending water over

Kirkland's nose. "You think they're looking for oil down there?"

Paul wiped his face and chin, spun the cap down tight on the canteen. "Beats the hell outta me."

Logan pried gently. "I thought this was Kirkland territory."

"It was! Up until the time I sent our bony friend down there to Austin for a positive ID. Then all hell broke loose." Paul swept a hand to the wash and the soldiers working in the hot sun.

Ernie said aloud, "The guy must have been a Congressman or something."

"I wish it had been that simple. We had no ID at all, but there was this West Point ring, so we sent a dental chart off to the Army, Navy, Air Force, and the Marines to see if he had a service record. The Army made him as Lieutenant Will Beck of Norman, Oklahoma. Three hours later the Air Force identifies him as radar specialist Gene Medford from Austin, Texas."

"If that don't beat all," Ernie said in surprise.

"You don't have to be a real smart sheriff to know there's a funny odor in the air. So I got to thinking and I called Dallas, San Antone, Fort Worth, and Austin to see if either Medford or Beck had a civilian record on file. I even tried Norman, Oklahoma. . . ." The sheriff tipped the hat down low, tilting his head back to see out from under the bill. "That was when this whole thing was taken out of my hands."

Absorbed in the rapidly changing identities, Logan asked hesitantly, "What about the vehicle? Who was that registered to?"

"Michael Curtis"—Kirkland sighed in defeat—"resident of San Antone. Checking that out brought me the FBI, the CIA, the Justice Department, the Texas State Police . . . I don't know *who* all. Whoever he was, he was one busy son of a bitch. The Army has him off to Vietnam in October of 'sixty-three and the Air Force has him returning the following month, in November of 'sixty-three. Three days after Medford returned, this Curtis fellow shows up to buy this jeep in San Antone. Then the three of them just upped and disappeared by the end of the year. All that ties in with the coroner's report for the estimated time of death. He says it could be six months either way. Doesn't make a hell of a lot of sense, does it?"

Logan shook his head as Ernie whistled impressively. "Sure don't."

Logan offered. "They probably have the guys all mixed up. Typical government screw-up."

"Maybe. . . ." Kirkland frowned. "Except that neither branch of the service knew what the other had told me. One guy drops from sight and the other takes over."

Logan fought to restrain his eagerness. "But there must be training records?"

"The lid's already down on that. Matter of fact, when I asked, the Army began to ask about *me!* They've been checking through the state capital already on *my* record!"

"If that don't beat all," Ernie repeated.

Logan deftly turned the sheriff's attention from the wash by asking, "So how's the crime situation in Moss County?"

"Quiet. You guys had a big narcotics bust up on Alianza mesa and didn't tell anyone about it. What the hell gives?"

Logan held his hands aloft in surrender. "Peace, brother. That was none of our doing. It was all coordinated by the powers that be. The federal drug people called all the shots. We were mere spectators."

"They're supposed to *tell* us when they come into our area like that!"

"There was nobody there from the state or county," Ernie explained.

"Damn people!" Kirkland growled.

"Easy!" Logan warned, waving a finger between him and Ernie. "Big brother's listening to everything you say."

The sheriff held his hands high above his head. "I give up! Jesus, I wouldn't want the dynamite duo after me!" The sheriff dropped his hands slowly, already tired of the game. "I gotta go. There's a couple of kids lost in the foothills, airmen from the local base."

Ernie came alive. "How long?"

"Two days now, but the report just came in this morning. I've got a dozen of the local ranchers out there and a couple of Indians."

"City boys?" Ernie asked intently.

"Seems like it."

Logan explained, "What Ernie's trying to tell you is that, if you ask Brook or Hudson, they just might let Ernie tag along."

"You want to go?"

"Hell, yes!"

"What about that knee?"

"It'll be okay. C'mon, Paul, I haven't had a good track in a week!"

Kirkland went to the radio in his dune buggy. "You want to go?" he asked Logan.

Logan shook his head. "Somebody has to guard the shore against the Brown Peril." He laughed.

They listened as the call was relayed from the Moss County sheriff's office to the Immigration headquarters in Del Amo. Moments later Brook himself approved the loan of Border Patrolman Ernie Wheeler to the sheriff's department.

"Hot damn!" Ernie shouted as he hobbled to the sheriff's buggy.

The two drove off to the north, leaving Logan to watch the arrival of fresh Army troops. They shed their fatigue jackets and relieved their sweaty companions in the wash. One moment Logan had the details sorted out comfortably in his mind, the next they began to nag at him, chipping away at his "solid" theories. He'd been perfectly content to accept the reasoning behind the Army payroll robbery. Now, after talking with the sheriff, that explanation seemed too simple.

The other disturbing factor was the Army itself. They seemed determined to dig up the whole state of Texas if need be. With all that available manpower, it wouldn't take them long to realize the money was not in the wash. There was one more day, possibly two before the Army confirmed it. "Then what?" he mumbled. Would they begin to question everybody connected with the area? How long before they narrowed it down to the two Border Patrolmen, in whose domain the money had lain for many long years?

For a moment it appeared that all the diggers were resting on their shovels and looking his way. Logan nervously turned the ignition key and sped away. He had to rid himself of this urge to return each day to the digging site. Curiosity in itself was suspicious.

Logan gassed the jeep, checked the water level in the radiator. He topped the gas can and the water container, placed the battery-charger leads under the hood and set it for trickle charge. He was leaving the maintenance shed with the clipboard under his arm when he saw Ray Chadney, the local FBI agent, moving toward the parking lot.

"G-man!"

Chadney spun around in time to see Logan's hand flash toward the holster. The agent dropped behind a fender, opening fire with his own invisible weapon.

Logan blew the nonexistent smoke from the end of his index finger. "You're dead, Chadney." Logan smiled as he moved to the auto. "What the hell you up to?"

"Chasin' 'em down and lockin' 'em up." Chadney's

heavy Texas accent belied a degree in law that saw the local Del Amo boy graduate in the top ten percent of his Harvard class of 1960.

"I didn't think they ever let you out of San Antone."

"I'm guardin' the Alamo." Chadney grinned, pumping Logan's hand warmly. "Where's that shadow of yours, that good ol' boy Ernie?"

"The half-breed's up in the woods, looking for a couple of lost kids."

"Now *that's* something he can handle."

"What are you doing so far from home?" Logan asked again.

Chadney planted his butt against the fender. "We've got us a Russky across the border we're keepin' an eye to. Also had to do a little paperwork on the guy you boys found in the arroyo."

"I heard about that." Logan feigned a casual interest. "I saw the Army out there today; they're digging up the world. What the hell they up to, Ray?"

Chadney narrowed his eyes and whispered, "You been cleared for top secret?"

Logan crossed his heart. "Got me a secret decoder ring in my locker."

"A Captain Midnight Secret Squadron decoder?" Chadney asked in amazement.

"That's before my time," Logan admitted.

"Aw hell . . . it ain't nothin' special. They guy in the wash was jes' a case of simple mistaken identity . . . that's all."

Logan nodded, trying to hide the fact that he was visibly disappointed. "That's what the sheriff's been saying. . . ."

"Jes' a big mix-up, really . . . I'm more concerned with Rudy the Red, who went across the border."

Logan settled against the opposite fender, listening attentively. "Who is he?"

"Supposed to be jes' an ol' farm boy, one of them agricultural experts. But we think he's KGB. I have a couple of boys on his tail." Chadney patted Logan for a cigarette and Logan dug out the pack and shook one loose. "If we catch him doing somethin' we'll take his picture and send it on to the Russky Embassy. They'll send Rudy the Red home once his cover's blown. Then we sit back and wait for the next one."

Logan knew that charges of espionage were almost impossible to prove. The FBI couldn't afford to go into court and reveal secrets that had changed hands. Unable to reveal publicly the information the Russians desperately sought, the bureau would resort to blowing the spy's cover. A picture was ample evidence of the man's true mission. His usefulness to the Russians at an end, the farm expert, weather scientist, space administrator, or embassy servant was sent home. Tomorrow or the next day, another man would arrive. He might be a lowly stagehand with a touring Russian dance company or a press representative. Then the whole system of shadowing and detection would begin all over again.

"You know," Logan mused, "we're both in the same boat. I catch them coming across the border and send them back to start again. You guys throw them out and wait for the next one."

"It's a lot better for you ol' boys, believe me. We have to be very careful who we go after. But those wetbacks are nobodies! You can throw 'em out, you can kick hell outta them, and there's nobody to complain to. But when I go to the old man and tell him that a visiting Russian astronaut is taking pictures of everything he can lay his hands on, then I'd better be damn sure I'm right! Otherwise I end up in Washington washing staff cars! The press's breathing down our necks . . . suddenly everything we do is suspect!"

Logan felt a certain empathy for Chadney. He'd

known the agent since graduation at the Immigration Academy. Chadney had been a guest speaker on several occasions and still was actively involved with reaching the local high school students and Border Patrol classes. Everyone felt a deep respect for the man and his job. Teachers pointed him out to their students, Border Patrolmen counted him among their friends.

Logan twanged, "Maybe we ought to get us a couple of head, a small spread and set it out on the prairie."

Chadney's eyes narrowed on a distant scene. "My pappy did that for a whole lifetime. I didn't see how he could stand it. Now it seems so damn sweet. I wish I could jes' reach out and touch it once again. I'd make a hell of a cowboy."

"Maybe it'll get better."

"Sure." Chadney grinned wistfully. "I'll bust the Russky only to find out that he's over here buying Rolaids because of his own pressures. Who the hell knows anymore?"

"How much longer do you have to go?"

Chadney rolled his eyes to the sky. "Too long. Ten more years for full retirement. That works out to be about three cases of Excedrin and three of Tums."

"Hang in there," Logan said as Chadney slipped into his auto.

"I have to speak at a high school in Batesville tonight. I've got a whole list of things I want to tell them, but all they'll be interested in is Watergate, opening people's mail, and who do we keep files on."

"Don't let them kick you around." Logan's attention caught on the oddly shaped medallion swinging from the ignition.

"I have to get my ass back to Sani-flush," Chadney announced as the car slipped from the stall.

Logan gave the agent a brief wave, his concentration on the empty parking space. It took a long agonizing moment before Logan would admit that the medallion in Chadney's hand and the one belonging to the skeleton of Michael Curtis were one and the same.

It was a staggering moment of affirmation. He felt faint and had to lean against a nearby auto for support. That Curtis, Medford, Beck—whoever the hell he was—had been somehow connecteed to the FBI office was as difficult to accept as the soldiers' sieving the wash.

He stood in the late-afternoon sun, clipboard pressed against his chest, his mind gathering data, discarding them again almost as quickly. Piling fact on fact, rearranging them, only to reshuffle them in confusion. When he was absolutely certain none of it made any sense at all, he allowed his feet to lead him to the patrol room.

Changing into his secret clothes following a shower, Logan was overcome by a tremendous depression. Each moment seemed to be taking the money farther from their grasp. Yet there was no rational explanation for any of it. Multiple forces were converging on the wash, turning it into a very complicated situation, defying the coolest reasoning.

Logan placed a coin in the slot and dialed the number. He asked for special operator twenty-seven. He felt warm when he heard her voice.

"Good morning," he said.

"It's afternoon, silly."

"I had to talk to you."

"I'm glad you called."

He listened to the empty pause before saying, "I want to see you tonight."

"I'd like that. . . . Is anything wrong?"

"No. Ernie's out on a witch-hunt. I thought that maybe you could come down here. We could have supper, you know. . . ."

"Are you sure you're all right?"

"I'm just tired . . . that's all. . . ."

"You can't come to Odessa?"

"I was hoping you could come to Durbin. . . ."

"It's a long way, Robert."

"I know." Logan exhaled painfully into the receiver. He knew there were words that would send her flying to Durbin, but he was too tired to play that game. "I just don't have the energy to drive all the way to Durbin and then go on to Odessa. I'm drained, babe."

"Then maybe you need your rest."

"I don't want to be alone tonight."

When she didn't answer, he said, "I want to make love to you . . . and hold you all night."

Her voice sounded husky. "I'll be there as soon as I can—tell me how to get there."

Logan gave her instructions to the apartment, closing with, "Drive carefully, huh?"

He hung on the phone as Hudson, the chief patrol inspector, made his way down the hallway. The gray-haired veteran cupped Logan's chin with a hard, rough hand and turned the face to him. "You lose your partner for one day and you look like you lost your best friend."

Logan forced a smile to his lips. "I just made a date for tonight, and I was wondering what I'm going to give her for supper," he lied.

"That should be the least of your problems. I thought you might like to know that the drug-bust figure has risen to almost one hundred million. You and Ernie should be real proud of yourselves."

Logan shook his head. "That's a lot of dough. . . . They had a ton of it there."

"Real good work. If it hadn't been for you boys, I'm sure they'd have blown the whole thing."

Logan felt the hand rapping gently against his shoulder. He nodded self-consciously. Like many of the patrolmen, he idolized Hudson. The chief patrol inspector had been a legend at the academy. To be assigned to him at Del

Amo was a stroke of luck for very few of the new patrolmen. It had been Hudson who set the tenor of training for all Immigration neophytes. His tips on tracking and cutting signs were still the bible. Shot six times in a career spanning almost thirty years, Hudson had also provided the more humorous episodes of the Border Patrol's history. Trainees were enthalled by his tracking of aliens wearing horses' hooves, cows' feet, and stilts. Every possible trick had been tried on Hudson, and each one became a lesson in the training manual. The record for the longest tracking in patrol history belonged to Hudson, four hundred and fifty miles in pursuit of seven aliens leading him on a chase across five counties over a two-week span.

Everyone in the bureau had been pulling for Hudson to make district chief before his retirement, but the vacancy three years before had gone to Brook, an outsider, a transferee from California. The Del Amo patrolmen took it harder than Hudson, who shrugged it off as being "best for the department." A new patrolman's reward was to work with Hudson at Del Amo and maybe to someday have the big man put a hand on his shoulder and tell him, "You did a hell of a job out there, son." It more than justified the long hours, the patience, the deadly routine.

Logan wanted to tell the man of his conversation with Grillo. He wanted to explain what he'd been told. It was important that Hudson know why the recent raids had produced so few results.

"The exams are coming up in another month, Bobby. You going to take them this time?"

No one had ever called him Bobby except his parents, and he found the name flattering and awkward. If Hudson hadn't called him Bobby, he might have had the courage to speak his mind. But the term sent a flush of sympathetic pain through him. He couldn't look Hudson in the eye and announce that a traitor was among them. That there was one in their midst whose personal ambition did not serve the good of the department—that one man, in a very high position, was undermining the efforts of more than a thousand hardworking, dedicated men.

How can I tell him we have a dangerous cancer here? he thought.

"Will you be taking the test, Bobby?"

"Oh, I don't know, Stan. I don't know what I'm going to do."

"It's the fence, isn't it?"

Logan looked up into the tired old face and said, "Yes, I never expected it would be like this."

"I understand," Stan said seriously. "But you and Wheeler are fine young men. You have a good future here. I've seen a lot of patrolmen in my time and the pair of you are among the best mavericks I've ever seen. All the good ones were mavericks. You just promise me you won't make any hasty decisions before you talk to me, you *or* Wheeler."

"I promise." Logan smiled.

"Good." The inspector gave his shoulder a last gentle pat before continuing down the hall.

It was almost dusk when he steered Ernie's Lincoln out smoothly onto the highway. The radio played softly, the air conditioner hummed above the tires on the roadway. The sand was afire on the horizon as he flipped the visor down to block the glare. Bits of conversation, out of the past, buzzed about his head. He heard his name in his father's voice, heard his mother calling from far away in his life. He thought of the police picnic when he was just a boy, the portly police chief with mustard on his lips. "Bobby's going to be a policeman!" his mother announced for all to hear. He saw his father wince, and the man with mustard on his lips pinched his cheek in reward. It had been a marvelous day, with pony rides, swimming, and plenty of food. Green-ticket numbers were called every fifteen minutes and someone always yelled in surprise.

Men in sleeveless T-shirts dragged others across a large muddy puddle with a heavy rope. Kids wore red strawberry-stained faces. The chrome handle on the beer keg was wired down while large paper cups paraded under the foam. The police band played or slept in the gazebo, the music interrupted occasionally by an impromptu speech pledging undying support for the department. The chief, hardly able to stand now, his shirttail trailing, toasting his men, singling out his father, only to stop short when it was obvious to everyone the chief didn't remember his father's name. His father had been half frozen in a crouch, his seat inches above the wooden chair, bent at the waist like some half-strung puppet. "Bob Logan," his mother called out in anger, then she started to cry. Others laughed. His father stared straight ahead, oblivious to the laughter. The picnic ended when his father rose to scattered applause.

It was dark when his father drove away, leaving him pressed against the screen door.

"Good-bye, Bobby, see you soon."

"Good-bye, Paw."

He never did understand the situation that kept his father from their home. His parents grew into two tired old warriors, respectful of each other's abilities to cripple and injure. Wary of the blows, they skirted each other at every meeting, defensively waiting for the first assault. The war ended at Fort Worth's Rose Hill Cemetery with his father's small funeral.

Logan toyed with the idea of returning the money to the wash under cover of darkness. He dismissed the idea as often as it recurred. The money was missing. Good or bad, it was now their money. With it came the uncertainty and promise of life beyond the border. Without it bureau stagnation, obscurity, eventually bitterness. The money meant life. He needed it now more than ever. Without it he didn't know if he could survive.

The revelations of the past few days had been staggering. He laughed sardonically at his own naïveté. He'd been content to tool along in his jeep, oblivious to the power struggles, unaware of pressures shaping the everyday decisions. Three days away from section seven had opened his eyes to the world that existed outside his desert sanctuary. A world he strolled through absently, like a sleepwalker. His world view had blamed the Mexicans for conspiring against him, ignoring the thought that the conspiracy went far deeper. This new world was unmanageable. It went beyond Brook, beyond the bureau itself. It infected Grillo and the Drug Enforcement officers. It ambushed Chadney and the FBI. It was a cotton-candy web of duty and service, clutching tenaciously at all takers, pulling them deeper into the pocket of bureaucratic conformity, until even the most idealistic among them was doomed.

He shuddered at the thought. Surely it hadn't always been this way! There must have been a time in their lives when men went about their duty, doing the best possible job they could under impossible conditions. *When had it all changed?* he wondered. *When did the Grillos come into our lives? When did they cease to function as servants of law and order and become tools of political favor?*

Logan began to laugh at the absurdity of it all. Here he was worrying anxiously over the honesty of others, when he himself was the recipient of four hundred and twenty-five thousand dollars of someone else's money! Logan turned the radio louder to drown out his own dishonesty.

Why did I take that money? he asked himself. *Why?* He, Robert Logan, a boy who had stolen only once in his life and had been caught. A boy who played hooky only once in his life and had been caught. How did he suppose he could take this money and just walk away scot-free? What had possessed him to even consider keeping it?

176

He shook his head in dismay. *I don't know who the hell you are, Logan! Who the hell do you think you are?*

Logan slid the small preroasted chicken into the oven to keep it warm. There were still forty-five minutes before Julie reached the apartment; he figured the ninety-mile trip would not bring her in much before seven.

He popped the top of a Pearl beer and took it into the closet. On the upper shelf, above his uniforms and clothing, lay the mementos of his life. A small green album housed the pictures of his youth, family and friends. It was thick with uniformed pictures taken in Vietnam, uniformed pictures of his graduation from the Immigration Academy, and his own personal two-and-a-quarter snapshots of the war. He'd always intended to file those away in some special book for his own reminiscence.

Atop the album lay a book of Capa photos, the collection of several wars. Robert Capa had been the first American photographer killed in Vietnam, and the man and his pictures occupied a special place among Logan's souvenirs. Atop the Capa book lay a single *Life* magazine, the November 29 collector's issue with the color Karsh photo of the slain President Kennedy. Standing beside the books, an expensive pair of Tony Lama Western boots, specially made for Logan's feet by the renowned boot company of El Paso, representing a month's discharge pay.

Logan brought down the left boot, fished inside to find the small .38 wrapped in cloth. He dumped the boot and caught the buck knife that fell. He replaced both, but not before he buffed his brass initials on the handle of the knife. Shaking the other boot brought forth the small plastic-bag container. He carried the package to the table, spreading the items out in order. All the items from the wallet were placed in one row, the driver's license on top, beneath that the two phone numbers, the Dunhill Realty card, two air-mail stamps in a cardboard holder, and one hundred and sixteen dollars in bills, five twenties, a ten, a five, and a single dollar.

He inspected the faded pink license, examining both sides carefully for scribbled notes or markings. Finding nothing, he replaced it and scrutinized the realty card. It was a plain business card, the type that listed only the firm's name, not the person representing the company. He searched the back for telltale writing, numbers. Finding that blank, he returned it to the table. The two air-mail stamps were plain, no marks or writing on the gummed side or within the folder that protected them.

Logan fondled the wallet before he went to the closet, returned with the razor-sharp buck knife, and sliced the stitching away. It unfolded into several pieces of imitation leather. Satisfied there was nothing hidden in some secret compartment, he slid the dismembered wallet to the bottom of its pile.

The articles from the glove compartment were next, placed down the right side of the Formica tabletop. The parking tickets were almost illegible; only the impressions of the punched times were readable. He examined both sides several times, holding them to the light in desperation. Curtis had arrived in one lot at seven ten A.M. and departed at ten forty. The next ticket showed Curtis punching in at eleven twenty with no checkout time punched.

Julie had provided him with the outdated phone numbers and he now began to wonder if each of those places had a metered lot outside. Curtis must have gone to the Dallas Police Department, for whatever reason he had, gone inside, then left without paying. Why Curtis would leave the lot without paying bothered him tremendously. The parking tickets bothered him. The phone numbers bothered him. Everything bothered him. Yet he didn't know why.

When he couldn't explain the annoyance, he slid the parking slips aside and turned his attention to the gas slip from Uvalde, Texas. The only legible item was the station's name and address at the top of the slip. He examined both sides before he was forced to set that aside also.

Logan examined the stiff, rotten gloves. The cotton was decayed, the fabric separating, making it impossible to tell whether or not they had ever been used. He took the buck knife and slit the fingers open to convince himself they were empty. Logan threw the fabric down on the table, cursing the items for their lack of significance.

The only object left was the map. Logan slipped the other items into the plastic bag, clearing the table completely. Then he spread the map out on the Formica top, a beer can holding down one corner, the buck knife the other. He inspected the borders for notes or doodles. He flipped it over to the northern half of the state, examined it carefully, then turned it back to the southern section. Convinced there were no hidden clues, he carefully refolded it to the position in which it had been found.

There were no special marks for Dallas or Fort Worth, no symbols at San Antonio, which was due south of both cities and the supposed home of Michael Curtis, if in fact the man *was* Michael Curtis. He traced the route from the Dallas police station to San Antonio, a straight shot south on Highway 35, through Waco and Austin. He sent his finger toward the closest route to the Mexican border; his nail led him through Uvalde, halfway between San Antonio and the border crossing of Del Amo. The slight elation quickly vanished when he realized that in itself, it told him nothing. The body had been found west of Del Amo, miles from the closest highway, sixty rugged miles west of the easiest border crossing.

Logan slammed his palm into the map. "Damn you, Curtis-Medford-Beck! Whoever the hell you are!" Angrily he doubled the map and stuffed it into the plastic bag. The container was forced into the toe of the expensive hand-tooled boot; the buck knife was closed and thrown inside the ornate boot shaft.

11

Toots bent at his map, leaning away from the shadow caused by his head. The map had been carefully marked where each area of the Cretaceous rock formations existed. Each thoroughly combed area was dated as to entry and findings. Above the map he had written, *"135,000,000 Years!"* with arrows leading to the suspected canyons. On the wide plain of Mexico he had drawn the large claw mark, the object of his search. The sketch eliminated the two metatarsal bones of the toe that were seldom visible unless the print was extremely deep.

As he did each night before retiring, he recorded the day's search, the area covered, wind conditions, sand deposits, before he turned to the next day's arena, the Galinda arroyo area. He studied the elevation, traced the imaginary line that would have existed before man and the highways had altered the course of the arroyo. Satisfied with his plans, he folded the map. The section facing him had been scribbled in angry red marks, an area rich with ancient Indian artwork submerged by a new government dam. "Waste," he had written. "Grievous loss!" He noted the area with a sad shake of his tousled hair before placing the map on a metal milk crate he used for a shelf.

The dog growled as he reached to blow out the candle. "Necho!" he hushed the dog named after the great pharaoh of Egypt who fought against Nebuchadnezzar. Hamoudi, the other animal, slept on.

Toots held Necho with his hand, stroking the dog silent until he, too, heard the vehicle in the distance. Pulling on his laceless boots, he peeked from the tin door of his makeshift cabin.

It was a fairly new sedan, headlights rising in the air as it bucked and bounced over the washboard terrain. Toots held the candle in his hand as the headlights spun toward him. He closed his eyes against the brightness as the sedan roared forward, fastening him against the tin shed. Toots protected his eyes with one hand while the other softly closed the door against his pets.

He heard one door slam, then the other as the men emerged from the car and the dust wafted up through the headlights. Two men came to the fenders, just a few feet away, yet the blinding glare made it impossible to see their features.

"Who are you?" he asked them.

A hand came forward into the headlight; an object glistened in the palm. "Is this yours?"

Toots took a half step closer to see the object, squinting against the luminous dust. "Yes . . . but it wasn't mine. . . ."

"Did you trade this in Durbin for some groceries?" the same man asked, the man on his right with the palm extended into the headlight.

"If you call a simple can of peaches groceries, then, yes, I did trade that item."

"Where did you get it?" the same man asked.

He couldn't understand why the other man hadn't spoken. He knew there were two of them, he'd heard two doors open and close. "As I told the grocer, I found it. It's just a harmless replica of an ancient Spanish piece of eight. It has no value whatever, except as a curio."

The man's voice sounded angry. "Where did you get it?" he repeated impatiently.

Toots would have liked to see the man's face, to see the skull formation, the line of the forehead. One could tell a great deal about people by studying their bone structure. Ironically, it also revealed a great deal of the person's background.

"Where did you get it?" the voice snapped.

Toots heard the crunch of sand as the man on the left took a step toward him. He answered quickly, "There was a body . . . in the Merida wash . . . that bauble was on a small key ring. It has no value!"

"Why didn't you report the body?" The man on his right pressed slightly closer, avoiding the headlights, his voice now hard and uncompromising.

"I am a simple man!" Toots cried, feeling suddenly threatened. "I wanted no trouble! I didn't believe that taking the coin would be a hardship to the man in the wash—he was quite beyond caring. . . ."

"How do you know it was a man?"

Toots nervously swept a forearm across his eyes. "It's quite easy to tell, believe me. . . ."

"What else did you take from the wash?"

"Just the coin . . . a cheap copy . . . brass and tin, I believe. . . ."

"Nothing else?"

"There was nothing of value!" he said, ashamed as soon as it left his lips "There was a ring—I left that! The man's family would want such a memento. If you think they would like the coin. . . ?"

"What do you have inside? Why are you holding the door?"

"My pets are there. They're old animals—they react foolishly to strangers. . . ."

"We want to see what you have inside."

"It's just my work!" he said, ashamed of his quarters, embarrassed by the wretched hovel that was his home.

"We want to see inside."

The man on his left was already moving toward the rusted, rope-hinged door. "Be careful of my pets!" Toots pleaded. "You never did identify yourselves!" he begged of them as they brushed him aside.

They made love while the frozen package of scalloped potatoes bubbled in the oven. They sat at the table naked, pulling the cold chicken apart with their fingers, washing it down with wine. She passed him dark meat of the leg between ivory wet teeth, using her tongue to disengage a portion of white meat from the hair on his chest, returning it to his mouth with greasy lips, giggling with abandon.

They took their slippery bodies to the shower, leaving the foil dish of scalloped potatoes untouched, the brown-orange crust unbroken and cold.

She made them coffee and mocked the poses of the brown-skinned girls in the black velour. He laughed and wrestled her atop him. They fell asleep with her head on his chest, their legs intertwined.

Logan heard the key in the lock and flipped the covers over them in a last tremendous effort. Ernie appeared in the doorway, haggard and drawn. The porch light threw deep purple shadows under each eye.

"Doctors Johnson and Masters, I presume."

Logan closed his eyes, a smile of contentment his only answer. He heard Ernie limp into the room, moving past to the shower. "How did it go?"

Ernie bent and painfully retrieved Julie's pants. He hooked them over the chair, searched for the signs of her bra before he realized she probably hadn't worn one. "Kirkland had three Indians out there helping us. Mescalero Apaches. I found the boys about ten at night, but it took me three hours to find the fucking Indians!"

Logan laughed, the blond head bouncing against his chest. He wanted to talk to his friend, but it took all his energy to even nod or laugh. The opportunity slipped by and Logan's mouth went slack as exhaustion overcame him.

"We're going to lose one of the boys," Ernie said to no one in particular. "I don't think he'll make it through the night." Ernie pulled the leather chest strap loose that went from the right side of his waist and across the left shoulder. He dropped the belt, hanging the revolver and tools on the bathroom doorknob. He stripped the shirt off in the doorway, dropped his boot. He slid Julie's foot from the corner of the bed as he sat heavily and pulled his other shoe free.

"He fell in a canyon—he was almost dead when we found him. I don't think he'll make it. Just a kid, too—couldn't have been more than eighteen. . . ." The deep rhythmic breathing told him he'd lost his audience. He rubbed the swollen knee, flexed it several times before he rose and limped stiffly into the bathroom. He gave the figures on the bed a last look and whispered, "Nobody gives a rat's ass about a kid anyway."

The early-morning flyover of section seven disclosed no alien trespassers in the area and Logan and Wheeler were reassigned to a sweep operation hitting the local carrot farmers in Moss County. "Clean Sweep" began ninety miles east of Del Amo with the two patrolmen scheduled to join the operation on Green Road, a thousand yards short of the White farm entrance.

Ernie slept against the door of the Lincoln while Logan drank coffee from the thermos. Julie had been gone when they awoke, leaving messages about the apartment, an "Ugh" perched on top of the discarded scalloped potatoes. Bright lipstick kisses adorned his body and took considerable scrubbing to remove. "Call me soon. I love you," with dozens of little X's across the bottom, was pinned to his pillow.

Logan set the thermos cup on the dashboard, watching the way it steamed the windshield. Across the road sheep worked the grass outside the fence, their woolly necks craning toward breakfast. He wished he had a long-lens Canon camera. He saw it as a shot through the steam on the windshield, the long lens catching the sheep's head in the center of the frame, the edges soft and fuzzy with mist.

A white-on-white photo, the type Richard Avedon popularized in his fashion photography.

Farther down the road a swaying vehicle crested the hill and rolled slowly toward him. Logan recognized the shingled home of Amarillo perched precariously above the pickup. He left the car and held his arms aloft to wave the man down.

Amarillo slowed the truck opposite the desert willows. The dog was on the front seat. The old man looked apprehensive; he could barely meet Logan's eyes.

"How you doing?" Logan beamed.

Amarillo's lips quivered in fright. "Pullin' out."

"How come?" he asked in surprise.

"After what happened to Toots"—the old man shook his head—"no one's safe anymore. . . ."

"What happened to Toots?"

Amarillo and the dog cast a baleful eye in his direction. "They burned his place! Killed him and the dogs! Burned it right to the ground!"

Logan couldn't believe it. "Who would have done a thing like that?"

Amarillo pulled his lips tight across his teeth, started to speak, then shook the thought away.

"That's really terrible!" Logan said. "Do you think it was kids?"

"Kids?" the old man scoffed. "Kids? You know who it was!"

"I really don't," Logan said in confusion. "Who could have done a thing like that?"

"They're your friends!" Amarillo blurted.

"*My* friends?"

"Immigration people—just like you!"

"You're kidding!"

"There was two of them, Roget and . . . Lama—"

"Lombasino?"

"That's right. They seemed nice enough, too. They

traced him to the store in Durbin and then they came up on the mesa and asked me where he lived. I told them I didn't know for sure. I said he was some kind of a crazy guy—he moved around, living in abandoned huts and mines. I told them there was a shed about six miles away, an old tool shed. Maybe he lived there. That's where they found him, all right—burned the shed and him and killed the dogs."

"Border Patrolmen?" Logan whispered incredulously.

"It was Roget . . . and that other fella, who asked me where he lived. If they didn't do it, then they told someone who knew where to look. It's not right what they done—not right. . . ."

Logan watched as Amarillo's eyes misted over, the man rocking himself softly against the steering wheel. "I'm really sorry about this," Logan mumbled. Out of desperation, out of pity, he found himself reaching for his wallet. He removed two twenties and stuffed them in Amarillo's shirt pocket. "This is something for the other night. You helped me and my partner pull down a big bust—we wanted you to have this."

Even the dog seemed tearful. "You don't have to do that, son."

Logan shrugged. "It's just a little something."

The old man nodded, the rocking stopped, the eyes fastened on the far-distant black roadway painted to the horizon.

"What did you do with those burros?"

"Turned them loose," he said helplessly to the windshield. "Don't know who's going to watch out for them."

"I'll go up there in a couple of days and chase them down to Raeford Springs—there's plenty of water there."

"That would be nice. They're not afraid of people—now they might even come to the hunters. They're real friendly, you know—maybe I shouldn't have cared so much for them. . . ."

"They'll be all right."

The man blinked several times, slipped the truck in gear, ending the conversation. Logan took a step back, waved his hand before touching it to the stiff brim. The camper rolled away, its wooden shell swaying gently in place.

"Did you hear any of that?" he asked Ernie as he slid behind the wheel.

"Most of it." Ernie yawned. "Who were the Border Patrolmen he was talking about?"

"Roget and Lombasino. Hudson sent them out to chase down the prints found in the wash. They must have traced Toots to Durbin, but hell, they wouldn't have *killed* him!"

"Maybe they thought he had the money."

"But they wouldn't have known the money was missing!" Logan shouted in irritation. "Nobody knows that except us and the civilian investigators! Even the Army doesn't know what it's digging for!"

Brook roared the bureau car to a halt beside them, motioned them to the driver's side of the auto. "We're running a little late," he said in annoyance, "and we've just picked up a visitor—Pinedo. If he follows us to the White farm, I want you boys to detain him and see he doesn't get up there."

"Sure," Ernie agreed.

"Who's Pinedo?" Logan asked.

"One of them fucking Mexican attorneys. Give them an education and they're nothing but trouble. Now this Pinedo's been causing some real trouble for the department. He's been monitoring our calls and shows up everywhere. He just arrived at our last bust and I'm certain he'll tail us here to the White place. If he's still with the group, you boys stop him and shake him down real good. I'd love for him to try something. You get my meaning?"

"I think so." Ernie nodded.

"Rough him up good, then book him for obstructing

justice. Just keep him away from the White place. I'll leave you this auto and I'll ride in with the lead car."

Logan started to ask why this Pinedo should be busted, but resisted the impulse.

"If he has a camera—and some of the boys think he's always carrying one—you take it away and bust it up real good. We don't want our pictures in any of those spik papers." Brook laughed.

"We just saw that old guy that lives up on Alianza mesa," Logan said. "This one who helped us with the drug bust, and he says someone killed Toots, the old guy whose prints Roget and Lombasino tracked away from that skeleton in the wash—"

"That damn thing!" Brook groused. "You'd think we found Henry Kissinger down there with Martha Mitchell, for Christ's sake!"

"I saw Ray Chadney in Del Amo. He's working on it, too."

"It's a big deal, all right," Brook agreed.

"What the hell's the FBI want with an old body?" Logan pressed.

"Learned a long time ago to never ask questions." Brook grinned. "Do what you're told and everything takes care of itself."

"One hand washes the other." Logan sighed.

"That's it exactly. You boys spend so damn much time out in section seven that I sometimes even forget you work for us. This your first roundup?"

"My first time," Logan said dryly.

"My third," Ernie announced.

"They can really be something, especially when all them spiks start running. It's the closest you'll ever come to chasing rabbits!"

"Here they come," Ernie said softly.

Brook stepped from the car, waving the lead car of the Immigration caravan abreast of him. Whispered instructions were passed; then Brook said, "Pinedo's in the last car, all right. You boys know what to do."

Brook climbed into the rear seat of the lead vehicle as the four bureau sedans moved slowly up the road. Logan took the wheel of Brook's auto while the rest of the caravan cruised slowly past. The last official vehicles were the empty Immigration buses used to haul away the illegal aliens rounded up at the White farm. Immediately behind them trailed a light blue battered Mustang. Logan sent his auto across the road as the last bus went by, effectively blocking the Mustang. Logan got out slowly, his hand on his revolver, the leather snap unhooked, freeing the hammer. Ernie moved softly to the passenger side.

A weary young man rolled the car to a halt, snapped off the two-way radio, and stepped carefully from the auto. Pinedo was in his late twenties, with shoulder-length dark hair; owl-eyed sunglasses covered the small nose suspended above the thick black mustache. He kept his hands well away from his thin body and moved cautiously onto the roadway.

Logan asked, "May I see some identification, please?"

Pinedo left his right hand hanging limply in midair as he sent two fingers of the left hand to a rear pocket. He held it gingerly for Logan to retrieve. Instead Logan left the arms hanging in air and stepped in close, passing his hands over the young man's clothing. Pinedo was jacketless, a tie pulled loose from the collar. His cheeks were coarse and pockmarked, white teeth showing in a perpetual smile. Through the window, Logan could see Ernie going efficiently under the seats and cushions.

"What's your name?" he asked the man.

The man continued to smile fearlessly. "Mario Pinedo."

It amused Logan to see the man wasn't afraid of them. He took the wallet from the fingers and went through it slowly. Pinedo's age proved to be twenty-nine, and all his papers appeared in order. There was even a small copy of a birth certificate in one of the plastic windows. Only people used to being harassed carried this additional protection.

Logan passed the wallet back and asked, "What can we do for you, sir?"

"You can let me pass to the White farm."

"I'm sorry, that will be impossible at the moment."

"Ah . . . you're worried about my safety, that's very considerate. May I put my hands down?" The smile was almost a challenge.

"Of course," Logan replied, answering with his own broad grin, sensing immediately that in another time or place they might even have been friends.

"What do you do with this, friend?" Ernie asked as he came around the car, a camera swinging from a small strap hooked over his finger.

Pinedo watched as the camera advanced to within inches of his face. He looked the object over solemnly, smiled, then announced, "I take pictures with it."

"Pictures of what?" Ernie demanded.

"Pictures of you and the growers busting my people." The smile of white straight teeth with the large center space publicly proclaimed they had no secrets from one another.

"We just bust the illegal aliens," Logan explained.

"And right at the end of the season." Pinedo smiled. "Precisely when the last of the great emperata carrots are off to market and the workers are to be paid."

Ernie stepped forward threateningly. "What the hell is *that* supposed to mean?"

Pinedo smiled his reply.

"I asked you a question, friend!" Ernie shouted.

The smile fell from Pinedo's face; the voice hissed angrily, "I am not your friend!"

"Easy," Logan advised them. "What's your beef with us?"

"My beef?" Pinedo laughed sardonically. "My beef is that your people swoop down and bust these aliens, my people, on the last day of harvest. Since that man Brook arrived this has been going on! Year after year they round them up and send them back across the border just when they are to be paid! *That* is my beef!"

Logan stared at the young man. Pinedo removed the sunglasses and hung them from the front of his pants, his angry dark eyes awaiting the patrolman's denial. Logan felt his courage waver; a sick feeling of cautiousness crept over him. The terrible possibility that there might be a wedge of truth in what the man was saying prompted him to ask foolishly, "Can you prove that?"

Pinedo seemed surprised by the question, by the uncertainty in Logan's voice. The eyes softened, the anger slipped away. "It happens year after year, man. You think Immigration does not know when the carrots are ready for harvest? The farmers harvest the same time every year."

Ernie spoke out of the same growing doubt. "You're a lawyer? You could have picked a better clientele."

"They have no money." Pinedo shrugged. "They have nothing. If one of us does not look out for those who have nothing, who will?" He was bewildered by the apparent softening of these two new patrolmen.

Logan said firmly, "You can't go up there, Mario."

The attorney jerked his head once in understanding. He crossed his arms on his chest and leaned comfortably against his auto. He glanced at both patrolmen, then threw back his head in laughter. "You do not know what is going on up there! Diogenes! Where are you, my friend? Is this your first day? I have not seen you here before. Allow me the privilege of knowing your names."

"Bob Logan."

"Ernie Wheeler."

"Logan and Wheeler, yes." Pinedo smiled. "I've heard

of you. The desert patrolmen, of course. This is not new what you are doing. It happens so often now that it has become a minor industry. I am just one of many who are trying to end this collusion between Immigration and the employers. You have stopped me today and I have not succeeded in doing my duty. Perhaps I shall never be so fortunate as to be called *el jefe,* or leader of my people, but others will be right behind me—others will follow."

"You're going to buck the whole thing with this?" Ernie asked as he swung the camera in front of the attorney's face.

Pinedo smiled sadly. "A meager weapon at best, but a weapon nonetheless."

"You're fucking crazy!" Ernie decided.

"So are you, my friends. You should have me in your car by now. I should have a large bruise here." He indicated his eye. "I should be bleeding here." He pulled down his lower lip. "It will be you who will be crazy if you don't place me in handcuffs and smash that formidable weapon of mine. Señor Brook will be very upset if he does not see me in handcuffs. You gentlemen are interfering with an ancient custom. I think it's called 'Rip off the wetbacks!' There's a great deal of money involved."

"So you're part of the Brown Revolution," Logan stated.

"A small part." Pinedo grinned. "A minuscule, infinitesimal pimple on the behind of the great Brown Revolution you gentlemen so obviously fear."

"We're just doing a job." Logan sighed.

"And your job is to stop me from seeing what is actually going on up there. Just as you gentlemen will not see with your own eyes that I am speaking the truth. You, too, will miss the prearranged signal between the farmers and the government. You will not see that the savings will be sent on to—certain people. It reaches certain pockets, keeps certain friendly people in office. Of course you understand what I'm saying."

Logan nodded. He wanted to turn off the young man but he was powerless to do so.

"That money reaches Congressmen and Senators. Our people should be proud to know their hard-earned wages—wages cheated from them by *your* employers—will travel all the way to Washington. Their stolen wages will elect Senators, Senators who will kill any bill restricting employers from hiring illegal aliens. For they cannot have that, you see. They need the aliens, just as they need you to round them up at pay time. Ask yourselves, why wasn't this roundup done earlier? Why wasn't the White farm raided sooner? Mr. White harvests at the same time every year, just as his father has done and his son will do after he's gone. No, gentlemen—the crop must be *picked* first! The labor of bending in the hot sun must be completed! The carrots must be on their way to market before the government is allowed to sweep in!" Pinedo looked first to Logan, then to Wheeler. "I think now you may want to hit me here." He indicated his eye, closing it and steeling himself for the blow.

"You're full of shit and you know it," Ernie dismissed him. Pinedo turned his attention to Logan. He searched the patrolman's face before saying softly, "Your friend knows I am speaking the truth."

"I don't know anything," Logan said.

"He's full of shit!" Ernie insisted.

"If I let you go," Logan whispered, "will you promise to leave?"

"Do I get the camera back? It is an inexpensive model, but the funds of the Brown Revolution are not what you would call—extensive."

Logan reached across to take the camera from Ernie. Wheeler held it a moment before relinquishing his hold

194

on the strap. "You should stay away from this," he warned the attorney.

Pinedo plucked the camera from the air. "Lettuce harvest begins in three weeks. I will stay away three weeks, that is all I can promise."

Logan nodded as if he understood.

Pinedo reached for the door handle of the battered Mustang. He thought a moment, then turned back to Logan. "On August 20, 1952, President Truman presented a bill providing stiff penalties to those who employed illegal aliens. It was defeated in Congress by powerful Texans. On June 26 of that same year Senator Johnson voted against a bi'l to give the Border Patrol more money to expand their fight against my people. And Johnson became President. . . . So you see, my friends, you are in good company. But those are facts, gentlemen. Thank you for your courtesy." From a shirt pocket he withdrew a card and pressed it into Logan's hand. "I may be reached at home at any time. Please call me if you ever need anything. *Vaya con Dios.* . . ."

"How can you believe any of that crap?" Ernie asked as the Mustang sped off down the road.

"I don't know what I believe anymore, Ern! I don't know where the lies end and the truth begins! I don't know anything anymore!" He thought of Pinedo, one of the little men caught up in the grinding out of justice, and he wondered what chance the man could possibly have. "You know, it's true what he told us. *That's* what sticks in my gut. Down deep I know he's telling me the truth. Just like Lou Grillo telling me we only bust the factories after they've been warned. Damn it! I knew it was true even while he was talking!"

"It's probably just Brook. Once he's gone the whole thing will straighten itself out."

Thinking back on all the areas in which illegal aliens had been captured, he realized they'd infiltrated everywhere. One had been nabbed tending gardens for the Nixons at San Clemente, several others in Washington, working on the same floor as the Immigration and Naturalization headquarters. One of Nixon's Cabinet members openly employed them in her Gardena, California, factory. Eighteen were busted in the kitchens of the Military Academy at West Point. Others were arrested working for the bureau itself. Two more were caught guarding the New Jersey office of the FBI; Chicago's O'Hare Airport had two in the Immigration Service offices. Two illegal aliens were arrested while painting the Statue of Liberty. Two hundred and seventy-seven were arrested in the employ of Las Vegas hotels. Even as he thought about it, Logan knew there was no hope in sight for either them or the aliens. "What the hell we doing here?" he asked Ernie. "Why don't we take the money and tell them to stick it in their ear? What the hell's happening to us? One day we were chasing each other across the desert, content playing grab ass, oblivious to all the inner workings and foreign intrigue of Immigration life, the next moment *everything's* suspect, no one can be trusted. What the hell's happening to us?"

"Quit," Ernie suggested. "You quit and then I'll follow you in in a week. We'll take our chances with the money."

"How would that look?" Logan stormed. "The Army and Navy's out there looking for that dough, and we up and quit—with a bundle yet! You know, it's got me scared, Ern. I watched those kids digging in the wash, and I hate to say this, but they're not going to be happy until they find what it is they're looking for. Now this thing with Toots. Who the hell would harm an old geezer like that anyway?"

"It couldn't have been Roget or Lombasino—they're as honest as the day is long. Neither one of them would harm a flea."

196

"Then who?" Logan demanded.

"You got me, pal. . . ."

"Where the hell's Pinedo?" Brook shouted as he scanned the rear of their auto.

Logan gave it only a moment's thought. "I let him go."

"You *what?*" Brook shrieked.

"I let him go," Logan repeated.

"I wanted him!"

"Sorry. . . ."

"Sorry? That greaser's a troublemaker! I told you that!" Brook threw the door open and thumbed them out of his auto. Flinging himself behind the wheel, he spat, "What the hell did you think I meant when I said he was a troublemaker? It means he's no friend of the bureau's and it's your job—your duty—to see the book is thrown at him! Don't I speak English?"

Logan gave Brook a long, hard look before he turned away in distaste and settled his attention on the sheep grazing by the roadway. The peaceful setting of tall grass and woolly necks stretching through the fence cleared his mind.

"You answer me when I talk to you, God damn it!"

"I understand you perfectly," Logan said evenly.

The caravan moved silently down the road, two busloads of dark, fearful faces pressed against the glass. Logan watched the straw-hatted workers pass silently by.

"I don't know what the hell's the matter with you!" Brook continued. "You have your head up your ass or something?"

"It was my fault, too," Ernie said. "I agreed with Logan to let Pinedo go free."

"I always thought you guys were bananas and you've just proved me right! You get your asses back to seven before I decide to press charges against you! I don't want to see your faces! You got me?"

"Yes, sir," Ernie mumbled.

"Get the fuck outta my way!" Brook yelled, spinning wheels in gravel as he swung into a wide U-turn.

They watched the auto race away to the caravan. "Fine mess you've gotten me into this time." Ernie sighed.

12

They exchanged the Lincoln for two jeeps at the Del Amo station, hurrying out to section seven as quickly as possible. Logan took the southern route past Cardoza Canyon while Ernie went north, circling through the Merida wash and the Army excavation.

Logan stopped to admire a large rattler sunning itself atop a rock table. He wished his own troubled existence could be traded for a simple, peaceful nap on a barren rock. He positioned his imaginary camera and shot several stills until he was satisfied with the final product. Dismounting from the jeep, he smoked a cigarette in the shade of the canyon, the dedication of the Pinedos flitting through his mind. "If we are to be called the Immigration and Naturalization Service," Ewing once remarked, "what service do we provide?"

What service do we provide? Logan thought. Throwing people out of the country wasn't much of a service. Tracking desperate men through killing terrain wasn't much of a service. Thwarting the ambitions of those who wanted to make a place in America wasn't much of a service either. Where did service enter into it?

Ernie's voice on the radio brought him back to the hot afternoon. He stabbed the Marlboro into the sand and went to answer the call.

"Do you read me all right?" Ernie asked.

"Loud and clear," Logan responded to Ernie's request to rendezvous.

"I've been getting a lot of breakup," Ernie explained.

Breakup was their code—signifying that area in section seven where the desert floor pushed its way skyward, leaving a trail of stony projectiles hunched against the sand—a place where they could meet unknown to the bureau's desk warriors.

"I'm at Cardoza Canyon and I read you loud and clear."

"Ten-four," Ernie signed off.

Logan drove his jeep carefully over his own footprints, a precaution each patrolman took, preventing others from discovering footprints that were old and previously tracked.

"I saw Kirkland," Ernie announced, "and he's really pissed! He thinks it was Chadney's boys who went up there to Toots's hut."

"Chadney?"

"Kirkland insists Roget and Lombasino went up there first, after tracking Toots to the store in Durbin where the old man traded something he found for some food. Roget and Lombasino took it to Brook and Brook told Chadney about it. Kirkland's so pissed he can't see straight. He just came back from the fire and says there are prints and car tracks all over the place. The steel-belted radials we use are there, but there's another set on top of that, from another auto—and a lot of street-shoe tracks."

Logan held up a hand to slow Ernie down. "Wait a minute. Roget and Lombasino went up there first and then there were tracks on top of that?"

"Right on, pal. Kirkland thinks it was Chadney's people up there sometime during the night because Roget and Lombasino went off shift in the late afternoon."

"How many prints did he say?"

Ernie held up two fingers. "Count 'em. Maybe there are two others who want that money as bad as we do."

Logan shook his head. "You know what I don't understand?"

"What's that?"

"How can they be so sure the money went to the wash?

We're the only ones who know for sure it actually got there. Hell, the guy could have stuck it in a locker somewhere along the way!"

"Except"—Ernie balled a fist and held it in front of his own face—"except . . . except . . . for some reason . . . somebody knows Curtis had to have had it with him when he went into the wash."

"The only people who could know that—"

"Are the people who gave it to him. . . ."

"Because they saw it loaded aboard the jeep. . . ."

"Far away from the city. . . ."

"Knowing he had no chance to stash it someplace. . . ."

"Then they know that it has to be here somewhere," Ernie said helplessly.

Logan exhaled sharply. "Yeah."

"They can't tie it to us." Ernie sounded unconvinced.

"We covered our tracks pretty well," Logan agreed.

"We were up on the mesa with that kamikaze pilot when Toots stumbled onto the thing."

"There's no way they can tie it to us," Logan said.

"Absolutely no way," Ernie agreed.

The two exchanged quick, worried glances. Section seven had been their own personal domain for over six years. Few others had ever negotiated its arroyos or mesas. The troublesome reality of it passed wordlessly between them.

"Aw, *caca*," Ernie said in disgust.

Ernie was in the shower when the phone rang. "Hello!" Logan shouted over the noise of the water.

"Logan?" the familiar voice asked. "Jim Wells here."

Logan hadn't talked to the sheriff of Hadley County since asking the man to trace a license number that no longer seemed important. He cursed his own stupidity for not following up on the call. How long had it been? He

201

couldn't remember. Weeks? Days? "Hey, Jim! How are you?"

"I'm not calling you boys to bullshit," the old sheriff growled. "You boys dug me a nice little hole with that license number."

"Whatta ya mean?"

"You want to tell me what the gag is?"

"No gag," Logan said weakly.

"Don't bullshit your old sheriff, boy! I been around too long for that! You boys fed me that license number three days before Ewing sighted that vehicle in the wash down there. I was doing you boys a favor and chasing down a license number that hadn't even been found! You boys fooled your old sheriff. . . ."

"Hey!" Logan protested. "I gave you that number because it was the one Amarillo gave to me! Now if he's wrong, then he's wrong. But I didn't know anything about the wash until a few days later. If you don't believe me, ask Amarillo. He gave me the number!"

"I can't." Wells sighed. "They just found his body about forty miles from Del Amo."

"But I just saw him this morning!" Logan said in disbelief.

"His camper went off the road and burned near McCann. The Brookins County sheriff's says he never had a chance."

"Jesus."

Wells was silent for a long, terrible moment. "That's the second one of my people to die in as many days. You boys set me up, and I don't take too kindly to that."

"It *wasn't* a setup!" Logan insisted.

"You boys have me and Kirkland in a dry wash," Wells replied, his voice tired and a long way off. "They came into Stone Hill yesterday, lots of 'em—them cleancut boys with their Harvard and Yale haircuts and English. They're asking a lot of questions. They want to know why I asked for information about that license number before the jeep was even found. Oh, I passed it on to Amarillo, but now it's going to bounce right back again. You boys fooled the old sheriff and that doesn't sit too well with me."

"But we didn't!" Logan protested unconvincingly.

"Then how come *you* didn't run that number through Immigration?"

Logan swallowed so loud he swore Wells heard it over the phone.

"I don't think it's going to take them long to trace it back to you boys." Wells sighed. "I hope you have a better story ready than the one you fed me."

The receiver clicked loudly in his ear. Logan stared at the closed shower door, the buzz in the receiver drowning out the spray. He replaced it gently in the cradle, his mind racing through the avenues open to them. They could take the money and run. Or they could sit still and maintain their innocence. No one could prove they knew where the money was. Even a jail sentence would mean that after the statute of limitations ran out, the money would be theirs to do with as they saw fit. A small price to pay for eight hundred and fifty thousand dollars? Mightn't the time specified by the statute have already passed? The English bank robbery was solved within days of the expiration of the statute. Mightn't the money already be free and clear?

The phone rang within his palm and the shock of it sent his heart into his throat. His hand trembled as he picked it up and placed the plastic against his ear.

"Hello?"

"Logan? Stan Hudson. Sorry to bother you, but we're calling up all units. Someone's snatched Roget and Lombasino from a road check at the Ignacio turnoff on Highway Ninety."

"When?" Logan exclaimed.

"We don't know for sure, late afternoon sometime. We're scrambling everybody to that location now."

"Wheeler and I will be there in less than thirty minutes."

"Good, hurry."

The direct intersection of the Ignacio turnoff and the asphalt highway was lined with cars from the Immigration Service, highway patrol, Moss County sheriff units, and state police from the Texas Department of Public Safety. Immigration investigators and Border Patrolmen huddled worriedly, their badges pinned to their off-duty windbreakers.

Logan asked Hudson, "What do we have?"

The chief patrol inspector indicated the discarded stop signs being carefully dusted by investigators. "Somebody grabbed them while they were working the traffic check. Took them away in the bureau sedan. It doesn't look too good."

"Any sign of a struggle?" Ernie asked.

"No, but you'd better check in with Brooks. He's personally assigning each team."

Logan nodded as he and Wheeler threaded their way through the groups to the district supervisor. Intelligence officers from the Texas State Police were reading Brook a list of subversive antibureau enemies as potential suspects.

Wheeler shook his head in anger as they waited; sixty men were tramping over the area, handling what little evidence existed. "If they find anything here after this," he whispered to Logan, "it'll be a goddamned miracle!"

Sheriff Kirkland stood off to one side, conferring in whispers with his deputy. Logan looked around for Sheriff Wells, but could see no sign of the former Texas Ranger. "Mario Pinedo," he heard the intelligence officer say.

"That's a damn good one!" Brook snapped. "Bring that bastard in!"

"Pinedo was with us today," Logan heard himself say. "We stopped him at the White ranch. He was with us."

"What time was that?" the Texas investigator asked.

"Ten . . . ten thirty. . . ."

The investigator turned to Brook. "That still gives him plenty of time to run up here and grab these guys. We've got a pretty big file on him."

"Get him!" Brook ordered.

Logan warned, "You're making a big mistake with Pinedo!"

"That file's a mile long," the officer stated. "He's a Commie bastard and so was his old man. Hippie type with a college degree in home economics."

"He's a lawyer!" Ernie interjected fruitlessly.

"Wait a minute!" Logan shouted. "Damn it! How could he have driven his own car off and still taken their car? What did he go, pull a weapon and order them to follow him?"

"Nobody said he was alone." The investigator smiled.

"Go pick him up," Brook hissed menacingly.

Logan felt the eyes within the small circle swing his way, awaiting any new challenge he might offer. Reluctantly he backed off.

Hudson was standing with several of the officers. "Ernie and I are going to track the highway to the west," Logan announced angrily. "We'll check all the side roads and see if we can shake something loose."

"What did Brook say?"

Logan stared at the chief patrol inspector. "He's too busy cleaning house to give a rat's ass about what happens to Roget and Lombasino."

"Okay," Hudson said slowly. "Just keep in touch so we know where you are."

Ernie was bent at the roadside, examining tracks in the headlight of a state police car. Logan dropped to one knee beside him. "I'm going to call Pinedo and warn him," he whispered softly.

"Oh, Christ," Ernie moaned, "leave us out of this. The roof's falling in, man!"

"I can't," Logan replied, "I just can't, Ern."

Ernie rose slowly and kicked at the ground. "There's nothing we can do here anyways. There's been fifty cars over this ground. Whoever snatched them went northwest probably."

"I'll call him from the first pay phone we come to."

In the hot, stifling booth he listened to it ring once, twice, three times. A woman's voice asked hesitantly, "Hello?"

"May I speak to Mario Pinedo, please?"

"Who would be calling, please?"

After a moment's hesitation Logan replied, "A friend."

He heard the phone placed on a hard surface. Seconds later Mario's voice. "This is Mario. May I help you?"

May I help you? Logan thought. *My God,* he wanted to say, *everything's caving in on us and the man is asking,* "May I help you?"

"Mario, the Texas State Police are on their way to pick you up—"

"Who is this?" Pinedo asked, his voice calm and unruffled.

"What the hell difference does it make, damn it! Didn't you hear what I said?"

"Ah, of course. The blond one, Logan."

"Mario! God damn it, man, get out of there! Right now!"

"I appreciate this, my friend, but I cannot run. That is exactly what they would like me to do, isn't it? But I will use your warning to send my family away—"

"Don't be there alone!" Logan warned.

"If I call friends, they will accuse us of holding a meeting to plot against them. No, I will meet them on the front step, reading the evening papers like any other citizen."

Logan stared through the glass of the booth at Ernie patiently waiting in the jeep. "I'm sorry about this."

"I know—thank you, *amigo*."

"Good luck. . . ." Seconds later the phone went dead in his hand and he stabbed it into the cradle. It took a great effort to pull the door open and step out into the headlights. He stopped momentarily when he realized he hadn't phoned the girls. He should have called Julie to tell her something had come up. But how could he explain it? How could he tell her that people even *remotely* connected with the money were dying like flies and that a silken noose of federal assassins was being slipped over their heads?

"What the hell you doing?" Ernie called.

"Nothin'," he said as he stared absently at the empty booth. "I don't like it," he told Ernie as his partner sent the car back onto the highway.

"I know what you mean, pal. Somebody desperate enough to snatch two border guards is crazy enough to kill them."

"I went through the academy with Roget. He's a good ol' boy." Logan cupped his hands against the wind as Ernie drove slowly along the shoulder of the highway. The flame from the Zippo burned Logan's fingers before he managed to light the end of his Marlboro. He locked his eyes to the ground spilling before the headlights, senses keened for the telltale mark of a bureau sedan's steel-belted radials.

Immigration jeeps were specially wired to allow the high beams and low beams to be on at the same time. It made tracking at night that much easier. They covered twelve miles with Logan hanging from the vehicle, peering intently at the road's soft shoulder. When his neck became cramped, Ernie switched positions as Logan drove methodically to the northwest.

The radio crackled with calls as the FBI launched its own investigators into the field. Reports came in from the north, south, east, and west as federal agents, Texas State Police, and highway patrol took to the bushes and seldom-used roadways. Immigration autos zipped past their crawling vehicle as they sped up the highway to investigate the reports that began to trickle in.

"They're missing the boat," Ernie agonized as the units raced off in all directions. "If you held a couple of kidnapped border guards, would you take them toward a town where they might be spotted? Hell, no! You'd want to get rid of them as soon as possible and get the hell outta there! Would you take them south toward the border?"

"No," Logan replied.

"That's right! You'd want to take them as far *from* the border as possible!"

"Away from the desert, where they'd be easily spotted. I'd want rough country, someplace where I could hide a couple of guys for as long as possible."

"You'd want to buy as much time as you possibly could! You'd want a gully or a canyon where they could scream their heads off and never be heard. . . ."

Or where they could be shot without anyone hearing a thing, Logan thought. Ernie fell silent and Logan knew the exact same thought had been briefly shared.

The first set of steel-belted tracks led them off a well-traveled road to an International pickup located in a dimly lit farm-yard. They cursed the farmer and wound their way back to the highway.

"Y'know that damn Roget would do anything for a laugh. One day, at the academy," Logan said, chuckling, "we had to run a mile race and he dropped his sweat pants and ran the race bare-ass naked. Everybody he passed fell on the ground when they saw his bare-ass going by. We didn't have a chance. . . ."

"Lombasino fixed me up with his sister-in-law, a divorcée from Tulsa. God, what a man eater. He told me what a sweet kid she was and how this rotten son of a bitch she married had screwed her around. Hell, she was all over me! She practically *raped* me! Tony said, 'Nice kid, isn't she?' What the hell was I supposed to say? Jesus, was I glad when she went back to Tulsa. I was sore for a week."

"I always liked Roget."

They'd reached the highway when they realized they'd already written the men off and were thinking of pleasant memories to hang onto.

A set of steel-belted radials led them to a boy scout camp-out, the frightened chaperons caught in sleeping bags. Each time they returned to the highway, doggedly following the winding road into the rough high plateaus of West Texas. They waved hellos to the honking sheriff's cars that whipped past, reporting in hourly on their slow progress. At four fifty-three Logan found the third set of prints, leading up a deserted dirt road. Ernie pulled the jeep off the highway, hiding it in the brush as they went cautiously forward on foot. Logan walked the west shoulder and Ernie the east, their flashlights playing about the tracks. At one point Ernie dropped painfully to one knee and whispered, "There's another set of tracks; they cross the steel-belteds. . . ."

"How old do you think they are?" Logan was going to ask. A common joke between them, for the television and movie hero always looked down at the tracks and said, "They went this way twenty minutes ago." There was no way for a person to know how old tracks might be. But Logan found he was unable to joke with his partner, for he felt a stinging wetness creep into his eyes and he knew he was perspiring in nervous excitement.

Logan saw that the other set of tracks had been moving rapidly, the tires throwing sand about, leaving them a clean set of front tires, well worn on the inside.

"Which way do you think they went when they reached the highway?"

Ernie shrugged his indecision. "We ought to double back and see why that bastard was in such a hurry."

"I'll do it," Logan offered. "You rest your knee."

He trotted back to the highway, observing that the tracks of the second vehicle headed south, toward Del Amo. He brought this puzzling news back to Ernie.

"Getting back below the border before all hell breaks loose," Ernie guessed aloud.

The steel-belteds were crossed in several places by the auto with the two worn front tires. The worn tires sped in and out of the area while the steel-belted remained wherever the road was leading them.

A mile and a half from the highway, the steel-belteds stopped in a grove of desert willows and led to a partially hidden bureau sedan. Logan felt a stab of anxiety and exchanged worried looks with his partner.

Ernie slipped soundlessly forward to inspect the auto. He gave Logan a grim "no" and indicated the nearby darkened cabin. The men moved wordlessly through the dark, pistols drawn, Logan moving off to scout the cabin itself while Ernie thrust the pistol forward with both hands.

Logan avoided the rickety steps, placing his feet carefully as he went along the side of the house. The interior was dark, and after listening carefully, he moved on to the rear, where he scouted the intense darkness through a broken window.

He emerged in front of the house and gave Ernie a shrug. Then he tapped his chest and indicated the door. He waved Ernie to the front window to cover him.

Ernie readied his magnum and flashlight as he crept silently into position, waiting for Logan to crash through

210

the door before he snapped on the beam to flood the room.

There was no way that Logan could reach the door quietly; the rotted steps were sure to squeal in agony, the door bound to shriek. He decided to rush it from a distance, taking it down with his shoulder after clearing the steps in a single bound. He took a deep breath to steady himself, then dashed forward, snapping his beam on against the door, hoping against odds that it wasn't barred by a two-by-four. He braced himself for the shock of impact but the door gave way in a hush of air, the momentum throwing him off-balance, sending him forward into the room, where he crashed into the opposite wall and fell helplessly on his side.

Ernie's flashlight sprayed through the window, blinding Logan, whose own flashlight rolled in the dusty corner. Logan jabbed his weapon at the two figures standing between him and Ernie's intense light. In the split second before he pulled the trigger he noticed they weren't moving toward him but swaying in some bizarre, threatening pose. He held the shot, his finger a hairbreadth away from sending the hammer about its business.

In the eerie light that rimmed the figures, Logan could hear his heart above the insects feeding on their find. He sank to one knee as Ernie walked the light into the doorway to reveal Roget and Lombasino.

Logan fought the gagging nausea that overcame him. Lombasino's hands were cuffed together above a rafter, his body hanging slack, the toes dragging across the floor as the body swayed slowly back and forth. Lombasino was fully dressed, unlike Roget, whose shirt had been pulled loose and hung about the waist like a tattered skirt. Roget's belt was still in place, as was the narrow strap that went across the shoulder. The mouth was open in surprise, the head squeezed between muscular arms that ran straight up to a rafter, where they were held in place by handcuffs cutting deeply into the wrists.

Someone had cut Roget about the chest; thin dried rivers of crusty blood ran into the trousers, trailing from the toes in a large sticky puddle. Under the left armpit was the fatal wound, a deep thrusting gash that poured out the patrolman's lifeblood.

Ernie sent his light to the small neat hole at the base of Tony Lombasino's skull. The light led them where the bullet had emerged above the right eye, leaving a large flap of skin and tissue hanging above the bloodied brow.

"Jesus," Logan said, "Jesus."

"God," Ernie said faintly.

Logan fought the urge to cry in outrage. Sucking desperately for clean fresh air, he lurched for the door. Across the clearing he stumbled, dropping to his knees by the tall grass, where he breathed rapidly and loudly, his head between his legs.

"They executed them," Ernie mumbled, "just killed them like animals."

It took a long time for Logan's voice to settle down, to reach that controllable moment when he could say, "I'll phone it in." With a great effort, he staggered to his feet and began the long walk to the highway.

The microphone trembled in his hand as he held it and formed the necessary words. Then he pushed the button under his thumb and made a brief statement to Del Amo. The radio came alive with rapid instructions from the dispatcher. Logan dropped the handset to the floor, heard the forces of the federal government and the state of Texas being called to the suddenly important site. He started the jeep, wheeled it angrily across the road to prevent the caravan from driving over what little evidence they had. Then, leaving the lights burning as a beacon, he walked numbly back to the cabin.

Logan waited outside, an unlit cigarette stuck between

his lips. Ernie squatted on his haunches a few feet away. Neither man spoke directly to the other. "God almighty," Ernie would cry.

"Jesus." Logan sighed in disbelief.

The first sirens shrieked their way up the highway and neither man moved. Lights bouncing up the dirt highway splashed over them and the area in front of the cabin grew bright with the headlights of a dozen cars.

"God damn them!" Ernie screamed as he ran forward to wave them off the few precious tracks remaining. Brakes locked, cars slid to a halt in front of the apparition that appeared out of the darkness, arms flying, lips cursing the drivers.

"Why the hell do you think we *blocked* that road?" Ernie demanded of the autos. The occupants spilled out, ignoring the madman who confronted them. The dust gathered about the headlights as Ernie ran around beating frantically on the fenders of the rapidly emptying cars.

Hudson and Brook ignored him as they tramped into the cabin, followed by dozens of uniformed and civilian-clothed investigators.

Logan turned away from the scene in disgust, leveling his gaze on the eastern skyline with its first hint of a new day.

Ernie staggered to his side, his hand going out to indicate the mass invasion taking place.

They had become spectators, watching in shocked silence as thirty men from several different agencies touched, walked, handled the evidence. Ernie counted the men aloud who handled the abandoned auto, palming the door handles, fingering the steering column and doors as they leaned curiously inside. An FBI print expert arrived with Ray Chadney to dust the bureau sedan. By that time Ernie had counted *thirteen* investigators who'd handled the auto.

Chadney was puffy-eyed from lack of sleep. As the

agent in charge of the case he took statements from all agencies. It was daybreak when he made his way to the despondent patrolmen. Logan was staring silently to the east, his hands across his chest. Ernie had taken a seat on the ground, his arms around his knees.

"Now I come to the stars of the show." Chadney sighed.

Logan shrugged indifferently. None of it seemed to make any difference anymore. He kept his attention on the long line of cars winding back to the highway. In the distance he could see the coroner's wagon crawling forward past the cars parked along the road.

"We'd been cutting signs since we left Ignacio Road, looking for any sign of a steel-belted radial—they're fairly easy to spot. They're brand new—all our cars have them. . . ."

"We found a couple of others that didn't pan out," Ernie offered. "Then we found this set."

"And they led you here?"

"Yeah."

"Nobody was here? The place was deserted?"

"That's right," Logan said painfully. "I took the door. Ernie covered me, and there they were—just hanging there by their wrists."

"We didn't touch anything," Ernie explained. "We didn't touch the car or the bodies. I even kept my hands off the cabin door."

"And you phoned it in?" Chadney asked Logan.

"I phoned it in. I ran the jeep across the road to keep everybody off the tracks we had."

"What about you, Ern? You notice anything?"

"What difference does it make! *Everybody's* fucked around with whatever we had! There were good tracks here! Street shoes! Three guys went in and out of that cabin! The car they left in has a front-end alignment problem! They headed south at the highway. But you'd never know it now!"

"And none of you touched the car?"

Logan turned angrily to Chadney. "We're the *only* ones who didn't!"

Chadney seemed embarrassed by the line of questioning. He gave Logan a grim smile. "Maybe we'll get something from it anyway."

"Fat chance!" Ernie grumbled.

A moment later they heard Brook say. "Is this yours?"

The patrolmen looked around to see Brook exhibiting a flashlight.

Logan looked himself over carefully before replying, "It's mine."

"I found it inside," Brook said. Chadney's eyes narrowed in curiosity.

"I must have lost it when I hit the door," Logan explained.

"And you were the boys who found the tracks leading to the cabin?"

"That's right," Logan said evenly.

A smile broke across Brook's face. "Convenient, wasn't it?"

Logan caught Ernie as his partner exploded past him. "What the hell's *that* supposed to mean? That's a shitty remark!" Ernie screamed.

Logan snapped, "We checked every damn set of steel-belted tracks for the last twenty miles!"

"I see." Brook continued to grin.

"You don't see a fucking thing!" Ernie raged. "You're some kind of asshole, you know that?"

"Wheeler!" Hudson snapped. "Knock it off!"

"You're a fucking psycho!" Ernie raged on uncontrollably.

Hudson pushed Ernie away from Brook while Logan tugged his partner to a safe distance. "I'd advise you boys

215

to get back to Del Amo," he warned them. "You go on duty in less than an hour."

Logan started to protest. He wanted to tell Brook and Hudson that they'd been up all night, that they badly needed rest. But he realized that everyone had been up all night. They all needed a good night's sleep. Grudgingly he pulled Ernie away as the coroner's wagon made its way to the front of the cabin.

"Where the hell does he get off talking to us like that?" Ernie shouted back as he was led away. "We bust our asses and what thanks do we get! They were our friends, not his!"

At the jeep Ernie growled, "You'd better drive, because I'm starting to feel homicidal!"

13

They were well into section seven before they stopped for breakfast. They parked the jeeps side by side and ate cold ham-and-egg sandwiches and drank coffee from steaming stainless-steel thermoses. They'd showered and shaved at Del Amo, picked up their vehicles from the maintenance shed, and headed out before reporting in.

Logan lit a cigarette and enjoyed the after-breakfast smoke while Ernie picked his teeth. "We'd better do it."

Logan nodded, picked up the mike, and pressed the thumb switch. "Logan here, Del Amo."

"Hey, Logan," the dispatcher called, "you guys did a hell of a job last night. Or should I say this morning?"

"I don't know myself. Half the guys are just checking back in; no one's been to bed in the last twenty-four hours. I guess you heard Richart caught one in the leg?"

"No, when did that happen?"

"Early this morning or last night. Like you said, they all run together. He was caught in the leg during the smoking of that suspect. Hudson seems to think the doctors pulled a three fifty-seven from his leg. My guess is he pulled the trigger while it was in the holster or one of the other guys hit him in the leg. A little embarrassing, huh?"

"What suspect was smoked?" Logan asked fearfully.

"Some spik—I don't remember his name. I've been on this all night myself."

Logan looked across to Ernie and swallowed noisily. "Could it have been Pinedo?"

"That's the guy!" the dispatcher said brightly.

Wheeler snatched up the mike and shouted, "How could he have taken their car and driven his own off at the same time?"

"Beats me," the dispatcher replied. "The Mex fired a shot and they opened up on him."

Logan closed his eyes slowly; his head fell back against the roll bar. "They killed him," he whispered to the sky.

"That's been confirmed?" Ernie asked slowly.

"Absolutely," the dispatcher answered. "You ready for your assignments? Wheeler, Brook asked that you check out Castle Canyon. Somebody reported activity in the area. Logan? Brook wants you up on Seminole mesa, a couple of fresh tracks east of the sotol grouping. If you ask me, you guys have a real soft touch."

"Yeah, sure," Ernie replied glumly. "We're moving on it now."

"Ten-four."

Ernie asked Logan, "You all right?"

"I don't know. I don't feel anything anymore. I'm too old to cry . . . I'm numb—it's got me all twisted up inside. . . ."

"I'll race you to Seminole mesa for our pink slips?"

"You'd sell your soul for a good set of prints," Logan grunted as he threw the rest of his coffee on the ground.

"Damn right!" Ernie agreed, capping his thermos, revving his engine as he bent low over the wheel.

Logan tried to laugh, but he couldn't. He started the engine and looked across at his partner. Ernie's ridiculous posture and the engine sounds sent a smile to Logan's lips. "I'm not going to race you," he said firmly, realizing the tremendous effort it took for them just to wipe Pinedo from their lives.

"You heard about the Texan whose son was born weighing seventeen pounds but after the circumcision he weighed only ten?"

Logan shook his head and snorted.

"How about the Texas farmer who was stopped on the street and asked what he did for a living?"

Logan continued to shake his head, feeling the laughter forcing its way up his throat.

" 'I raise bees,' the farmer said. 'How many bees do you have?' the man asked him. 'About twenty-five or thirty thousand.' 'Where do you keep them?' the man asked. 'Right here in this cigar box,' the farmer replied. 'Wait a minute,' the man says. 'You mean to tell me you have twenty-five or thirty thousand bees in that cigar box?' 'Yep,' the farmer says. 'Doesn't it get a little crowded?' the man asks. 'Fuck 'em,' says the farmer." Ernie was waiting for the first sign of breakthrough, and Logan rewarded him with a grin.

"I hate a sour-ass partner!" Ernie called as he let out the clutch, leaving Logan to eat the large dust cloud that enveloped him.

"Smile, you bastard," Ernie snapped when they'd reached Seminole mesa. Logan gave his partner a smile and said, "Keep in touch."

Seminole mesa was a large shelf rising some three hundred feet above the floor of the Rio Grande. It covered almost two hundred square miles of triangular desert, spreading northward some thirty-one miles. The mesa's face bordered the drag road, the steep sides cut by two ancient rivers, presenting a steep face some six miles across.

It had been two years since anyone had crossed the Rio Grande and attempted to scale the steep sides. On that occasion, he and Ernie had busted a wax ring smuggling in the precious candelilla wax used in churches and especially fine candles. Its import duty was high, and as contraband it enjoyed a wide market. The smugglers had exhausted themselves reaching the mesa and were easy targets for the patrolmen.

Logan drove the drag road parallel to the mesa face,

searching for the signs of entry in the soft sand. He drove the road several times without cutting a sign. Then he reasoned that the wetbacks had entered to the south of the mesa, traveling one of the washes to reach the area. Realizing the wetbacks were smarter than most, he began to examine the dry riverbeds on either side of the wedge to determine which one had been used for entry. In less than forty minutes he was certain no one had entered from either of the arroyos. Footprints on the top would have to mean someone came in via the northern route, possibly someone searching for another landing strip.

Logan left his vehicle hidden in the wash, slung the canteen and binoculars over his shoulder, and gathered up the two sandwiches that were his daily lunch. It was a rough climb over the sandy soil, the footholds tumbling out from under him and racing to the canyon floor. He was thankful the western arroyo had been in the shade, for he found his uniform soaked through, and the dust clung to the wetness, turning the green a muddy brown.

Reaching the summit, Logan stayed low to the ledge, scooped a tray for his possessions, and kicked a firm platform for his feet. The binoculars were removed from their case and hung around his neck. A white linen handkerchief wiped across his face and the back of his neck. Only when the sweat had been wiped away did he place the glasses to his nose.

The area was as flat as a plate for ten miles to the north. Then it rose slightly at the northern tip, becoming a thin point thirty-one miles away. Scanty brush clung to several of the gullies that ripped across its plains. Two hundred yards to Logan's left was a large sotol patch, thick with the ankle-tearing plants bunched together for their own protection. Once sotol had been roasted and eaten by the Apaches, who cooked the trunks for food, whereas the Mexicans used it to make a mouth-searing liquor. And sometimes it had even been used to make soap, a practice still common in many areas of the South.

Logan directed the glasses from the sotol thicket east one-quarter mile to the reported prints. From ground level it was impossible to see markings; there was nothing to interrupt his vision—just miles of flat plain dotted with an occasional greasewood bush or creosote plant, nicknamed chaparral by the Mexicans.

It would have been impossible for men to have walked the mesa undetected. If they were foolish enough to climb to the plateau, they would have found themselves entirely without cover. A small dry creek ran diagonally through the center, carrying off rainwater in a northeast to southwesterly direction, leaving a few bushes clinging to the last vestiges of moisture.

Having already ruled out the wetbacks, Logan now hoped to find signs of another runway being built or of one already in use.

For a brief instant the sun glinted off a reflective object in the distance. Logan focused the glasses in that direction, but it had disappeared. He scanned the shallow creek bed and the few bushes that served as cover. Could they be hunters, local boys out for a day's target shooting with Daddy's rifle? Logan lowered the glasses and placed them on the ledge before him. He removed the sunglasses and checked himself for anything reflective as he prepared to wait them out. The badge was slipped from the shirt and placed on the ledge, the watch and ring beside it. He lit a cigarette, ducking beneath the lip as he did so. Patience was a lesson Ernie had taught him well. Often the wetbacks took cover at the sound of a patrol jeep and simply stayed there until they were reassured that all was well. Eventually they'd expose themselves and continue north. The patrolmen would be waiting. Ernie claimed he could outwait a fossil, and Logan had never had cause to doubt him.

Logan smiled to himself as he nestled comfortably on

221

the side of the mesa. Most of his body was in the shade, unlike whoever it was who lay down there in the shallow creek bed. The hot noon sun was just beginning and he knew whoever was out there would become extremely uncomfortable and show himself before long.

He thought of Ernie tracking the Castle Canyon area, a stone flooring, the very thought of which would have made most of the patrolmen blanch. It would be a tremendous challenge for Ernie, an adventure to compensate for the lousy setbacks they'd experienced over the last few days. Logan envied Ernie that as he set his attention on the small clump of brush a thousand yards away. He was met by a pinprick of light from the same cluster. Raising the glasses revealed nothing. Again it had eluded him. Again he settled back to wait them out.

The sun moved slowly behind him, scalding his back with its intensity as the clump gave up frequent glimpses now. He had ruled out the hunters theory. To be a hunter one must shoot at something. Whoever lay patiently waiting in the creek bed never fired. He was now firmly convinced that the men were waiting for something. A plane. A vehicle. Timing Ewing's flyovers for a drug run? This last solution pleased him most, for it would explain the men on foot, men who'd walked the area to check the surface for suitable landings.

Technically, Logan's hands were tied. He couldn't arrest the men for scouting an illegal airport. They couldn't be arrested for simply planning a crime. He didn't have the authority to run them off the mesa. He didn't have any authority whatsoever unless they were caught in the act of committing a crime. Yet his curiosity had been aroused. He wanted to know who they were, how many there might be, and why they remained hidden.

The corned-beef sandwiches left him drowsy and he began to nod off in the late-afternoon heat. He hooked his thumb in the chest strap as his head fell against his shoulder. The sun beat against his back, the perspiration raising large damp spots on his clothing. He opened his eyes to tiny slits, saw the glint from the brush, and nodded off in satisfaction.

The shadows of the sotol grouping crept cautiously out across the mesa floor, and still the men did not show themselves.

The light turned yellow to warn of the approaching blackness just hours away.

Far to the north a small dust cloud appeared. It wormed its way onto the mesa as Logan dozed against his shoulder. When the first sound of it crept into his subconscious, he heard it as the incoming motor of a dust-off. He heard the VC firing their Mossin-Nagant 7.62 rifles into his position. A VC K-50 opened up on his left somewhere above the drone of the chopper. He woke with a start when the bullets slammed into the ground beside him. He was breathing rapidly, the sand was orange, the tiger cloth uniform was gone. The air was still except for the far-distant sound of a motor vehicle. Logan sighed with relief and lit a cigarette with trembling fingers, grateful it had been a dream and he did not have to relive the awful conclusion of the rotor blades of the chopper hitting the ground as it spilled its occupants into space and exploded. He puffed eagerly on the tobacco, fumbling for the canteen as the dry heat brought him back to the mesa.

He was startled to see a dust cloud approaching. Pulling the glasses to his eyes, he focused on the advancing vehicle. Logan briefly glanced at his watch and was surprised to see that it read seven fifteen. He'd been on the mesa almost eight hours. Eight hours of patient waiting, to be rewarded with a vehicle.

Three men rode in the open jeep to the clump of creosote. Two emerged from the brush with rifles and boarded it. Logan saw canteens and food supplies passed inside as the jeep continued south, directly toward Logan's position. Logan gathered up his belongings and crabbed his way along the western wall, sprinting in a crouch for the cover of the sotol brush.

He followed the men with his glasses as they drove past him, rifles held between their knees, muzzles to the sky. The driver wore a sports jacket but was tieless. The others were clean-cut young men, dressed in new jeans that Logan thought made them notably conspicuous.

The jeep made a wide swing of the face of the mesa; the occupants disembarked as they walked the lip overlooking the drag road. Logan was grateful he'd taken the time to hide his own jeep. Grateful that the men who cradled rifles didn't see an empty Immigration jeep right below them.

The driver whistled and the men readjusted the rifles and carried them back to the jeep. The four-wheel-drive vehicle made a wide swing north and back to the closest highway. Logan stayed in his position, following the dust cloud until it was obvious the jeep was headed to the highway and out of the area.

He visibly relaxed and noted the time once again: seven forty-five. There'd been something odd about the men. Whether it was the way they rode with their rifles held so casually skyward or the persistence of their waiting. Varmint hunters possibly. Out for a day's shooting of prairie dogs or rodents? But whatever they'd been expecting hadn't arrived.

Logan crept and slid to the floor of the wash. He settled himself in the familiar seat, lit a cigarette that burned his throat, and wiped the sweatband of his stetson. He snapped on the radio and waited for it to warm up as he puffed punishingly on the burning tobacco. He faced the setting sun, sunglasses firmly in place. He thumbed the switch on the handset. "Hello, Del Amo. This is Logan in number seventy-four."

The voice that answered belonged to Brook. "Logan? Where the hell are you?"

"Seminole mesa."

"You were supposed to check out the mesa!"

"I did! Has Ernie checked in yet? I haven't seen him all afternoon."

"You were supposed to check out the mesa!" Brook repeated.

"I did!" Logan insisted before the terrible reality of it hit him. A shock so numbing he could only choke back the words before asking, "How do you know I *didn't*?"

"Where are you?" Brook demanded.

Logan stared at the microphone as all the pieces fell inexorably into place, cluttering his brain as they vied for attention, demanding that he inspect each dread bit of logic. There could have been only one way Brook would have known he actually didn't show himself on the mesa. Only one other party would have known it—the men who had waited for him. That he should be sent to the remote mesa where two men waited with rifles was suddenly more than coincidence.

"Where are you?" Brook's voice dropped its command and the words were meant to be soothing, to lull him off guard.

Logan thumbed the switch. "Where's Ernie?" he asked, trying to control the panic that gripped him.

"Ernie checked in about two hours ago," Brooks cooed. "So where are *you*, Logan?"

Logan placed the handset on the hook. Ernie wouldn't have gone in without stopping by the mesa. There'd been tracks leading to his hidden jeep. Ernie would have discovered them and tracked Logan to the mesa.

He spun the tires in the soft sand as he headed for Castle Canyon. "Where are you?" Brook asked in annoyance before Logan snapped the radio silent.

Suddenly the small details of the day took on new significance. Hudson hadn't given out the assignments, the dispatcher had said "Brook wants." There was also the coincidence of his and Ernie's being sent to two isolated locations. Two locations seldom traveled, ideal spots for ambush. Also, there'd been no afternoon flyover by Ewing. Why hadn't Ewing covered the area as usual? Had Brook assigned him elsewhere? And if so, why?

It was forty long miles to Castle Canyon and darkness moved in swiftly once the sun slipped below the horizon. Logan drove recklessly across the desert floor. A new fear propelled him forward—fear for Ernie, fear for himself. He was so terrified he drove without lights—every wash was suspect, every bush hid a possible sniper.

Snatches of conversation and details swarmed. Wild, random thoughts took hold of him. Roget and Lombasino assumed new importance. Their grisly tableau haunted him as he realized that their killers and the men on the mesa might be somehow interconnected. But he was at a loss to explain Pinedo or the why of *any* of it. What was it Brook hoped to gain? How many were involved and who were they? Was it simply a coincidence that Roget and Lombasino were killed? Who were the men waiting on the mesa?

His vehicle rocketed into the air with a grinding tear of metal. The impact threw him against the steering wheel as he fought for control. The jeep teetered on two wheels before righting itself. Moments later the red oil light flashed its warning. Logan cursed his stupidity, his thoughtless daydreaming. He headed the jeep for a distant group of desert willows, the engine protesting the dryness by rapping loudly under the hood. He covered the frame with brush, only to realize that the tracks led straight to the willow clump. He was wasting valuable time like a fool—time better spent escaping with Ernie. He was tired, he reasoned. He wasn't making sense. It had been almost forty-eight hours since he'd had a good night's sleep. His foggy brain was betraying him into stupid mistakes. It prevented him from thinking clearly. He'd never given any thought to escaping. How did one escape and where?

He spent valuable time sweeping his tracks as he lashed himself forward on foot, canteen and binoculars over his shoulder, toward Castle Canyon.

14

Ernie's empty jeep stood against the dark canyon walls. In the moonlight it resembled an empty coffin. Logan had been hoping against all odds it would not be there. That Ernie had indeed gone on to Del Amo as reported. He clutched the jeep for support, his heart racing with exhaustion. He was too tired to think. Too tired to run one more step. Too tired to inspect the canyon. He noted that Ernie's canteen was missing and felt a certain relief in knowing his partner had had the good sense to take water. It was the only glimmer of hope in an uncertain situation.

Tracking the canyon was extremely difficult in the daytime and impossible at night. Logan gave it little thought; he went forward blindly, picking his way along its floor, stopping periodically to listen for any sign at all. The only sounds he heard were the beating of his heart and the hoarse rasping breath that escaped his parched lips.

At each bend he expected to see Ernie, a finger to his lips, admonishing Logan for the noise he was making as he stumbled up the canyon. If Logan had been wise to the men on the mesa, Ernie would have been even smarter. Every few yards he expected to come across Ernie patiently outwaiting his quarry, playing the deadly game of wait-and-see.

Then Logan began to fear he might pass his partner and stumble into the trap laid for Ernie, if there was such a thing. He wasn't sure *what* he thought anymore. What seemed important one moment was completely forgotten the next. The men on the mesa were a long way off in time. What had been hours before now seemed like days past. Time ran together, then split away, leaving him exposed and naked. Had someone tried to kill him? Had there really *been* a trap? When was that? Yesterday? The day before? Today? This afternoon? *What day is this?* he asked himself. Was it just this morning he'd stormed the door to a deserted cabin and found his old friend Roget?

Logan realized both his hands were empty. He was picking his way through the dark, expecting an assault at any moment, yet he had his weapon holstered. He withdrew the magnum and filled his other hand with the flashlight. This seemed to make more sense, though he had to admit he wouldn't use the beam of the light unless absolutely necessary. He held the weapon ahead of him as he worked his way past the cathedral-high walls bordering the rock floor, plunging the canyon into pitch blackness. He felt as if he were wandering through one of Ernie's black velour paintings, his fingers guiding him through the pockets of inky darkness.

He desperately needed a cigarette, desperately needed a rest. Yet he was afraid to uncap the canteen, afraid even to rattle it to splash the water that might be heard by someone waiting just ahead.

Each mile became harder than the last. The nerves of his body had worked their way to the outside layer of skin, tingling in anticipation, making him acutely aware of the pockets of warm air given off by the rocks. When he found the second vehicle, it was empty. A four-wheel-drive jeep standing in a clearing. There were no canteens or keys. The tracks around the area were those of men in street shoes. A separate set of lug-boot tracks told him Ernie had found the vehicle, too.

The street shoes went down into the canyon, the very same avenue he himself had just taken. They emerged again from the stone floor, mingling in the sandy-soiled clearing before they went out the exit road to the west.

He followed the tracks in the moonlight until he came to signs of another vehicle which had picked the men up and driven them away. *Why would they leave their jeep?* he wondered. He made his way back to the abandoned jeep and followed the tracks into the canyon again. The floor became hard and the signs disappeared into the stone basin.

Satisfied the others were gone, he moved much faster now, panting with fear, dashing with bone-jarring agony into each rock labyrinth, flashing his light around recklessly as he searched for his partner.

Ernie rested against a stone couch, arms flung wide, one foot tucked behind the other leg. The familiar mouth was wide in a grimace of pain, the eyes dull and clouded. Logan cried out in agony as his light reached the other large mouth beneath the chin, a gaping, crescent-shaped wound brutally severing the windpipe and spinal cord, causing the head to fall back at an unnatural angle.

Logan squeezed his lips tight, forcing the sobs deep into his chest, where they broke loose in a torrent of choking moans. The sounds were magnified by the canyon walls until a hundred Logans were moaning and crying on their knees.

Logan cried aloud for his partner, his friend. He cried in anger at the way they had mutilated Ernie's body. He cried for his own irreplaceable loss. The deep sorrow he felt was exhausting, punishing his weakened body until not a sound of grief was available. He crawled forward on his knees and rested a hand on Ernie's leg as the rage took hold of him. With clinical detachment, he forced himself to spray the light on Ernie's body. The jacket had pulled loose from the chest, the belt and chest strap left intact. There was a similarity to the wounds and cuts drawn across the breast, a marked resemblance to the ritual markings left on Roget. Between the legs lay a dark sandy puddle, dry with the caked blood from Ernie's body. On the far side, tucked into the folds of the green blouse, was the weapon. The handle of Logan's buck knife protruded from the cloth, the blade buried deep between the ribs as a last gesture of contempt.

Logan recoiled in shock, crawling on his knees to the far side of the tiny nook, where he stared unbelievingly at the knife. The knife he had hidden in his boot. The knife that had rested with the papers of Curtis-Medford-Beck.

Logan fumbled with Ernie's keys until he found the one that fitted the jeep. He pumped the vehicle to life and spun it around swiftly. It was thirty-three miles to the Kaufman chimney. Thirty-three long miles, if Ernie had told them where the money had been hidden. Thirty-three miles to make some sense of the carnage that had come to section seven. Thirty-three miles to plan the rest of his life.

He'd been foolish to leave the papers in the apartment. Foolish to trust a pair of old boots. Death warrants hidden in the toe of Tony Lama hand-tooled boots. Curtis-Medford-Beck had brought them all down, as surely as if he'd fired the weapons or wielded the knife.

The tired brain tried to reason it out, but there were so many things requiring a clearer explanation. So many puzzles whose pieces shifted around and defied assembling. Roget and Lombasino floated in and out of the reasonable theories. Toots and Amarillo confounded logic. Brook was totally inexplicable. Chadney? What part did Chadney play in all of it? The Army? What the hell was the Army's goal? The money? That federal Immigration employees would be killed for a sum of money that, once split among the various agencies, wouldn't amount to a year's salary was unthinkable. That people wouldn't grow curious at the death of three patrolmen in less than twenty-four hours would be hard even for Brook to alibi. And who did Brook report to?

"It was Toots' misfortune that he stumbled into the wash," Logan reasoned aloud as he peered into the fast-moving darkness. "And what was Amarillo's misfortune? That he knew Toots? And Roget and Lombasino? They only tracked Toots in and out of the wash. Which they reported to Brook. Who did Brook report it to? Chadney? Why Chadney? It was just a body. All this led someone back to Toots. Did that someone think Toots had the money? Did that someone think Roget and Lombasino had the money? Why would they be killed if it *was* thought they had the money? Killing the patrolmen wouldn't get them the money—so why kill them?"

Logan turned up a small canyon, his eyes swimming with fatigue. He thought he'd figured out why there'd been no flyover during the afternoon. Ewing could not be sent aloft or he'd spot the men waiting at Seminole mesa and Castle Canyon. Brook had set them up and didn't want Ewing to spot their hunters. "But why?" Logan persisted. If the papers had been found in the boot, there was enough evidence right there to link the two patrolmen to the body. Why not simply charge them with theft? Why not call them down and charge them?

He wondered if Ernie's murder would prompt the department to continue their housecleaning, rounding up another group of literate Mexicans who might one day challenge their authority. No, the knife left at the scene was an attempt to link *him* with Ernie's murder. To blame another patrolman for the death of one of their own. *But no one would buy that.* Logan scoffed. Ewing and the others would see right through it. Hudson knew how close they'd been; it would be inconceivable he would kill Ernie.

There wasn't an ounce of logic left in him. He was too

exhausted even to formulate a plan of escape. His only thought was to find the money and somehow race with it to somewhere. The confusion and weariness brought him back to Ernie's body, and the tears spilled down his cheeks, making driving almost impossible. He cursed those responsible, vowing to see that they not be allowed to profit from any of this. He felt it important that someone know about Brook. He felt it important that the bureau know about the Brooks among them.

He had the feeling he was sitting in a darkened room and some prankster was flashing random images on the screen for him to explain. Just as he was in the middle of an explanation, another picture would be thrown out to confound him.

He saw Julie, eyes closed, teeth clenched in passion. She was in love with him; the kisses and notes told him so. She would do anything for him without asking a lot of foolish questions. If he could reach a pay phone, she could meet him with his treasure at some deserted spot. Her car could take them to safety. He tried to remember when they'd last shared his bed, had played their games and sweated noisily over each other, greasy hands pulling the chicken apart, prompting Ernie to observe the following morning, "You ever stop to think, if our ancestors had landed in Australia instead of Plymouth Rock, every Thanksgiving our mothers would have been stuffing kangaroos?"

Damn them! He began to weep, jerking the jeep to a halt in confusion. Another thought had raced by him and escaped into the blackness before it could be deciphered. He lit another cigarette in the darkness, feeling the chill that warned him he was making a terrible mistake. He stared numbly at his hands on the wheel, the quiet desert night caught in the coughing of his engine. Then he knew what had eluded him. He'd been leaving tracks to the chimney. He'd driven along, head swamped with weariness and sorrow, leaving a four-wheel trail that would lead his pursuers straight to the chinmey. He drove to the nearest clump of brush, cut numerous branches, and fastened them behind the rear bumper.

He drove on, leaving a wide swath of scratches up the arroyos that followed, moving at a crawl as he dodged the boulders and soft sand. He drifted back ten years to Nam, powerless to stop himself, unable to reason why. Faces and voices danced in his head. Visions of dead and dying, laughing and crying comrades fogged his mind. Then he knew the parable. He'd vowed to himself that he would never come close to anyone, would spare himself the grief that accompanied each loss. Yet he'd violated that rule with Ernie, and for good reason. Nam had been another time. After Nam it was safe to love someone again. It was safe to make new friends without concern they would abandon you. "Damn you, Wheeler!" he cried as he sent the jeep up a steep embankment to harder ground.

The brush had been worn to thin, trailing sticks by the time he reached the Kearney Plateau. The sun was an hour away from peeking out at the chimney. Logan left the jeep and climbed the sheer sand face. The chimney stood against the thin line of light creeping into the horizon. He searched in all directions before he estimated the time needed to reach the stone marker. A long mile separated the money from the secure spot he held on the lip of the plateau. A long mile to run, stagger, and worry that they might be waiting. His hand began to shake as he thought of the long, exposed run. If Ernie had told them anything, they'd be waiting. If Julie had told them anything, they'd be waiting. It was the first time he reasoned that she, too, might already have been traced to the phone numbers. If the license numbers had been traced to Sheriff Wells, might not Julie be suspect? Was not *everyone* suspect?

Logan took several deep breaths, fighting the urge to close his eyes and take a well-deserved nap before he began this last phase of escaping. He would need all his energy to drag the box back to the wash and secure it in the jeep before heading south over the border. He needed all the strength he had, and he had very little.

With a last look skyward, he burst over the lip onto the flat terrain and began to run for the stone sentinel. In less than a hundred yards his legs began to go rubbery and a sharp pain stabbed at his side. He slowed to a walk, spinning around in all directions, trying to see behind him and at all sides at the same time. He pirouetted across the desert, ears keened for the slightest sound, eyes whipping about in ever-widening circles.

"What the fuck am I doing out here?" he whispered through teeth gummy with dust. He hugged his side to ease the pain, the projectionist busily flashing the insane images again, ripping his mind from one subject to another. "I can't call you!" he said to Julie. "They may be wise to you. Your line may be tapped. These guys play for keeps!"

He had been walking backward, staring intently to the rear, when he slipped into the slight depression at the foot of the chimney. He dropped to both knees, his breath rasping in his chest, his heart tripping rapidly against the shirtfront.

Kaufman had built a large cement hole at the base of the fireplace, an ingenious contraption for catching the ashes. Kaufman himself must have been quite proud of it, for it allowed the fireplace wastes to be emptied from outside, eliminating soot or dust from the house.

Logan uncovered the cement pit, digging rapidly with his hands until he found the first container. It had been Ernie's idea to bury the money deep at the bottom, thinking, if someone did discover the hole, they might be satisfied to find a metal box containing two fishing rods and a rifle and not dig further for the money that lay beneath.

Logan pulled the first box out of the hole, then continued down to the money box. He tugged it loose, drawing it to his side. He felt no exhilaration when he saw the money. The very fact that he'd been allowed to reach it told him Ernie had revealed nothing. Instead a bitter anger swelled within him, souring his stomach, spoiling the moment of discovery. The relief that the money was still there gave way to rage. That Curtis-Medford-Beck had triggered the diabolical happenings of the last few days incensed him. The furious resentment at Ernie's death sent him railing at the metal fishing container. He broke the lid back, provoked by its bland presence, infuriated with himself for understanding so little of what had happened. Suddenly consumed with rage at this Curtis-Medford-Beck for destroying everything around him, Logan yanked the poles from the box and demanded, "Who in the hell are you?"

He smashed the poles against the fireplace, snatching at the pieces for some yet undiscovered clue. Certain now that the mystery to the trinity of Curtis-Medford-Beck had been within his grasp and he had simply failed to see it, he assaulted the rods, inspecting each part.

He broke the reels open and looked for something—anything. In frustration he threw the broken parts away, snatched up another section, examined it, discarded it to the desert until the rods themselves were all that was left. He inspected the hollow fiberglass tubing, cracking the rods across his knee. Each section was scanned thoroughly, then flung away. Then he turned his anger on the box itself, dumping the rifle on the sand and swinging the container against the stone formation, battering it with wild, furious swings. Hammering it out of shape, the lid coming loose, the sides collapsing. And still it revealed nothing.

Logan inspected the cuts in the palms of his hands, inflicted by the sharp edge of the metal. He cradled them against his body and wept in fury. There had been so many clues, so many little bits to make up a satisfactory explanation, and still he had nothing. He sobbed as he reached for the rifle, drawing it across his lap as he noticed the first rays of sunlight striking sharply across the flat. He reached for the sunglasses that always hung from the front of his shirt. His hand patted the empty place where they should have been. He blinked in dismay, the tired lids involuntarily closing against the bright assault from the east.

The rifle lay across his lap, the sling hanging to the sand. Logan squinted down at it, passed a dirty hand across its rough stock and rusted barrel. The cheap telescopic sight hung loose from its mount. He rolled it over and tried to pull the clip loose. It refused to cooperate. He withdrew his pistol and used the butt to break the rusty hold. He raised it in the air to shake it free.

He was holding the rifle in the air, the muzzle against the sky, when the projectionist came back to work in his brain. Logan swung his head from side to side, the pictures being replaced one after another, rapidly now, too fast for interpretation. The first was the Capa photo of a Spanish Loyalist at the instant of death. The rifle was in the soldier's right hand, the arms flung wide, the white shirt bright against the sun as the man died. The next was of Trotsky, the first published picture of Capa's from Copenhagen, 1931. It was all there in his own collection of Capa's photos.

Logan tried to shake it away. The projectionist was driving him crazy with pictures, single frames flashing rapidly back and forth, too quick to be explained. Logan narrowed his eyes on the rifle, sorting through the flashes for the one picture that kept returning. Not Capa, no. Not the Spanish Loyalist, but another man. A man with a hat, holding a rifle in the air. And then another man, small, slight, a newspaper in one hand, a rifle in the other.

The answer began in a tight ring around his forehead and swept his body in a tingling of warmth. His skin prickled as he dropped the weapon to the sand and closed his fists against his chest. He saw the detective holding the rifle in the air. Knew the man with the newspaper who posed for the young wife, rifle in hand, as the shutter clicked.

Logan drew the rifle gently to him; he brushed the sand away with fascination. He took the key from his pocket and began to scratch the rust away from the inscription. "Made in Italy" confirmed the terrible suspicions. He scraped "Cal 6.5" clear. Found the serial number, "C1339," and the year, "1940." It was not a Mauser, as Ernie had thought and as others had thought. It was a Mannlicher-Carcano 6.5.

Logan wrested the clip and counted the rusted bullets. One was missing.

Dazed by this, he held the rifle to his chest. He knew now why everyone had died, why it was so important that the possessions of Michael Curtis be found.

The 7.65 Mauser that both he and Ernie had mistakenly identified, as had the deputy constable from Dallas, was in fact a 6.5 Mannlicher-Carcano, equipped with a four-power scope. Identical weapons.

The telephone numbers of the Dallas Police Department and the Texas Hotel in Fort Worth became suddenly clear. The President had been staying at the hotel before leaving on that fateful morning for Dallas.

The parking tickets for Fort Worth and Dallas, timed accounts of a man tracking the President of the United States. Tickets that remained in the man's possession. The nagging item that had been bothering Logan. Curtis had retained possession of the tickets. Parking tickets were always returned to the attendant. They were the only source of company records.

The newspapers, filled daily with the accounts of that November day in Dallas, right before their eyes and they failed to see it. That Curtis had been the man on the grassy knoll immobilized him. His body felt as if it were filled with poison, that Curtis had polluted him with his simple existence.

He hastily reconstructed the other facts. Curtis-Medford-Beck had been in Nam in late October and early November. The coup against the Diem brothers had begun at 1 P.M. on the afternoon of November 1. Curtis had been there. Curtis had returned to the States in time to purchase a jeep and wait in Dealey Plaza for the President's auto. "But the money," he wondered aloud. Why did Curtis-Medford-Beck run with the money? Was he afraid of a double cross? A mysterious accident? Another convenient heart attack? "How many have died?" he asked aloud. "When will it stop?" The number had to be almost fifty, if one counted all the witnesses who had suffered fatal ailments over the last ten to fifteen years.

Logan stroked the weapon he held in his arms. He knew he should feel a certain revulsion, but the rifle was proof. Proof that there *were* others involved. Proof that the snapping head shot that the authorities discounted had indeed been fired by someone else.

Logan sat in the rising sun, contemplating how he could relay this staggering information. The sun was too bright, making it impossible to think clearly of all the facts.

The impact drove the rifle from his hands and sent him sprawling. Seconds later he heard the loud report.

Chadney had the same gold medallion as Curtis.

In the distance Logan saw the man lower the rifle and climb into the jeep. He felt a numbing in his chest, felt the cool sand at the corner of his mouth. To his left he heard the *whump* of helicopter blades. With a great effort he dragged his head across the sand in time to see the chopper rise from the arroyo. The man in the doorway sent bursts of flame in Logan's direction. To the rear Logan heard a second chopper, more distinct than the first. He felt the whack of hot rivets in his back as the sand stitched its little spurts nearer and nearer. He rolled himself into a protective ball as the dust kicks reached him.

"This the last one?" the thin man asked.

"The last one," the heavy man answered.

"You sure?" the thin man asked.

"Christ, I hope so," the heavy man answered.